SWEDISH
REFLECTIONS

SWEDISH REFLECTIONS

From Beowulf to Bergman

edited by
Judith Black and Jim Potts

A

ARCADIA BOOKS
LONDON

Arcadia Books Ltd
15–16 Nassau Street
London W1W 7AB
www.arcadiabooks.co.uk

First published in the United Kingdom 2003
Copyright © The British Council, Sweden and the contributors 2003
Foreword copyright © Michael Holroyd 2003
Introduction copyright © British Council 2003

A catalogue record for this book is available from the British Library.

ISBN 1–900850–76–1

Typeset in Scala by Northern Phototypesetting Co. Ltd, Bolton
Printed in the United Kingdom by Bell & Bain Ltd, Glasgow.

Acknowledgements

Arcadia Books acknowledges the financial support of the British Council
Sweden, the Arts Council of England and London Arts.

Arcadia Books distributors are as follows:

in the UK and elsewhere in Europe:
Turnaround Publishers Services
Unit 3, Olympia Trading Estate
Coburg Road
London N22 6TZ

in the USA and Canada:
Consortium Book Sales and Distribution
1045 Westgate Drive
St Paul, MN 55114-1065

in Australia:
Tower Books
PO Box 213
Brookvale, NSW 2100

in New Zealand:
Addenda
Box 78224
Grey Lynn
Auckland

in South Africa:
Quartet Sales and Marketing
PO Box 1218
Northcliffe
Johannesburg 2115

Arcadia Books: *Sunday Times* Small Publisher of the Year 2002/03

Contents

Memoirs and Biography

Foreword

Michael Holroyd

Though I never lived in Sweden, my mother would regularly take me over to spend part of my school holidays in Stockholm with my grandmother; and also, during the late 1940s and the 1950s, for visits to Borås and Göteborg to see my Swedish cousins. I was always happy to disembark at Göteborg, not least because I could leave the savagely rocking boats, the *Suecia*, *Saga* or *Patricia*, that had bucked me so remorselessly over the North Sea all the way from Tilbury Docks. As they started out on their three-day journeys, creaking and groaning, swaying and heaving, I would go down to my cabin and begin groaning and heaving with sympathetic sea-sickness.

Ulla, my mother, was never ill. She was immensely popular on board, never missing the music playing, the sun shining, the splendid smörgåsbord and the company of strangers. Occasionally I would crawl up on deck and see her talking to some admirer and exchanging addresses. I remember only one of these gentlemen, a Mr Smith, who wore his watch with its face on the inside of his wrist. I was so impressed by this novelty that I turned my own watch round, and have worn it so ever since. Later, 'Mr Smith on the boat' became a generic term, and I would tease my mother about this ever-recurring gallant on her travels round the world.

My mother and father had been divorced at the end of the war, and from then on my mother was constantly travelling between new liaisons and towards new marriages. But what I did not know was that my parents had actually met on board one of those Swedish boats sailing to England early in 1934.

My father's family were the agents in Britain for Lalique Glass, and my father, who specialized in glass lighting, was attempting to form an amalgamation with Kosta Glass. My mother, then aged seventeen, was coming over to improve her English. She possessed an adventurous spirit, and though she loved Kaja, her mother, she was looking forward to a more free and independent life. Kaja, as one of the team at Countess von Schwerin's fashion house, Märtaskolan, was something of a martinet on matters of dress and decorum. When Ulla said she was going out to a party in Stockholm, Kaja would dress up and come along too. And what a power dresser she was! She had such a sharp eye and was so strikingly smart that her presence became increasingly oppressive to her daughter. They appeared like two dancers forever treading on each other's toes. Kaja, then in her forties, seemed quite old to her teenage daughter who was annoyed when people at these parties mistook them for sisters – though Kaja herself looked delighted. So, though mother and daughter were close to each other, Ulla felt happy to be going abroad alone.

Kaja had arranged for Ulla to be seated at the Captain's table on board the *Suecia*. What neither of them had bargained for was the presence of my father. Everyone dressed for dinner in those days. There were formal toasts, a clicking of heels, a bowing of heads. Altogether a dignified atmosphere prevailed – that is, until my father's loud and persistent British voice began to be heard. It sounded unpleasantly raucous because, as he later explained, he had been smoking too many Gauloises. On the second evening, with exaggerated correctness, he came swaying up to my mother's table and requested the Captain's permission to ask her for a dance. So Ulla found herself waltzing, and then quickstepping, in the arms of this jovial Englishman (actually he was half-Irish and a quarter Scots – but such nuances meant nothing to Ulla). My father had what the Irish call 'the gift of

*Michael Holroyd with his mother, grandmother and cousin Mary at
Marstrand, August 1946.*

the gab' – which is to say he had a silver tongue and, when
enthusiastic, was extremely eloquent. 'He could talk anybody
into anything,' Ulla remembered. He soon talked her into
giving him her address in England (she was staying with a
Mrs Malmburg who provided English language tuition in
Beckenham). Then, in no time, having enriched her English
with some contemporary slang in London (they used to meet
at the Hyde Park Hotel where King Gustave often stayed), he
talked her into marrying him. He had, however, neglected to
inform Kaja of their marriage – possibly because my mother
was already pregnant with me.

They sailed over to Sweden in time for Christmas 1934,
when my father, in *Alice Through the Looking-Glass* style, formally asked his mother-in-law's permission for her daughter's hand in marriage. Over the next couple of days, while
she was pondering her reply, Kaja noticed how sick her
daughter was in the mornings. Her sharp eye quickly perceived the truth, and after an hour of frowns, she happily

gave her retrospective approval – arriving in London the following summer for my birth which my father (who was playing golf) missed.

It was partly the war which, after seven or eight years, broke their marriage apart and caused my childhood and adolescence to become so radically fragmented between Britain and Sweden. Would I have learnt more than rudimentary Swedish if there had been no war and no divorce? I do not know. What I do know is that my Swedish eventually vanished and that when I now try out a few words of it, all the Swedes who hear me break into spontaneous laughter (quickly destroying their collective reputation for being humourless).

I eventually took to wearing two watches, both facing inwards like Mr Smith's, and when asked for my reason, would sometimes answer that one kept London time, the other Stockholm time. Was this true? It is so difficult to tell with non-fiction writers, especially novelists manqués. But I daresay it symbolized a need for unity between my parents and their countries.

My Swedish connection made me a figure of some mystery and exotic interest at school in England. It was unusual for boys to travel much abroad after the war. So when I returned from Sweden, like some mariner disembarking from a piratical voyage with his booty (a Lapland knife in its multi-coloured leather-and-fur sheath, a vast marzipan pig with chocolate features, a brilliantly exciting ice-hockey game or a magically tilting wooden maze through which you steered a silver ball) I found such treasure made me a wonderfully popular chap.

Because of my regular visits to Sweden and my grandmother's frequent trips to England, I became for a time almost as familiar with the names of Pär Lagerkvist and Selma Lagerlöf as I was with those of Tennyson and Wordsworth – indeed I developed a leaning towards the former because, unlike the latter, they were never made the subjects of my school exams. I was given *The Long Ships* to read, came to love the symphonies of Franz Berwald and grew familiar with the domestic paintings of Carl Larsson. My mother took me to see a couple of Strindberg plays, and I took myself to see many of Ingmar Bergman's films. The cross-currents of Swedish and English culture seemed a natural phenomenon to me.

The biographies I went on to write reinforced this feeling. I was not surprised to discover Augustus John's strong portrait of Percy Ussher in the Swedish National Gallery, or to find myself attempting to recreate on the page John's vexed and dramatic relationship with Frida Strindberg. I also enjoyed writing about Lytton Strachey's curious visits to Saltsjöbaden and recording (with the help of August Strindberg's biographer, Michael Meyer), Bernard Shaw's extraordinary encounter with the Swedish dramatist in 1907. I am delighted to see that both these adventures have found a place in this enterprising anthology.

Twenty years after his meeting with Strindberg, Bernard Shaw donated his money from the Nobel Prize for Literature to create an Anglo-Swedish Literary Foundation. In the deed, dated 21 March 1927, the object of this Foundation is set out as being 'the encouragement of cultural intercourse between Sweden and the British Islands through the promotion and diffusion of knowledge and appreciation of the literature and art of Sweden in the British Islands'. The funds have been mainly used to assist and reward the translation of Swedish books into English – the first of these translated works being those of Strindberg himself.

I am particularly pleased to be introducing this fine anthology which partly reminds me, and largely informs me, of writings by both Swedish and British writers, re-acquainting me with Swedish culture without the agony of crossing the North Sea. As I look through its contents, my two watches seem to be ticking away in marvellous unison. This book has been compiled very much in the spirit which first animated the Anglo-Swedish Literary Foundation almost eighty years ago. As Bernard Shaw's biographer, I welcome and applaud its publication.

Introduction

Jim Potts

The British Council opened in Sweden on 17 December 1941, although British Council programmes had been organized in the country as early as 1939 (essay competitions in schools, with the prize being a visit to the UK, following a visit by the Secretary of the Council's Students' Committee in January–February 1939). There had also been influential English Language Teaching Summer Schools held in Sigtuna. During the war the British Council organized a five-week lecture tour by T.S. Eliot (in 1942) which was judged a great success. He gave talks on 'Poetry, Speech and Music' and on 'Poetry in the Theatre', which received exceptional publicity and detailed coverage in the Swedish press.

This anthology marks the sixtieth anniversary of T.S. Eliot's British Council tour of Sweden, and was conceived to celebrate the sixtieth anniversary of British Council projects and full operational activity in Sweden.

In September 1941 the chairman of the Council's executive committee reported in the minutes that 'H.M. Legation at Stockholm had urged the Council to appoint a representative in Sweden to organize Council activities there. The Foreign Office were strongly in favour of expanding the Council's work in Sweden'. Modest expenditure was approved by the Treasury which would 'allow it to be taken from savings in the Balkans and Finland'. (Following the dramatic changes in Eastern Europe after 1989/1990, funding priorities in the region would shift in favour of the Baltic States, Central and Eastern Europe and beyond.)

An influential exhibition of Modern British Watercolours ('Nutida Engelsk Akvarellkonst') at the Swedish National

Museum in 1943 and other centres like Gothenburg (total attendance was 12,600) was probably as close as the Council ever came to 'cultural propaganda'. The opening at Stockholm was attended by T.R.H. the Crown Prince and Crown Princess of Sweden and Prince Eugen.

Political propaganda during the war was the responsibility of the Ministry of Information. The Council did organize window displays on the social services, hostels for factory workers, community centres, modern developments in British schools, British provincial towns, the historical development of the English book, the English theatre and other subjects.

Other activities in the 1940s included lecture tours by Sir Howard Florey, Sir Lawrence Bragg (whose 'unusual ability to interpret science to laymen made him a most popular

Grand Hôtel, Stockholm, 14 December 1948. In customary fashion, the year's Nobel Laureate in Literature, here T.S. Eliot, is woken early one morning during the Swedish Lucia celebrations by the hotel's own Lucia.

visiting lecturer'), Dr Malcolm Sargent (who also conducted concerts), Sir Kenneth Clark, Erik Linklater, J.B. Priestley as well as T.S. Eliot.

The Council was almost the only means of cultural contact between Britain and Sweden during the war and

> difficulties of transport from September 1943 onwards did not prevent its work from increasing rapidly, for Swedes now know better what the Council can do for them, partly by reason of the publicity its activities have received in the Press, and partly on account of the distribution of 16,000 copies of a brochure in Swedish describing the work of the Council in Sweden. Expansion has been noteworthy in the Anglophile Societies, in English teaching, in the publication of English books in Sweden, and in the distribution of periodicals. If the increase in the Anglophile Societies is a symptom of Swedish sentiment, the expansion of English teaching is not less so. A Gallup poll taken during the year showed that 17 per cent of the Swedish public can read English, while only 16 per cent can read German, and the figure for English is far greater among those under forty. (*BC Annual Report 1943/44*)

Courses in English literature, music, history, geography and language were given at the Council's offices in Stockholm, as well as popular English language circles for young people. A monthly periodical called *Things English* was produced by the Council for secondary schools and for younger students of English. Six thousand copies were sent out (and 2,500 annual subscriptions were quickly taken out; by 1944/45 there were initially 7,374 annual subscribers, with 54,700 copies sold during the year). Council staff contributed to School Radio English programmes and 'Mr Snodin did film teaching, using *Pygmalion* and *Good-bye Mr Chips*, in the Stockholm, Uppsala, Gothenburg and Skåne areas, and had about 10,000 attendances'.

It is interesting to speculate that the tours by T.S. Eliot and Sir Howard Florey may have helped to reinforce their claims to their respective Nobel Prizes. Eliot was back in Stockholm

xviii   *Swedish Reflections*

in 1948 to receive the Nobel Prize for Literature, 'for his out-standing, pioneer contribution to present-day poetry'.

Whatever the impact of these tours by distinguished visitors, the English language teaching contribution by resident lecturers like F.A.L. Charlesworth, Albert Read and M.R. Snodin clearly had a major impact on the development of English language teaching in Sweden after the war, both at the elementary and secondary school level, in adult education (WEA/ABF, Folkuniversitet), at university level, and through the formation of Anglophile societies all over the country. The Sigtuna Summer Schools seem to have made a huge impact (there were eight courses in 1944 alone, and they were visited by the Swedish foreign minister on the closing days). Swedish firms donated a number of scholarships. In 1944 there were 638 applicants for places, participants were taught by a British and Swedish staff of 69!

The British Council's first office was at Birger Jarlsgatan 15 in Stockholm. The first Director, or Representative (1941–44), was the poet Ronald Bottrall (much praised by F. R. Leavis and T.S. Eliot). He was followed by Professor Michael Roberts, a professor of history, and then by Brigadier H.C. Travell Stronge, CBE, DSO, MC.

Early Assistant Representatives included Dr Arthur King, D.J. Gillan and R. Washbourn. More recent Directors have included Dr Patrick Spaven, Ann Hellström, Dr Sean Lewis, John Day, Raymond Adlam and David Thomas.

The Council's focus has changed over the course of sixty years. English language teacher-training and joint research programmes have virtually disappeared, as links are now largely self-sustaining. The arts and cultural relations projects remain an important area of activity; the focus has moved at times towards areas like cultural and public diplomacy and collaboration with the embassy and other partners in the creative industries (for example the *British Design Season* in 2001, *Scotland in Sweden* in 2002), to reaching a wider, younger public and aspiring young professionals, and to the development of projects in partnership with Swedish groups and organizations, in a spirit of 'mutuality'.

Creating a dialogue between the countries, and the creation of wider European networks is a priority, as well as the sharing of good practice, for example in public and social policy, science and technology, and combating intolerance.

In 1986 the Council was involved in a significant three-day seminar on 'Multiculturalism in Britain and Sweden' in partnership with the Swedish Academy (UK writers included Salman Rushdie, Kazuo Ishiguru and Grace Nichols). Cultural diversity remains a significant focus, one example being the 2002 Intercult project called 'Trans//Fusion'. The Council's new project, 'Discovering Diversity', aims to provide teaching materials and on-line resources for use by teachers and pupils with the objective of exploring issues of diversity and tolerence.

Information work has changed in line with developments in electronic communication. With trends towards increased use of the Internet, towards study abroad (up to 4,500 young Swedes study in UK higher education and further education institutions) and greater ease of travel (not least by means of the Channel Tunnel and the Öresund Bridge and tunnel), the Council is well placed to develop new models of cultural relations to reflect these changes in society and the instant information needs of diverse groups.

Whatever projects we undertake in future, whatever the thematic or regional focus, such as *Scotland in Sweden,* or a focus on the Öresund or Gothenburg/Västra Götaland regions, we shall be concerned with the better measurement of impact (a comprehensive evaluation report on the 2001 British Design Season was produced in September 2002). Not that it was lacking in the past. In 1945, for instance, articles in the Swedish press based on Council material amounted to 3,568 column inches (circulation 3,394,142) and references to the Council's activities to 12,243 column inches (circulation 11,211,914). Press space connected with the Council totalled 15,927 column inches (circulation 15,559,740).

Whilst our impact was being measured even in the early days, it is a pity that we cannot now go back and measure the effectiveness of all past events, like the impact of T.S. Eliot's 1942 lecture tour on the development of Modernism in Swedish literature[1], or the impact of the Sigtuna Summer Schools on the successful spread of the English language schools and business, or the full impact of Council lecturers on the teaching of English in adult education.[2]

As the current British Council Director, I look forward to continuing this conversation, this mutually rewarding tradition of dialogue and exchange, and I am confident that we will be able to demonstrate and measure the impact of our future projects and partnerships. I have faith that the Council did play an important role in spreading the teaching of English in Sweden after the Second World War, even if we can't take credit for the astonishing levels of fluency achieved by Swedes today![3]

The Nobel Prize in Literature

I once calculated that, in just over 100 years of the Nobel Prize in Literature, around twenty-five per cent of winners had written their main works in the English language. Those winners that we tend to consider as British or as representing 'English Literature' (however defined, but including *belles-lettres* and works of literary value) – regardless of nationality or personal sense of identity – are Rudyard Kipling (1907), W. B. Yeats (1923), George Bernard Shaw (1926), John Galsworthy (1932), T. S. Eliot (1948), Bertrand Russell (1950), Winston Churchill (1953), Elias Canetti (1981; emigrated to England 1938; British citizen from 1952), William Golding (1983), V. S. Naipaul (2001), and we might lay some claim to Seamus Heaney (1995) and Patrick White (1973), since they were born and educated in the UK. If we wish to stretch the point, we may also wish to express our pride in other winners born in the former British Empire: Derek Walcott (1992), Wole Soyinka (1986; educated at University of Leeds), Rahindranath Tagore (1913), and Nadine Gordimer (1991).

Personally, I would take even more delight in my own favourites among the prize-winners: Albert Camus (1957), George Seferis (1963), Odysseus Elytis (1979), and Jaroslav Seifert (1984), but that may be because I have lived and worked in Greece and in Prague, and because I deeply respect the view and criterion of Alfred Nobel, that 'No consideration whatever shall be given to nationality'.

British translators like Rex Warner, Philip Sherrard and Ewald Osers played an important part in the Swedish Academy's deliberations, one can assume, just as translators such as Joan Tate, Paul Britten Austin, Robin Fulton, Robin Young, Michael Meyer and Sarah Death have played such an important part in bringing Swedish literature to the English-speaking world.

Issues of national identity and the sense of belonging are not always easy. It seems the Swedish Academy does not always find it so easy to decide on the prize-winners either. Over the years, there has been surprise in some quarters that figures like Thomas Hardy, James Joyce, Henry James, Joseph Conrad, Virginia Woolf, Graham Greene, W.H. Auden, Lawrence Durrell, Anthony Burgess, Vladimir Nabokov and other deserving English-language authors at the height of their fame and reputation, were not awarded this high (the highest) international distinction. Kjell Espmark and Sture Allén admit, in *The Nobel Prize in Literature, An Introduction* (Swedish Academy, 2001), that the Academy was criticized for ignoring Graham Greene, 'a frequently praised candidate until around 1970'. At least he is one of the few foreign writers who has a 'Literary Stockholm' plaque, with a quotation from *England Made Me*, near Stockholm's North Bridge. It has been suggested that Artur Lundkvist opposed Greene, whereas Per Wästberg supported him over the years (see Michael Specter, 'Letter from Stockholm, The Nobel Syndrome', *The New Yorker*, October 1998).

There has always been gossip and speculation about the reasons why specific writers are overlooked, about possible personal vendettas or vetoes, and members of the Academy have occasionally spoken out or even 'resigned', for example when Kerstin Ekman and two other members of the committee 'resigned' (or rather, there are three empty chairs since, once elected, they are members for life and cannot resign) over the Academy's stand in 1989 about the *fatwa* imposed on Salman Rushdie. On another occasion, Lars Gyllensten revealed information about the voting and how he had intended to vote (for example concerning the occasion when William Golding was awarded the prize). According to Michael Specter (*The New Yorker*, ibid.), 'Artur Lundkvist, Neruda's champion, was the first to break the Nobel code of *omertà*, when he vowed to outlive Graham Greene, if only to deny him the Nobel. Lundkvist also denounced William Golding, who won in 1983, as a 'little English phenomenon of no special interest'.

It has been suggested (by Humphrey Carpenter, in *W.H. Auden, A Biography*, Allen & Unwin, 1981) that the reason that W.H. Auden was not awarded the prize was the way in which he had described Dag Hammarskjöld's character and ego in the introduction to the Auden/Sjöberg translation of Hammarskjöld's *Markings*, which he suggests Leif Belfrage found unacceptable. Most of the published accounts are based on pure speculation, I have been assured by Kjell Espmark, the distinguished poet and Chairman of the Nobel Selection Committee. One respects the secrecy of the Academy's proceedings and the policy that the Academy does not take a public position on controversial political issues.

Evolution of this Anthology

This anthology is not just about writers who have been supported in some way by the British Council. That may have been the starting point. It soon began to develop as an anthology representing the best of British creative writing about Sweden, and including some outstanding examples of Swedish writing about the UK, as well as translations of Swedish writers by leading British literary figures.

The final stage in its evolution was to include some important examples in English written by non-British writers, like Paul Durcan's wonderful poem about Stockholm, and Longfellow's translations of Tegnér. They are simply too important to leave out. Both Durcan and Heaney are published by UK publishers. It is worth pointing out that the Nordic region (Sweden, Denmark, Norway and Finland) is the second largest market for British book exports after the USA (DTI UK statistics for Exports of Books).

At the end of the day, it is the reader who comes first. I am grateful to all my Swedish friends and colleagues who have suggested writers and passages for inclusion, and I also wish to acknowledge the assistance provided by the British Council's Literature Department (especially with contact addresses).

I would like to thank all the generous Swedish hosts, who, over the years, have invited British writers to come as writers-in-residence (for example Jamie McKendrick, Carol Rumens, Barry Unsworth, Marion Lomax/Robyn Bolam, Clive Sinclair, Oliver Reynolds, Raman Mundair, Kevin MacNeil) to the Universities of Lund, Uppsala, Stockholm, and Gothenburg; to the English Societies at Lund, Uppsala and elsewhere, the International Poetry Days in Malmö, the Gothenburg International Book Fair, the Stockholm Poetry Festival, the International Writers' Stage at Kulturhuset in Stockholm, the Swedish Institute, the Swedish Academy, the Swedish-British Society, and publishing houses like Bonniers and Norstedts.

In the two years that I have been in Sweden, visiting writers supported by the British Council have included Tony Harrison, Jessica Mann, Jean 'Binta' Breeze, Dannie Abse, Adrian Mitchell, Jamie McKendrick, Katherine Pierpoint, Sophie Hannah, Ruth Fainlight, Stephen Knight, Diran Adebayo, Tony Parsons, Alan Sillitoe, Raman Mundair, Kate Clanchy and a wonderful line-up of Scottish writers came in 2002: Janice Galloway, Ian Rankin, Jackie Kay, Alan Warner, Kevin MacNeil, Roddy Lumsden and Gregory Burke. In recent years we have also supported Linton Kwesi Johnson, Benjamin Zephaniah, Caryl Phillips, Michael Holroyd, Claire Tomalin, Lawrence Norfolk and Tibor Fischer. Years after the event, people still recall really successful writers' visits under the auspices of the British Council, like those of T.S. Eliot and Angus Wilson, for example.

This is to thank the writers for giving up their time and for giving their audiences so much pleasure.

Most of all I wish to thank Dr Judith Black, my co-editor, who has done an absolutely outstanding job and assumed the lion's share of the work in editing this anthology.

Gary Pulsifer of Arcadia Books expressed his enthusiasm for the project at an early stage, and I feel sure that the readers will be fascinated by and delighted with the results.

Ever since the first English poem, *Widsith* (the oldest in English, probably the earliest of any Germanic people), British poets have been conscious of Sweden and the Swedes:

'Ic wǣes mid Swēom ond mid Gēatum
ond mid suð-Denum.'

Sometimes I think that the life of a British Council staff-member resembles that of Widsith, the wandering minstrel, travelling in foreign lands, far from his/her folk, friends and kin.

Jim Potts
Stockholm, January 2003

1 Gustav Hellström of the Swedish Academy remarked, prior to Eliot's acceptance speech, that, 'As a poet you have, Mr Eliot, for decades, exercised a greater influence on your contemporaries and younger fellow writers than perhaps anyone else of our time'.

2 Ray Bradfield, OBE, provided me in September 2001 with an invaluable account of the work of the British Council, of the Swedish-British Society and of the British Centre in Stockholm, especially in relation to the period 1945–55, 'the high-water mark of British-Swedish cultural relations'.

3 We must also share some of the credit with the Swedish-British Society, the British Centre, Sweden's English by Radio and Television projects, as Ray Bradfield has commented in a letter to me. Many others played an equally important part: teachers, lectors and lecturers, the Folkuniversitetet and other adult education organizations, and, not least, the Swedish Ministry of Education.

Two Twentieth-Century Novelists

Graham Greene

from *Ways of Escape*

I have always had a soft spot in my heart for my fifth published novel, *England Made Me* (a feeling which has not been shared by the general public), yet of the circumstances of its composition I can remember very little. I think of those years between 1933 and 1937 as the middle years for my generation, clouded by the Depression in England, which cast a shadow on this book, and by the rise of Hitler. It was impossible in those days not to be committed, and it is hard to recall the details of one private life as the enormous battlefield was prepared around us.

When the story came to me, when Anthony and Kate, the twins in the novel, clamoured for attention, and their incestuous situation (which was yet to contain no incestuous act) for exploration, I knew nothing at all of Sweden. I think it is the only occasion when I have deliberately chosen an unknown country as a background and then visited it, like a camera team, to take the necessary stills. (Many years later I visited the Belgian Congo for something of the same purpose, but the Congo was a geographical term invented by the white colonists – I already knew Negro Africa, in Sierra Leone, Nigeria, Kenya, the hinterland of Liberia.)

The photographs I brought back from Sweden were, I think, reasonably accurate, reasonably representative, and yet, now that I know Stockholm well in winter, spring, summer and autumn, I am a little afraid when I come to reread the book. That midsummer festival at Saltsjö-Duvnäs, a New Year's night when lead was melted over the fire to tell

Drawing of Graham Greene by Mark Boxer

the future and the piece I threw in the pan formed a perfect question mark – such impressions are not to be found here, nor the swans gathering on the ice outside the Grand Hotel, the taste of akvavit in the Theatre Grill, the lakes of Dalecarlia, nor that island in the archipelago from which in that later time I would row every morning to fetch water for cooking and where a lavatory seat stood like a surrealist object all alone in a mosquito-loud glade. These impressions are Sweden to me now, and it might be as distressing to reread this novel as an ancient letter containing some superficial critical estimate of a woman whom twenty years later one had grown to love.

I have few memories of that visit with my younger brother Hugh in August 1934; the clearest, because they have not been overlaid by the later memories, are attached to the speckless miniature liner which brought us up the canal from Gothenburg to Stockholm (and which I imagined falsely would prove a background for the novel), of waking to the soft summer brilliance of midnight and the silver of the birches going by, almost within reach of my hands, and the chickens pecking on the bank. I remember that my brother and I carried on a harmless flirtation with two English visitors of sixteen and twenty; we went for walks in separate pairs when the boat stopped at a lock, and once, for some inexplicable reason, considerable alarm arose because my brother and the younger girl had not returned to the little liner at the proper time, and the mother – an intellectual lady who frequently won literary competitions in the Liberal weekly *Time & Tide* – was convinced that both had been drowned in the canal. One evening in Stockholm, on the borders of the lake, my companion of the canal slapped my face in almost the same circumstances as those in which Loo slapped Anthony's in my story, for I had told her that I believed that she was a virgin. Afterwards we sat decorously enough in Skansen, Stockholm's park, among the grey rocks and the silver trees. (Her reaction was the only characteristic she had in common with Loo.) But August is not the best time of year to see Stockholm for the first time – what with the heat and the humidity, and the extreme formality of one dinner which we attended at Saltsjöbaden, we decided to move on to Oslo. I am amazed now at my temerity in laying the scene of a novel in a city of which I knew so little.

from *England Made Me*

Across the sky stretched the hillside lights of Djurgården, the restaurants, the high tower in Skansen, the turrets and the switchbacks in Tivoli. A thin blue mist crawled from the water, covering the motor-boats, creeping half-way to the riding lights of the steamers. An English cruising liner lay opposite the Grand Hotel, its white paint glowing in the light of the street lamps, and through the cordage Krogh could see the tables laid, the waiters carrying flowers, the line of taxis on the North Strand. On the terrace of the palace a sentry passed and repassed, his bayonet caught the lamplight, the mist came up over the terrace to his feet. The damp air held the music from every quarter suspended, a skeleton of music above an autumnal decay.

On the North Bridge Krogh turned up the collar of his coat. The mist blew round him. The restaurant below the bridge was closed, the glass shelters ran with moisture, and a few potted palms pressed dying leaves towards the panes, the darkness, the moored steamers. Autumn was early; it peeled like smoke from the naked thighs of a statue. But officially it was summer still (Tivoli not yet closed), in spite of cold and wind and soaked clay and the umbrellas blowing upwards round the stone Gustavus. An old woman scurried by dragging a child, a girl student in her peaked cap stepped out of the way of a taxi creeping up the kerb, a man pushed a hot chestnut cart up the slope of the bridge towards him.

DET LITTERÄRA STOCKHOLM

"*Regnet hade upphört, en östlig vind drev molnen i grå flockar över Mälaren, och solstrålar klatschade till Slottets, Riksdagshusets och Operans våta stenblock. Motorbåtarna som passerade under Norrbro piskade upp skum som vinden fångade och kastade som ett fint regn mot den tomma restaurangens glasveranda. Den nakne mannen på sin våta, blänkande piedestal stirrade över svallet av småvågor bort mot Grand Hôtel, med baken vänd mot bron och trafikanterna.*"

Ur romanen "De skeppsbrutna", 1954
Av Graham Greene, 1905-1991.
Graham Greene är en av de många utländska
författare som har skildrat Stockholm.

A literary plaque on Stockholm's Norrbro (North Bridge) with a quotation from Graham Greene's England Made Me, *describing the view from the bridge on a rainy, early autumn afternoon.*

He could see the lights in the square balconied block where he had his flat on the Norr Mälarstrand. The breadth of Lake Mälaren divided him from the workmen's quarters on the other bank. From his drawing-room window he could watch the canal liners arriving from Gothenburg with their load of foreign passengers. They had passed the place where he was born, they emerged at dusk unobtrusively from the heart of Sweden, from the silver birch woods round Lake Vätten [sic], the coloured wooden cottages, the small landing stages where the chickens pecked for worms in soil spread thinly over rock. Krogh, the internationalist, who had worked in factories all over America and France, who could speak English and German as well as he could speak Swedish, who had lent money to every European government, watched them of an evening sidle in to moor opposite the City Hall with a sense of something lost, neglected, stubbornly alive.

Krogh turned away from the waterside. The shops in the Fredsgatan were closed; there were few people about. It was too cold to walk, and Krogh looked round for a taxi. He saw a car up the narrow street on the right and paused at the corner. The trams shrieked across Tegelbacken, the windy whistle of a train came over the roofs. A car travelling too fast to be a taxi nearly took the pavement where Krogh stood, and was gone again among the trams and rails and lights in Tegelbacken, leaving behind an impression of recklessness, the sound of an explosion, a smell. In a side street a taxi-driver started his car and ambled down to the corner where Krogh stood. The explosion of the exhaust brought back Lake Vätten and the wild duck humming upwards from the reeds on heavy wings. He raised his oars and sat still while his father fired; he was hungry and his dinner depended on the shot. The rough bitter smell settled over the boat, and the bird staggered in the air as if cuffed by a great hand.

'Taxi, Herr Krogh.'

It might have been a shot, Krogh thought, if this were America, and he turned fiercely on the taxi-driver: 'How do you know my name?'

The man watched him with an air wooden and weather-worn. 'Who wouldn't know you, Herr Krogh? You aren't any different from your pictures.'

The bird sank with beating wings as if the air had grown too thin to support it. It settled and lay along the water. When they reached it, it was dead, its beak below the water, one wing submerged like an aeroplane broken and abandoned.

'Drive me to the British Legation,' Krogh said.

He lay back in the car and watched the faces swim up to the window through the mist, recede again. They flowed by in their safe and happy anonymity on the way to the switch-backs in Tivoli, the cheap seats in cinemas, to love in quiet rooms. He drew down the blinds and in his dark reverberating cage tried to think of numerals, reports, contracts.

A man in my position ought to have protection, he told himself, but police protection had to be paid for in questions. They would learn of the American monopoly which even his direc-tors believed to be still in the stage of negotiation; they would learn too much of a great many things, and what the police knew one day the Press too often knew the next. It came home to him that he could not afford to be protected. Paying the driver off, he felt his isolation for the first time as a weakness.

He could hear the siren of a steamer on the lake and the heavy pounding of the engines. Voices came through the mist muffled, the human heat damped down, like the engines of a liner flooded and foundering.

2

Krogh was not a man who analysed his feelings: he could only tell himself: 'On such and such an occasion I was happy; now I am miserable.' Through the glass door he could see the English man-servant treading sedately down marble stairs.

He was happy in Chicago that year.

'Is the minister in?'

'Certainly, Herr Krogh.'

Up the stairs at the servant's heels: he was happy in Spain. His memories were quite unconcerned with women. He thought: I was happy that year, and remembered the small machine no larger than his suitcase that began to grind upon the table of his lodgings, how he watched it all the evening, eating nothing, drinking nothing, and how all night he lay on his back unable to sleep, only able to repeat over and over again to himself: 'I was right. There's no serious friction.'

'Herr Erik Krogh.'

The room was full of women, and he experienced no pleasure at the way they watched the door with curiosity and furtive avidity (the richest man in Europe), their faces old and unlined and pencilled in brilliant colours, like the illumination of an ancient missal carefully preserved under glass with the same page always turned to visitors. The Minister attracted elderly women. He was absorbed now by the little silver spirit-lamp under the kettle (he always poured out the tea himself), and a moment later, after a nod to Krogh, he was picking up slices of lemon in a pair of silver tweezers.

'This is a great day, Mr Krogh,' a hawk-like woman said to him. He had often met her at the Legation and believed that she was some relative of the Minister's, but her name eluded him.

'A great day?'

'The new book of poems.'

'Ah, the new book of poems.'

She took his arm and led him to a fragile Chippendale table in a corner of the room furthest from where the Minister poured out tea. All the room was Chippendale and silver; quite alien to Stockholm it was yet like a cultured foreigner who could speak the language fairly well and had imbibed many of the indigenous restraints and civilities, but not enough of them to put Krogh at his ease.

'I don't understand poetry,' he said reluctantly. He did not like to admit that there was anything he did not understand; he preferred to wait until he had overheard an expert's opinion which he might adopt as his own, but one glance at the room had told him that here he would wait in vain. The elderly women of the English colony twittered like starlings round the tea-table.

'The Minister will be so disappointed if you don't look.'

Krogh looked. A photograph of de Laszlo's portrait faced the title-page: the sleek silver hair, the rather prudish quizzing eyes netted by wrinkles, the small round appley cheeks. '*Viol and Vine*.'

'*Viol and Vine*', Krogh said. 'What does that mean?'

'Why,' said the hawk-eyed woman, 'the viola da gamba, you know, and – and wine.'

'I always find English poetry very difficult,' Krogh said.

'But you must read a little of it.' She thrust the book into his hands and he obeyed her with the deep respect he reserved for foreign women, standing stiffly at attention with the book held at a little distance almost on the level of his eyes – 'To the Memory of Dowson' – and heard behind him the Minister's voice tinkling among the china.

* * *

It was true. He was not cut off in the white-panelled room, behind the vase of autumn roses; his prosperity was like a studied insult. He has not asked me to sit down, he is afraid for his tapestry chairs because my coat's a little wet. 'A dinner's a good thing,' Minty repeated, filling up time while he thought of some story, some joke, some rumour to leave the Minister less happy than he found him.

He said: 'I saw your book was reviewed in the *Manchester Guardian*.'

'No,' the Minister said, 'no. Really. What did they say? I never read reviews.'

'I don't read poetry,' Minty said. 'I only saw the headline: "A Long Way After Dowson". Did you say,' he went on quickly, 'that you'd been buying some of the new Krogh stock? You ought to be careful. There are rumours about.'

'What do you mean? Rumours . . . '

'Ah, Minty gets to hear a thing or two. They say there was nearly a strike at the factory.'

'Nonsense,' the Minister said. 'Krogh was here at tea. He advised me to buy.'

'Yes, but where did he go afterwards? That's what every-one's asking. Did he have a telephone call?'

'He had two.'

'I thought so,' Minty said.

'I bought a good deal of the last issue,' the Minister said.

'Well, well,' Minty said, 'there are rumours. Nothing that you can get hold of. They may send the price down a little, of course, but you can't expect every flutter to turn out well. Besides, you're a poet. You don't understand these things.' Minty chuckled.

'What are you laughing at?'

'"A long way after Dowson",' Minty said. 'You can't deny that's neat. Trust me always to tell you things. A diplomat can't be expected to know what's happening in the streets. But trust Minty.' He dripped his way towards the door. 'I'm always ready to help a fellow from the old school.'

In the long white passage he paused under the portraits of Sir Ronald's predecessors; in their ruffs, in their full-bot-tomed wigs, painted by local artists, they had a touch of un-English barbarity, a slant about the eyes purely Scandinavian, their breast-plates obscured by furs. Behind a Stuart courtier could be seen a pair of reindeer and a landscape of mountain and ice. It was only the later portraits which bore no national mark at all. Wearing official dress, knee-breeches and medals and ribbons, these models represented an art international-ized at the level of Sargent and De Laszlo. They were much admired, Minty knew, by Sir Ronald who would soon join them on the wall, and an unusual tenderness mingled in Minty's brain with the more usual bitterness, a tenderness for the framed men in wigs who had indeed been cut off, though not so completely cut off as he was cut off, a tenderness for the paintings which Sir Ronald called 'curious'. He walked gently to the door, leaving a trail of damp footmarks down the silver grey carpet, and let himself out.

The rain had stopped, an east wind drove the clouds in grey flocks above Lake Mälaren, and darts of sunlight flicked the wet stones of the palace, the opera house, the House of Parliament. The motor-boats passing under the North Bridge scattered spray which the wind caught and flung like fine rain against the glass shelters of the deserted restaurant. The naked man on his wet gleaming pedestal stared out over the tumble of small waves towards the Grand Hotel, his buttocks turned to the bridge and passers-by.

Minty went into a telephone-box and rang up Krogh's. He said to the porter: 'Is Herr Krogh still at the office? It's Minty speaking.'

'Yes, Herr Minty. He hasn't gone out.'

'Is he going to the Opera tonight?'

'He hasn't ordered his car yet.'

'Get me Herr Farrant on the phone if you can.'

He waited for a long while, but he was not impatient. On the dusty glass of the box he drew little pictures with his finger, several crosses, a head wearing a biretta.

'Hullo. Is that Farrant? This is Minty speaking.'

'I've just been out buying glad rags,' Anthony said. 'Shoes, socks, ties. We're for the Opera tonight.'

'You and Krogh?'

'Me and Krogh.'

Malcolm Bradbury

from *To the Hermitage*

One (Now)

SO: WHERE'S THE PLACE? Stockholm, Sweden's fine watery capital, laid out on a web of islands at the core of the great archipelago. Time of day? Middle to late morning. Month? Let's see, the start of October, 1993. How's the weather? Cool, overcast, with bright sunny periods and occasional heavy showers. Who's coming on the journey? I think it's best to wait a bit and see.

The fact is that the Swedish summer season – the super-physical, island-hopping, boat-building, skinny-dipping, crayfish-eating, love-feasting, hyper-elated phase of this nation's always rich and varied manic cycle – is reaching its dank autumnal end. Smart white tourboats with perspex carapaces still cruise the narrow canals of Stockholm's Gamla Stan, the Old Town. Noisy guides are megaphoning out their wonderfully gruesome tales of the Swedish Blood-bath. But now they are not very many, just an end-of-season few. On the ruffled waves of the city's inner harbours, dinghies with multi-coloured sails tack back and forth, hither and thither, up and down. But this is positively their final flurry; they'll all be winched out of the water and put into dry dock in a matter of a few more weeks or days.

In the neat windswept parks that surround the harbour, the leaves flop wetly, the last open-air coffee or sausage stalls are starting to hammer down their shutters. Here and there groups of men – some sporting summer shirts, but most in puffed-out winter anoraks – play chess with man-sized pieces. Small crowds of children and various time-wasting persons, walking little dogs, gather round as they menace black with white. On the benches, at the few final tables left outside the few final cafés, hopeful people sit with their chins elevated. Blank-faced, mystical, they're staring at the sky, hopeful of gathering a last sight of that most precious of all the northern treasure hordes, the sun. Aware of just how desirable it is, the sun keeps showing and then going, in a sequence of short sexy glimpses: now you see me, now you don't. It drops patches of gold dazzle onto the green-brown copper roofs and spires that cap and crown the grandiose national buildings over the water, the buildings of a big old empire: the Swedish Royal Palace, the Storkyrkan Cathedral, the Parliament Building. A bit further over in the panorama is the modernist City Hall, where the Nobel Prizes are awarded to the sound of a gunshot intended to celebrate Sweden's two most noted gifts to humanity: the sweet dream of universal peace, the big bang of dynamite.

A brooding Nordic gloom wafts through the air. Euphoria is over, winter depression starting. Yet why? Everything here is so neat, so satisfying, so wealthyish, so burgherish. Civic, that surely has to be the word. Everything suggests a common social virtue, a universal sobriety of mind, a decent respect for order, an open-faced moral clarity. Just democracy, expressive simplicity – the things of which so many people have dreamed. You'll find the same spirit everywhere you go. For instance, in the small clean efficiently modern bedroom of my nice little hotel on Storgatan, which looks out across the courtyard into the small clean efficiently modern rooms of innumerable well-fitted apartments. Both bedroom and bathroom are packed with gentle philosophical instructions – inspirations to citizenship and virtue, all couched in the liberal language of secular religiosity. 'Please help us save the world. In Sweden we love our beautiful lakes and seas and wish to protect them. Use only official soaps, and use your towels for at least two days.' 'Condoms and the Holy Bible are provided in your bedside drawer, for your physical and spiritual content and protection. Please make use of them with the compliments of the management.'

As I walk round, everything is like this. Liberal, simple, decent, without irony. The streets are clean, straight, neat, tidy. The food: crisp, clean, fresh, fishy. The coffee: dark, scented, thick, excellent. The air: brisk, sharp, pure, windy. Quality rules, yet not ostentation. It's the middle way. Nothing is too pompous, or too tacky; too blatantly conservative, or too vulgarly radical. This exactly matches what the Swedes like to say about themselves: nothing too little, nothing too much. There is plenty of wealth, but how very quietly it's spent. In the smart shopping streets the well-dressed shoppers stroll. Dark-coloured Saabs and leather-seated Volvos swish by. The cars have their lights on, the drivers have their belts on. The litres may be many, but the petrol's lead-free and the pace is sober; in fact everyone drives at a blatantly considerate, a truly *civic* sort of speed. The elegant pedestrians – tall girls in their leather thigh-boots, healthy men in their loden topcoats, universal cyclists theatrical in their arrowed helmets and Day-Glo Lycra (always in Sweden there are these reminders that it is healthy to be healthy) – stop, with the same consideration, to let them pass. Then suddenly, thanks not to some officious red light but to justice, reason, fairness and decency, the vehicles all stop in their turn. Whereat, with just the same polite consideration, the pedestrians and the Lycra cyclists, carefully, appreciatively, cross the road to the other side.

The crisp smart goods in the stores are just as well ordered, just as considerate. Don't imagine it was some chic fifties Swedish modernist with a doctorate in design from Paris who invented all these bleached white woods, pure colours, honest straight lines that deck the smart lofts of the known world. Swedish style was born from the Swedish soul: nature, the outdoors, the woods, winds, sea, rocks, spray, all of it shaped into function by the piney, craft-loving, ship-building, homesteading old Nordic soul. Look at it. Those carpentered chairs – so straight-lined and thoughtful. Those handmade tables – so crafted, sturdy, square-edged, crisp-grained. Those woven fabrics – bright yet so restrained. Everything modest, homely, truthful, under-stated. Yet, lest some unfortunate misunderstanding occur, all this simplicity is expensive beyond belief – especially if you're a wandering foreign tourist like myself.

But, as I'm discovering, the most expensive thing in this decent, pleasant, unpretentious liberal country is money itself. I'm in a bank in a clean tree-filled square at Storgatan, just up the hill above the harbour. An exceedingly nice bank – plain, modern, open-plan, white, computerized, smelling of fresh coffee, filled with nice people. So nice I know something is missing: the demonic rage of money, the danger of coin, not to say the angled security cameras, bullet-proof screens and Kalashnikov-toting guards that modern banking needs. The Land of the Bears is, I recall, famous for its banking. It went with a central role in the Hanseatic League, the mastery of Baltic trade, the role of financier of European wars. If my imperfect memory is right, it was Sweden that devised the notion of the national bank. Above all, it went with a decent supply of the things money is made of: minerals and paper. To use the mineral reserves of the Upplands, the Swedes dispensed with precious metals and invented the decent plain democratic copper coin: a great invention when you wanted a loaf of bread, though if you wanted to buy something really expensive – one of those Swedish tables, for example – you had to go out shopping not with a purse but a horse and cart.

So why (I'm asking myself) am I having so much trouble in performing a normal economic transaction, a simple act of rates of exchange? I've come to this handsome blonde bank because I want to change English pounds for American dollars. In the world of money it's a normal, rational request. At a handsome blonde desk a handsome blonde teller sits, tapping away at her handsome computer console. Like everyone else I've met since I flew into Arlanda airport this morning, she's serious, kind, courteous – civic, that has to be the word. That is the Swedish way. The Land of the Bears has always felt a bit like an enlightened Islington primary school, with tundra. First she asks me for my papers. Passport. Driving licence. Travel insurance. Health insurance. Social security number. Fine: I have paper, therefore I am. She enquires about the *traffik*, the *devise*, the *curso*, the *cambio*, the change I'm after. How will I pay? I hand her a splendid walletful: Visa, American Express, Diner's, Barclaycard, Master Charge, British Airways Executive Club. I have plastic, therefore I shop. But not, it seems, in modern Sweden.

'*Nej, nej,*' she says.

I offer bankcard, chargecard, Eurocard. I flash a gold this, wave a silver that. I lean forward against her scented blonde hair and murmur a splendid little secret: my pin number.

'*Nej, nej,*' she says, staring at me bemused, 'if you would like money, you must give me some money first.'

'But this is money,' I say. 'Money as we now know it.'

'*Nej, nej,* not in Sweden,' she says. 'This is not money, it's credit. I need good money. Don't you have proper English pounds?'

I look at her amazed. The year, as we've said, is 1993. This is a highly advanced nation. A glorious new millennium is to hand. Then, if computers don't crash and planes fall from the sky in the great turnover of numbers, we will all become part of Euro-Europe; that will be the end of the old age of rates of exchange. Francs will fade, Deutschmarks dissolve, escudos expire, lire lapse, the krona will crash. Even the great British pound will pass away, as in their season all good things pass away.

I for one will mourn its passing, shed a big wet fiscal tear. I madly love coin and currency, paper and print, guineas and guilders, sovereigns and sovereignties, ducats and crowns, farthings and forints, *cambio* and *curso*, cash and carry. True, here in 1993, Sweden has still not yet elected to join the European Community, but we all know it's just a matter of time. And true, with all those fir trees in the forests, all that paper in the papermills, all that copper in the Upplands, it has a vested interest in money as it always was and should be. But Sweden is modern, paper money isn't. Still, if that's what she wants, that's what she'll have. Money, yes, I remember I had some once. I dig deep into my wallet, and there it is: a small wad of British notes for general circulation. George Stevenson – Mr Puffing Billy – in his stovepipe hat looks proudly out from the fives. Charles Dickens, creator of one of the world's greatest fictional galleries of speculators and peculators, looks out from the twirls of the tens. Michael Faraday, who invented the electrical lighthouse, guards the security of the twenties. The Queen is present. Nothing could be more reliable.

'Will this do?' I ask.

'*Jo, jo*, tip top, *tack, tack*,' says the teller, smiling, taking and counting them.

There's quite a long line of people standing behind me now. But this is decent liberal Sweden, so nobody murmurs, and no one complains. The teller tip-taps her computer; presently she hands me a fresh wad of notes.

'*Tack, tack*,' I say, and look. They're Swedish kronor, elegant and colourful, not what I wanted at all. '*Nej, nej*,' I say. 'It's not right. I want American dollars.'

'*Jo, jo*, dollars, *tack, tack*,' says the teller, taking the notes back. She checks them carefully, to make sure I have not done them a mischief, returns them to the drawer, tip-taps her computer. The line behind me has grown longer, reaching into the street. Nobody utters, nobody shows the slightest impatience. The teller reaches into her drawer again, counts out a few crisp American greenbacks, and hands them to me.

'*Tack, tack*,' I say.

I look. And I look again. This wad seems curiously small. In a matter of minutes, a hundred British pounds have traded into forty American dollars, a very remarkable rate of exchange.

'I gave you a hundred, you gave me forty,' I complain. The line of people waits.

'*Jo, jo,*' says the teller.

'It can't be right.'

'*Jo, jo,* it's right,' she says. 'Tax. You made three changes. Each time you pay a tax.'

'I didn't make three changes, you did.'

'But in Sweden everything is changed through the krona.'

'Why is it changed through the krona?'

'Of course, so you can pay all the tax.'

Now in Istanbul or Athens, even in London's Edgware Road, this would look extremely suspicious. But this is Sweden: the higher society, the moral kingdom, the land of liberalism and utter honesty. I glance round. The line behind me reaches right across the street and is blocking the traffic; in fact this part of Stockholm has come to a total standstill. No horns bleep, nobody utters, no one even coughs.

'I don't want to pay the tax.'

'Everyone likes to pay tax.'

The teller smiles at me, the line of people behind me nod in agreement, all with that beautiful, open, Swedish reassurance that tells me money belongs to none of us, is granted on loan to us from the mother state. So don't we feel that much more human and decent, that much more . . . civic, when we know we're being swingeingly taxed?

Now what, you could fairly ask, am I doing here, in the world's most moral kingdom, trafficking British pounds for American greenbacks? Sweden lies on no familiar route from Britain to America. But America's not where I'm going – or not for many pages yet. In any case America long ceased trading in greenbacks. Even plastic is nearly finished; money in America is already virtual money, post-money, non-specie; it's plastic, smart chip, computer debit, electronic cash. But I'm on my way to the true land of the Almighty Dollar, the real nation of the greenback, at the far end of the Baltic: the CRS, what's left of the Russian Union and the great empire of the tzars. To prepare my journey I have carefully read, on the morning flight over from Stansted, a book by a famous eighteenth-century traveller there, the ubiquitous Comte de Ségur, French ambassador to Catherine the Great just before the French Revolution – which to her eternal disgust and dismay he warmly supported, at least for a while.

Even at that date, he was struck by the unusual nature of the Russian economy. 'Here one must forget the rules of finance one learns in other countries,' he noted. 'The mass of banknotes, the realization that there are no reserves to back them, the use of strange and unusual coinages, the kind of thing that in other lands would bring immediate collapse or revolution, here cause no surprise at all. The great Empress Catherine could, I've no doubt, turn leather into money should she wish.' Well, *plus ça change*; as it was, so it is now. To this day the rouble is a strange, only part-convertible currency, a set of roguish numbers, a con man's fancy that has never truly replaced barter in silks and camels, icons, part-worn dresses, Turkish drugs, old lampshades, surplus nuclear missiles, loaves and fishes, live or dead souls. In the hard heyday of Communism, the special shops for the nomenklatura traded, of course, in dollars – which then generally drifted westward to Switzerland or bought fine real estate in Nice. Now, in the fine new free-market era, when the nomenklatura prefers to see itself as the mafia, no smart Russian hotelier, sommelier, blackmailer, bribe-taker or capitalist oligarch would dream of trading in anything else. Avoid the rouble; it's dollars or nothing. That's what all the hardened travellers say.

And, someone has carefully warned me, it's best to carry your dollars into the country with you. These days nobody in Russia knows what money is worth; they just know it's a mad and ridiculous invention no one can get enough of. That's why it will be difficult to make a fair and reliable exchange in the grand and noble banks of Petersburg, and probably not even on the Russian ferry I'm booked on and which will be taking me there tomorrow night. Which is precisely why I'm standing here in the blonde bank at Storgatan, evidently rescuing without knowing it the entire Swedish tax system and it's fine welfare economy. I take my tiny wad of dollars and stuff them in my pocket.

'*Tack, tack,*' says the blonde teller, looking at me ever so sweetly.

'*Tack, tack,*' I say just as sweetly back, and walk out: out of the nice blonde bank into the fine bourgeois air; past the patient unending line of stalled philosophical customers which now extends almost as far as the harbour; into the tree-filled square at Storgatan, now completely gridlocked with polite Volvos, feeling different, poorer, wiser on the instant, as, for some reason, foreign travellers often say they do . . .

Modern English-Language Poets

Seamus Heaney

Ales Stenar [1*]

High summer. On the hilltop
The stone ship lies becalmed. Larks
Sing at the masthead.

from *Beowulf* [2]

Death of a Swedish King

Nor do I expect peace or pact-keeping
of any sort from the Swedes. Remember:
at Ravenswood, Ongentheow
slaughtered Heathcyn, Hrethel's son,
when the Geat people in their arrogance
first attacked the fierce Shylfings.
He kept hard on the heels of the foe
and drove them, leaderless, lucky to get away,
in a desperate rout into Ravenswood.
His army surrounded the weary remnant
as they nursed their wounds.

           All night
he howled threats at those huddled Geats,
boasted he would axe their bodies open
once dawn broke, dangle them from gallows
as food for birds. But at first light

when their spirits were lowest, relief arrived.
They heard the sound of Hygelac's horn,
his trumpet calling as he came to find them,
the hero in pursuit, at hand with troops.

The bloody swathe that Swedes and Geats
cut through each other was everywhere.
No one could miss their murderous feuding.
Then the old man made his move,
pulled back, barred his people in:
Ongentheow withdrew to higher ground.
Hygelac's pride and prowess as a fighter
were known to him; he had no confidence
that he could hold out against that horde of seamen,
defend his wife and the ones he loved
from the shock of the attack. He retreated for shelter
behind the earthwall.

                    Hygelac swooped
on the Swedes at bay, his banners swarmed
into their refuge, his Geat forces
drove forward to destroy the camp.
Ongentheow, aged, grey-haired man,
was cornered, ringed around with swords.
And it came to pass that the king's fate
was in Eofor's hands, and in his alone.
Wulf, son of Wonred, went for him first,
split him open so that blood came spurting
from under his hair. Still the old hero
did not flinch, but parried fast,
hit back with a harder stroke:
the king turned and took him on.
Wonred's son, the brave Wulf,
could land no blow against the aged lord.
Ongentheow divided his helmet
so that Wulf buckled and bowed his bloodied head

and dropped to the ground. But his doom held off.
Though he was cut deep, he recovered again.

With his brother down, the undaunted Eofor,
Hygelac's thane, hefted his sword
and smashed murderously at the massive helmet
past the lifted shield. And the king collapsed,
the shepherd of his people was sheared of life.

(lines 2923–2981)
translated by Seamus Heaney

Paul Durcan

The 24,000 Islands of Stockholm

How you do pontificate
About the politics
Of Stockholm –
About how too sedate,
Too predictable
Are the politics of Stockholm;
How the politics of Stockholm
Are like the citizens of Stockholm,
Too rational, too clinical.

On, on, you sermonise
About the Swedish Academy;
How the waters are awash
With bobbing condoms.
I doubt – but keep
The thought to myself –
That condoms 'bob',
Whatever their content
Or lack of content.

Have you nothing to say
About the islands –
The 24,000 islands of Stockholm?
Nothing?
About even, say, a single skerry?
A rock, a pine, a hut?
Nothing?
Not even about one of them?
One of the 24,000
Islands of Stockholm?

Nothing about skimming
With forefinger and thumb
Water-rolled slivers
Of infant granite?
Nothing about how oaks
Can conceive in crevices
On a rock in the Baltic?
Nothing about why
A man and a woman
Might choose to be sparse
On an island in Stockholm?
Nothing about how the Bergman
Question posed by the Garden
Of Eden is whether a human
Can handle leisure or not?
About the origin of deprivation?
About whether or not
The Goth has got it right
In the islands of Stockholm –
In the 24,000
Islands of Stockholm?

Ronald Bottrall[3]

Nordica

Here I stand on the northern outcrop
Stony for the ploughman, hard for the lumberjack,
Dry light feathering through the birches,
The sun's stroke oblique across the water,
A crayfish moon hanging like a red lantern
Over the churches preserved in an open-air museum
Over the gigantic palaces symmetrically opposed
To grotesque limbs of trolls and ogres.

I have turned my walk back
To latitudes of bitter memory
And waste-wood avenues tracking
Leaf and twig now an obsolete page
Or a fertile mould of years.

On the street men shuffle forward
From the cafeterias and the stainless steel
Snuffing enviously after
The never-to-be bargain in the ever-lost world,
Moving on the cloud of a cigar
From rack to pinion, hurl'd
On the rotation of their daily wheel.
The flaxen women wed and tread
Uneasily from bed to bed,
Craving the triumph of the freeing kiss
Over stylised gesture and boiled shirt.
The hum of generators and saws
Stuns the brash fluttering of heart
To heart, and enlightened laws
Enforce the cleft between love and deed.
The unspoken word, word to end wars,
Beats bloodily against the bars,

Fettered in anguish within the wall
Of its own skull.

Born of the soil they live earthy
Big-handed, heavy-footed,
Mouth to earth even
When silted up in the mud of cities.
Within them, flesh and name, are
Branch and leaf, lake and cataract.
Clothed in the woods, wood is their beverage.
And yet
Life is on a knife-edge
Staggering with raw feet
And the air flickers with sharp witch-wings.

Flying like a song over hilltop and stream
Is the blood of rovers cruelly spilt
Running like a rune in a dream
Heaving with madness and guilt;
The echo of death from the crowding sea.

Birth too is fierce and bloody
Whether in the hovel or in the fashionable recess
Of rectilinear and stream-lined cells.
Sap will rise for a time in the uprooted tree
But there is no new birth
In the rustic chair or the home-woven carpet,
No salvation in complacency with present hells
Or yearnings for past Valhallas.
Old strength lurks dark in the forests
Where sap is bubbling from deep wells
And in the liberating lonelinesses
Of waterfalls among the high fells;
Within the whirling daily round
Renewal is electric

In the radiant pressure of hand on hand
And the healing word springing to the quick.

Carol Rumens[4]

Swedish Exchange

When we entered the room it was white. The lampshade was
blue, circular, patterned with circular holes. A white half-
curtain at the window was printed with ellipses of different
colours. There was a flat mirror in a wooden frame that was
curved, lending the glass a faint concavity. A whitewood table
and two chairs. A red mat.

We made the red mat dirty. On the table we put a glass of
lilies-of-the-valley: they had cost thirty *kronor* on a street
corner somewhere near the Klara church. The woman who
sold them said: you must give them cold water! There is a
blue dictionary on the table containing 30,000 *ord och fraser*
and, on the window-sill, a lime-green tennis-ball containing
a finite but unknown number of bounces. The mirror is full
of badly hung clothes. Light sometimes leaks from the lampshade holes, the chairs refuse to sit at the table.

To make the room simple again we will have to leave it. We
ourselves will have to re-complicate. This is a pity. We'd like
to leave the room not as we found it but as we made it,
impressed with our favourite transfers. The room would be
grateful. And we would be white, clean, with natural wood
features and a few splashes of primary colour, an excellent
design for the modern human. We would close the door and
not invite ourselves back in.

Stockholm Haiku

For Eleanor Wikborg

*

motorway bank
– a family of violets
spreads its picnic

*

wind-flowers
– too white, too still –
moon-flowers

*

surprise picnic-guest
– one pine-tree's shadow

Kings of the Playground

All to get the Bully – who hid in a steel-clad cupboard –
The Bully Bashers stormed the trembling school.
They bullied the Bully's kit, his grubby blazer,
His sports-bag, his bully-beef flavour crisps.

They bullied the kids with the bruises
That showed the Bully's shoe-print.
They bullied the gerbils he'd teased, they bullied each
    computer
He'd slimed with his bully virus.

They bullied the prefects and teachers –
The nice ones first, then the bullies.
The kids who had conduct stars, the kids in detention, even
The football team, they bullied, yelling 'Ya bullyin' fairies!'

They bullied the books, though the Bully didn't like books:
They bullied the white-boards and black-boards,
They bullied the wall-charts, the registers, the sick-notes,
The pass-notes. They bullied the two-times table.

Then they thundered out and bullied the empty playground,
They bullied the big round sky that covered the playground,
They bullied the rain, the bushes, the used needles,
The trembling waiting parents, the tiny brothers and sisters.

Bully TV was launched. There was only one programme:
'How we Bashed the Bully.' Anyone who switched off
Was sentenced to 25 years community-bullying.
The Bully Bashers relaxed. Gave themselves medals. Flew
    home.

The Bully listened a while, and grinned in the dark cupboard.
He combed his hair. He opened the door wide.
He sauntered through the wrecked assembly hall.
Scared faces turned. Eyes that remembered his bruises

Clouded over, younger eyes grew shiny.
Suddenly someone shouted, 'Look, the Bully!
Them liars didn't get him! Three cheers for our Bully!'
And everyone yelled and stamped: 'Three cheers for old
    Bully!'

Old Bully mounted the stage. How tall he was,
What a lovely speech he made! The big boys lifted him high
And they all stormed into the trembling streets, yelling
'Make way for Old Bully, ya cunts!' And the people did.

Hugh MacDiarmid

Ballad of Aun, King of Sweden [5]

Surely Hell burns a deeper blue
With each noble boast of men like you.

With each noble boast of men like you
– Such men as all but all men it's true.

See what I'm doing for England, you cry,
Or for Christendom, civilization, or some other lie.

And no one remembers the story of Aun,
The Swedish king, who sent son after son

To death, buying with each another span
Of life for himself, the identical plan
All governments, all patriots, self-righteously pursue.
How many sons have *you* given, and *you*, and *you*?

Nine sons in succession was the grim
Record of Aun, till the people rose and slew *him*.

But when will the people rise and slay
The ubiquitous Aun of State Murder to-day?

Realizing murder is foulest murder no matter
What individual or body for what end does the slaughter!

Alan Brownjohn

Avalanche Dogs

At a whistling instruction from its trainer,
The little dog leapt at the large bank of snow,
Sniffed and barked and scratched, and its trainer helped it,
And through a hole they made the crowd could see
A face, that soon turned out to be Mrs Sundquist's.

My cat, and all my previous cats, have warned me
Against giving undue respect to any dog
Or credence to its talents. Did I listen too much?
This dog was thrown things for showing off its flair,
Though not many people seemed to value the sacrifice

Donated by Mrs Sundquist, who was covered
With snow again for a second dog to find her
– All this being done to show the ability
Of avalanche dogs to get Mrs Sundquist,
Or you or me perhaps, out of mountain snows,

In this case in the Lapland Arctic region,
Where every husky in the dog-sled teams
Knows left from right . . . And a third dog, and a fourth,
Mrs Sundquist being buried and reburied
Time and time again in the square outside People's House,

And people applauding the dogs, yet not Mrs Sundquist
When she finally came out from her hour-long incarceration
In the twilight drift.
                          I clapped my own soft gloves,
And one or two others took up the applause
– But which of us had brought anything to throw

To Mrs Anna Sundquist, dog's best friend?

Robyn Bolam[6]

Tobias and the Angel
from the painting attributed to Andrea del Verrocchio

In the pocket of my long, grey coat
Tobias is walking out with an angel
who is taller and broader than he is.
In one hand he grips a small scroll, and a string
which swings a fish along the inside of his thigh.
The angel catches the fish's eye or, perhaps,
what draws down the glance, is
a fingertip on top of that large, pale hand.

Tobias looks up expectantly, but has not yet
learnt a way of touching which is allowed.
His fresh-faced, feminine beauty fails to lift
angelic lids; his cloak, thrown up, makes
an ineffectual wing. He has not yet learnt
the nature of the journey. The angel strides, feet
strung only with the semblance of sandals.

Tobias's finger holds the stride in check:
the angel's red and black plumage rises –
they settle in a corner of my pocket.
In this city of fourteen islands it is easy
to think you are walking on water
at the heart of an archipelago
which has secularised its angels.

By the waters of Strömmen they walk briskly
along Kungsträdgården, taller than I am.
Gliding down a stairway through rock and water
to a train gusting light out of the darkness,
then staring from stained, faded seats –
any angels seem stranded on the surface.
What is the nature of the journey?

Roused by the movement of a fellow traveller,
I look up into a face which has no features.
Scars pucker in uneven pigments; eyes flit
to the exit for Valhallavägen. A downward glance,
coat flapping free as we begin to rise,
that large hand resting near to mine.
I reach out, but have not yet learnt
a way of touching which is allowed.

Two Springs

One north is not like another: one flight
north by northeast – under two hours
and I'm plunged back into winter;
snow still patches the dead ground.
The thermometer outside my window
reads two degrees when I mist the glass.

I know there are bluebells in England:
days ago, I walked through them
in a leafy wood. Here, trees are too bare
to imagine leaves – and the only blue
is a ship in the harbour, bigger than
millions of bluebells, blocking out a church
and a run of roofs with its cold bulk –
booming in the night, like a restless animal
taking sounds off Finland or Estonia.

Now we have rain from a grey sky
and the figures on the walkway,
half-way up a hillside, hurry,
walk stiffly, their eyes on the ground,
as if, by staring, they will warm it
and make the grass grow.

I live in eight tiers of single people,
draw the blinds when they do,
turn up the heat, boil a pot
on the stove to make some tea.
The radio tells me there are wolves
still – in Sweden. When the ship
booms again, I think I can hear them
calling down from the north
that winter is ending.

The Swedish Climate

Just yesterday, when the sun surprised us
by acting as if it had always been there,
and managed to trick a whole bed of croci
into opening before the middle of May,
we smiled in the streets, shed our ski jackets
and layers of clothing, phoned to say, 'Hej!
Come and have a beer. We're moored here in a bar
watching buds burst in the Djurgården trees.'
Today the temperature has dropped by
twenty degrees. Back in our coats, silent
in the rain, then underground, we have
Garbo faces: it's a serious business.
Our profiles lift to the distance.
We do not smile, want to be left alone,
as if we will risk abdicating our country
by riding the subway to New York or Rome.

Robin Fulton

Remembering an Island

'Island
what shall I say of you, your peat-bogs,
your lochs, your moors and berries?' Strange words
to remember on a Stockholm street-crossing – it's like
a dream where you find a door in a solid wall.

North-east, east and south-east
A top-heavy pile of thunderclouds,
west over Kungsholmen a glassy fire:
between, the city is a Dutch masterpiece,
still-life with evening traffic-flow.

And not a dream. I know where the walls end
and begin again. I touch doors on time.
The highland roads in my mind have been redeveloped –
a few old curves still visible, like
the creases in my birth-certificate from the thirties.

Dannie Abse

Blond Boys

In Stockholm
I saw my first shy love hobble by
hand in hand with her small blond grandson.

Eva Jones, remember me?
My acne. Your dimples.

When you rode your important Raleigh bike
to school, your skirt high,
I held my breath.
With heroic intensity of a fifteen year old,
dared by you, I climbed the glass-crowned wall
and stole Mrs Humphreys' summer apples.

Oh the forever of an August Sunday evening
when, near the back door's scent of delinquent
honeysuckle, forehead to forehead
I searched your searching eyes.

All the next week similitudes of love,
the jailer of reason until,

plain as the prose of a synopsis,
you bluntly said (with impressive sighs),
'You have a beautiful classy mind
but I find you physically unattractive –
and I prefer, um, blond boys besides.'

James Kirkup[8]
Swedish Exercises
The Dead Falls at Ragunda

This was where a river fell away
And left a useless fall of stones.
Where once a mountain flashed
With rushing water hangs today
A still cataract of rock, dead bones
Of an elemental life whose waters crashed
And stumbled with ungovernable force,
While over the black pine forest clouds of spray
Marked the continuous thunders of its own applause.

Now where the waters fountained trees have sprung,
Among the boulders stained with spreading sores
And rings of lichen, silver birches leap
Like phantoms of the spray that hung
And shivered with the smoke of catastrophic wars.
— But the dead falls only seem to sleep.
Under their arrested avalanches lie
Ancestral heroes, gods of the epic north, whose tongue
Lingers among the stillnesses, and cannot die.

Ice-hockey in Dalarna

The player's quilted shorts are red.
Padded shoulders and sweatered chest
    Appear to shrink that golden head.
He bears a different number from the rest.

    On booted skates he's tall.
Crimson stockings muscle knees and thighs
    And make his feet seem small.
Dark eyebrows draw a vizor on his eyes.

Over the open rink the forward leans and flies.
    He holds his stick in gauntlet clutch
And weaves the puck across the scoring ice.
    Like crabs the keepers in the goal-nets crouch.

Hard on the growling ice they thrust their blades,
    Scour the rink for danger and our rough delight.
Snow falls from the floodlights as the white sky fades,
    And captains shoot wet stars into the teeth of night.

In the Katarina Lift, Stockholm

The ground drops, the street lamps fall away
With the speed of divers slowly hurtling through
The sluices of the deep, flyover dark.
Gradually, with a decent readiness,
The city like a bride unfolds herself,
Her willingness made modest by the night
That yet more fervently reveals her fire,
Those radiating centres of desire,
The clustered lights of crossings,
The jewelled veins of squares and parks,
The looped ropes of doubled radiance down the lakes
On which the golden ferries burn
And move like hands intelligently down
The swan-clouded currents in the knocking ice
Whose opening and closing estuaries finally reflect
A distant fall of houses, every window bright.

Now, at the tower's top, and in the hanging
Gondola of stars we stand astride
The city of our admiration, she who lies
Profuse, and naked, passionate yet calm,
Inscrutably collected, in a brilliant pause
Before the swoop of love, the fall without a cause.

Gymnasium

The snowboots and the skis, the fur-lined hoods
That populate the coat-racks by the classroom door
Prepare me for an audience whose moods
Are those of warm relief and cold anxiety.
They have escaped the sharpness of the world outside.
Soon they must penetrate once more
The cruel street of ice, begin the homeward ride,
The battle with the snow, the wind's perplexity.

But for a moment all is warmth and light.
Pale-golden faces smile and laugh for me.
Their lips are pale, their perfect eyes are bright.
These boys are men with voices like the sea's.
Under the fragile desks their limbs are large,
Their laughter springs from huge
Good-nature that no winter night can freeze.
They are the giants of the forests that are men
Where legendary heroes lift their blond and massive
     heads again:
In their enormous hands a book
Tenderly flutters like captive birds,
And in their northern calmness is a generous look
Of level passion, stronger than any words.

Umeå

In the park emptied by winter
I tread the undistinguished paths of snow and dark.
The pale bandstand adrift on scrolls
Of wind-turned music, and the metal baskets
Packed with the overflowing wastes of snow
Are frozen ghosts of unimaginable summers.

A piled church warms the sky with orange brick.
The river shuffles neon alphabets of acid green.

– I do not care where paths begin and borders end,
But in the naked birch-grove that I saunter through
The snow's calm anarchy keeps off the grass
My steps that go where no one else has been.

Jämtland

The silver birch is papery, and veils
Its elbowed branches gloved with black
In a suspended shower of golden scales,
Its own slight leaves, that pattern a forest track
Like narrow starshine's riddled flakes
Or coins struck from the moonlight's hidden lakes.

A river is violet beneath the deep red clouds of dark.
The ash and aspen brandish sheaves
Of fireworks, each leaf a spark,
Along the forest's evergreen black eaves.
Rafts of logs lie on the sunset like an archipelago.
Mountains, pitched with pine, hang in the reeds below.

A green swan slings himself across the vacant air.
His rippling neck hauls on his feathered vanes.
Beyond the rowan drugged with berries, there
In a yellow sky along the lake he drags the water's reins,
Making the sheeted mirror flash and shake.
The washed reeds bow to the long processions of his wake.

He sails now among impenetrable mountains furred
    with larch,
Floats through the lake-reflected rainbow's double hoop
That frames the northern lightnings in its melting arch,
And over his own stern image seems to prowl and stoop;
While rosy distances of ice that draw him on
Still shiver through the birch-tree's page when he has gone.

To the Ancestral North

I

From that elemental land
Of iron whitenesses and long auroras
My Viking fathers sprang
In armoured nakedness.
The rock rang, and cold fire
Sparked at their striding heels.
Their prows plundered and struck the up-
Ending northern oceans with the smash
Of sword on stone, axe
Biting the pale flesh of the dark pines.
The wintered masts were holy,
Bore flame and fire from the gods,
And all Valhalla thundered in the mystic storm.

II

I love the archaic North,
The gothic loneliness,
The bare cathedral of the cold
Where, in the stunned ice,
The winter woods display
A stripped elegance, and frame the rare
Rose-window of the midnight sun.

III

There, in the blank fastnesses
Of frozen bays, on sands
Sheeted with stony ice,
By the frost-pleated firth, the glassy
Fjord scattered with ashes of snows;
Under the sea-mountain
In the wild moraine of stars

That haul the glazed oceans into heaps
Of shaggy ice, the ancestral ghosts
Of gods and heroes wander,
Melancholy, silent, and remote.

IV

O in the cold and grave and Carolingian forest,
In epic stillness, let me worship in their memory
The falling flake, the long
Larch grove, the lime-white lake
That burns in the trees' black lancets!

The twilight pauses like a stag at bay.
I hear a lost huntsman calling for a hidden castle.
And in the deserted valley
A sad horn echoes in a last, lingering *hallali*.

Raman Mundair[9]

Gamla Stan, 2001

In this part of the city you can turn
A corner and be in Venice,
Amsterdam or East Berlin
The man on the table next to me
Reads in Swedish to a woman
It sounds like he is singing, singing
His heart's truth to her
She receives the gift by moving closer,
Slipping off her shoes
And playing with his feet
Later in his ear she will whisper
Yes, yes, yes

The Transformation

Spring I am told is scheduled
For May 18th – We all wait
For someone to pull
The magic switch
That will transform this city green.
Outside my room, lithe yogic trees
Next door, a thin young man
Who wears black
Listens to dull song
And makes long phonecalls
Punctuated with a loud Ja! Ja! Ja!

Last night, it happened
Today the Sylla reach
Outstretched, open, open!
Like a book that reads
Joy! Joy! Joy!

Swedes open up like coy fans,
Shrug off winter and reveal
Bare flesh to the Sun
Who rewards worship with art
A grand collage
Using a transparent sheet of gold,
That covers all shades of pale
We now glisten and shimmy
Confident in our new attire

The True Bear Tale

The Bear came
from the North
looking for a mate.
We were all sentimental
watching the tv
reading the paper,
willing it to settle
find love.
For weeks it trekked,
we followed.
He travelled all the way down
South, almost crossed
the bridge.
And then, some trouble
With sheep, had to be
Shot. I cried. Dreamt
about him for weeks.

Partition Sketches I

A single line
Idly placed on a napkin
Fifty-four years ago

A seismic fault
That continues
To tremor

Partition Sketches II

May, in a modest flat in Sollentuna
A group of learned Indian and Pakistani
Men meet and excavate the details.

Waverley, Gandhi, Jinnah, Nehru
And Mountbatten bounce off the walls
In time with the retelling of the past

That created the present.
Families and fortunes torn
Apart in relation to the paper

Boundaries that poisoned the land
With li(n)es.
Fifty-four years later and the letters

Studied for in Indian and Pakistani
Universities account for worthless paper
Degrees, that turn exiled, educated men

Into part of the Swedish worker masses
Who now philosophize on the independence of India
As the May 1st evening draws to a close.

Skafferiet i Ekoparken, Stockholm

A little girl in pink
Watches me, no more
Than five years in age

And she has already learned
Not to smile back when I look
Up from my book and smile

At her. She holds my gaze
Steadily, and then walks away cool,
Disinterested, only to return again

With her eyes. I look down
And wonder if she sees me
As 'other'. Half an hour later

The light changes and beautiful,
Swedish, gay men gather in the sun and talk.
Tales of the troubles of bringing bananas

Through US immigration tickle my ears,
I smile and lean closer towards them.
My face lit up by the sun as one

Man began to speak of Swedish Immigration,
Where the more obviously looking Swedish
Are waved through, but he is always stopped

And questioned. 'But I shout at them,
"I am as Swedish as you!" His defiance
Touches me and I try to imagine

Shouting at the next UK immigration officer
That stops me when returning home.
'But it is safe to shout in Sweden, people listen'

The man declares and I wonder if he heard
My thoughts. I want to join their conversation.
A flash of pink catches my eye,

The little girl is back, goggle-eyed
I lean back and stretch, uncomfortable
Under the glare
Of the sun and try
To remember places
Where I belong.

W. H. Auden and Five Swedish Contemporaries

Dag Hammarskjöld[10]

from *Markings*

Tomorrow we shall meet,
Death and I –
And he shall thrust his sword
Into one who is wide awake.

But in the meantime how grievous the memory
Of hours frittered away.

*

The road,
You shall follow it.

The fun,
You shall forget it.

The cup,
You shall empty it.

The pain,
You shall conceal it.

The truth,
You shall be told it.

The end,
You shall endure it.

December 3, 1960

Haiku from 1959

Steep Swedish hills.
The coachman in front
Flicked the horse's sweating crupper.

*

Orgasms of bodies
On hot nights, lit
By flickers of summer lightning.

*

With a thrill of desire
His body sank, sun-drenched,
Into the salt wave.

translated by W. H. Auden and Leif Sjöberg[11]

Dag Hammarskjöld

Johannes Edfelt[12]

Summer Organ

Far beyond the scentless years
    the sacred aroma of summer:
cradling, intoxicating, gentle,
    it rose among the cherry-trees.

Far beyond the soundless years,
    the apple-tree's music:
the leafy tree-tops, swarming with bees
    were turned into organs then.

        translated by W. H. Auden and Leif Sjöberg

Harry Martinson[13]

The Cable Ship

On latitude 15 degrees North, longitude 61 degrees West,
between Barbados and Tortuga, we fished up the Atlantic
    cable,
held up our lanterns
and pasted fresh rubber over the wound in its back.
When we put our ears to the injured spot
we heard how it hummed inside.

One of us said:
'It is the millionaires in Montreal and Saint John who are
    speaking
about the price of sugar from Cuba and the lowering of our
    wages.'

Harry Martinson

In a circle of lanterns we stood there long and thought,
we patient cable fishermen,
then we lowered the mended cable
down to its home in the sea.

translated by W. H. Auden and Leif Sjöberg

Pär Lagerkvist[14]

Let My Shadow Disappear into Yours

Let my shadow disappear into yours.
Let me lose myself
under the tall trees,
that themselves lose their crowns in the twilight,
surrendering themselves to the sky and the night.

translated by W. H. Auden and Leif Sjöberg

Gunnar Ekelöf[15]

from *Dīvān over the Prince of Emgión*

In my dreams I heard a voice:
– Habīb, would you like this onion
Or just a slice of it?
At this I fell into great disquiet
This enigmatic question
Was the question of my life!
Did I prefer the part to the whole
Or the whole to the part
No, I wanted both
The part of the whole as well as the whole
And that this choice would involve no contradiction.

* * *

I speak to you
I speak of you
From deep within myself
I know that you do not answer
How could you answer
When so many are crying out to you!
All I ask is permission
To stand here waiting
And that you will give me a sign
From within myself of yourself!

translated by W. H. Auden and Leif Sjöberg

Swedish Writers on Britain

Per Wästberg[16]

Three-line poems with motifs from England

Country churches receive us like elderly aunts
long left unvisited. Nobody kneels before the altar
where thistledown eddies in the draught from the vestry.

*

Scraggy hawthorns in autumn's windfall light, a heather
    moor
facing seaward. Cows share the direction of our gaze.
AONB, the map's legend: Area of Outstanding Natural
    Beauty.

*

The Ashmolean Museum makes no connections. It
    celebrates
The Curiosity: poison phials made from turtle earbone,
    dragons' teeth,
shaving knives from Babylon, marten fur to warm the hands
    of nuns.

                              translated by Sarah Death

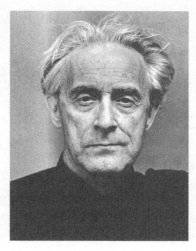

Werner Aspenström

Werner Aspenström[17]

What I noticed in London

A crumpled wind-cheater,
a man of indeterminate appearance
nailed to a concrete pavement-square
as if fenced in by questions.
I saw him raise his eyes, raise his foot
gropingly towards the next square
and abruptly, snake-bitten, jerk back

while the Thames and the human river
traditionally flowed by.

In the same street you could see Francis Bacon
step into the photo-booths, draw the curtain,
adjust the stool, insert his coins
and then be crucified by four flashes
and disappointed in advance await the answer to:
Who is Francis Bacon?

While the simple-minded but incorruptible machines
groaned and rattled and mangled his four faces.

In the same street in the same week the police lined up.
Behind the palisade of uniforms a president was glimpsed
accompanied by wife and mistress, The Black Box,
transported to a lunch in the royal palace.
In part to seek something, in part to ward off something
in one's own face, in one's own time,
in the district everyone belongs to,
on the journey everything makes through the world.

Hard! Hard! Hard! Hard!
repeats the rattling machine.

translated by Robin Fulton

Colour

The condor has verdigris-coloured legs.
Sylvia Plath was right.
She wasn't deceived that day,
that terrible day before Christmas:
the condor has legs the colour of verdigris.
She stubbornly clung to her vision:
London's condors have legs of Spanish green.
Such colours are contagious.
The panther in the next enclosure
is only jet-black to a certain extent.
The Bengal tiger has kept its black stripes
yet lost the tawny yellow of their background.
The rhino, too, has dipped its horn
in that poisonous copper-solution.
The children pulled by the llama in a cart
around the refreshment hut
have faces a sickly colour

as though they'd nibbled scarlet flycap.
Poetry is contagious.
The bouncing footballs in Regent's Park
can't escape from their tormentors.
What colour are the young footballers'
knee-socks? The condor's . . .
As yet it's only September, a day hazy with sunshine;
a long way yet to those terrible days around Christmas.
I take the bus down to Westminster.
Opposite me, a gentleman is sitting. The briefcases
gentlemen hold are the colour of verdigris.

translated by Robin Young

Eva Ström[18]

A to Z

A deadly fruit. A heart beneath your foot. Greedily the street
cuts in from Regent's Park Road, through the vertebral
avenue of fused, terraced houses. I have walked through tangled level crossings, confusions of blackened rails and grimy
viaducts to reach this empty, lonely street. On the outskirts of
the great rib cities, everything is ordinary, far away from the
beasts of prey with their bony, smiling jaws, far removed
from Chalcot Square and yet still in the same segment of the
A to Z. Tragedy always strikes as others browse round shops
for arty ceramics, saunter in the soft drizzle, notice squirrels
and narcissus. *A night arrives in one gigantic step*. A man puts
up a prophylactic lamp on your top floor, because forgetting
is the best cement. *Cast a cold eye On life on death*. I hurry
past, running, not daring to look to the side. Which heart is
it, beating now?

He

The coarse hands reveal the transvestite's disguise. He – or it could be she – has followed us from the lift at the underground. Now we sit in a Hampstead café drinking caffelatte and eating carrot cake. Freud, forsythia. And she – or could it be he – sits down beside us. And he – or could it be she – observes us from beneath a beret. Nose of bony horn, rounded eyelids. But the hands that she – or could it be he – brings up to rest on the marble tabletop at once catch the eye, glaring. Those are large, coarse, man's hands. *All things hang like a drop of dew upon a blade of grass.* Then he gets up and goes without a word, struck by that look as if by a scornful word. Or is it just that his disguise has been exposed, the game is over for this time and must now be tried on someone else?

translated by Sarah Death

The Outer Hebrides

If it's the case that you long for the Outer Hebrides
Or somewhere else, where you have the sea in front of you
And Europe behind you
And where the islands are only a thin film of rain
If it's the case, that you're yearning for these islands
Or other islands, of comparable unimportance

If it's the case that you're worn out with writing
Encyclopaedias
And reading them from A to Z
If you've absorbed all the knowledge that there is to be
    acquired
About the Jarrah forests and the Druids,
About Tantalus on to the Tatras

And if it's the case that the azaleas are fading
That their swollen pink petals have already dried
and dropped to the ground
And nothing is left of their hardiness,
their relationship to Ericacea, the heather on the moor;
hot-house flower, green-house flower –

if it's the case that you sense inside you the end is coming,
like a crack, or an idea emerging
if it's the case that you long to be changed
while you travel,
just as unripe fruit is changed as it travels
in the cargo-hold, over the ocean, beneath the Southern
    Cross,
a hull's-width away from the water

if that's the case and there's no other option –
if that's how it is –
you've already turned off the lights in the house:
you're on your way.

                        new English version by Jim Potts

Johanna Ekström[19]

Cotton Wool

You and I had a relationship. That's the first thing I've got to admit to myself. We had a short relationship. With each other.

The night before I first met you, the *Estonia* went down. That night I had a terrible dream. A school bus skidded off a coastal road on a bend and sank through the ice in a bay. It all happened in slow motion. People were standing up to their shoulders in water, immobilized, begging for help, but nothing happened. In the end they couldn't hold themselves upright any longer and sank down on their knees. A thin skin of ice formed on the water. Then they came floating up. They lay just beneath the surface, dead and almost transparent, like curled-up embryos, like dumplings. I dreamt I was crying and running. I tried to stop a taxi. My skin smelled of fish.

Johanna Ekström

I went with Sonja, my best friend. She said I was welcome to come along. I'd just arrived in London and she didn't want me sitting all alone on such a sad evening. It was the birthday party of the friend of a friend. In her face I could detect hesitation, a certain insight. But I wasn't sure. The catastrophe had affected her too. She said we ought to go in spite of how upset we felt. We hoped we'd be able to sit close enough to wink at each other if it got boring.

I happened to find myself sitting opposite you. A blank card at your own party. I tend to feel very sure of myself in uncertain situations. I extend, stretching like a lion. A move to disguise the fact that I'm sizing up the situation. I'm looking for codes, scents. I'm desperate for recognition. I'm prepared to turn myself inside out for a single word of approval. I stretch, turn into an elastic band.

Then shrink again. Go back to my usual self. But it must look like something new, in others' eyes. In your eyes.

No, you didn't turn me on. Not in any way that might make you proud or self-satisfied. Sorry, but it was your transparency that turned me on. And my own advantage. Having the advantage is so intoxicating at any given moment. It's like a camera flash. Blinding, eclipsing. Then it vanishes, leaving a bluish negative behind. An insipid, lustreless image.

I'm sorry about this. If you'd noticed my weakness, we could have derived some benefit from each other's company in spite of everything. I'd seen yours, you'd seen mine. I found something amusing in screwing you among all your soft toys. A grown-up, almost grown-up man among his belongings. The lion, the teddy, the cat, the kangaroo. The white seal. We laughed at them, ironically. But you didn't feel that irony, did you? You would have liked to cry.

You led the game, trying to find your role. You usually acted naïve. The man who said whatever came into his head. Who dared to blush. Who dared to collect things he found on the beach, to order an extra helping of custard with his apple pie. To lick his lips and have an appetite. Food came to play quite a central part in our story.

I meant something special to you. I was the first person to see you naked from behind. You were ashamed of your big backside. There was no dividing line there, between your buttocks and thighs. I didn't look that closely. I would've had to close my eyes if I had. I was absorbed in myself. Lay stroking my breasts while you went to the toilet. Found it embarrassing that you ran water into the washbasin while you were peeing.

We'd been together twenty-four hours when you suggested we could go to a country guest house for the weekend. You said you'd never done that before. You were afraid of seeming frivolous. It seemed to me that could only mean one of two things. Either I was the great exception in your life, which was flattering. Or I was the sort of girl who doesn't really count. The latter option made me feel lonely, but also as if I was letting myself go. If you don't count, you don't exist. You know that better than I do.

I recall so clearly my hand gliding over your thigh as we sat in the car. Such a simple action, but it made you wild with desire. This sort of thing only happens in films, you were thinking. Not to me, not in real life. I was curious. I was tremendously solid and slightly bored. I was idiotic too, though I didn't realize it at the time. I'd pressed play and couldn't stop the process.

I sat there beside you and started thinking about myself. Not on an analytical level. On the contrary, I was thinking only of my tastes and wants. I'm like this. I'm not like that. I like this style, this attitude. This makes me laugh, but not that. It was like a poison in me, that chilliness. A numbness I tried to mask with false expectations. Yet also an offer of redemption. Offer. Offering.

A sacrificial offering.

The hotel with its unkempt garden. Boggy ground, a badly lit conservatory. The owner, in a tweed skirt and a blouse tied in a bow at the neck. Old fashioned fire-extinguishers in the corridors. We made love quickly and you had your dressing gown on. I shivered as I touched you. A wave of nausea. The overhead light was on. We were hungry afterwards. We fantasized about tuna sandwiches and fish and chips. A mischievous look came into your face and you crept down to the kitchen to hunt for food. You came back with some tiny peppermint meringues. The fridges were all padlocked.

There's one thing I can't really remember. We were driving along a road and you were telling a story, some local folk legend. It was about sudden, violent death and a gate leading down to Hell.

By the roadside was a pump with a sign saying the water had health-giving properties. You stopped and I got out. Cupped my hands and drank messily. Was it nice, you asked. I said I liked it. It tasted of blood and iron. Then I choked, coughing so much I had to hold onto the car door. You were so unnerved your whole body shook. I could see you were genuinely scared. You want me to come with you to see your father and his new wife. Since we're going that way anyway, you say. We stop in a village on the way. Buy cheese and some tulip bulbs in the market. I pretend I'm your future wife. Who will see the tulip bulbs coming up in your garden. It occurs to me that if we happened to get separated, we'd never find each other again. I don't know your face. I've never looked properly. Why don't I want to look at you?

You grow nervous as we get closer to where your father lives. You grow quieter. You want to fill up with petrol, clean the car, fit new windscreen wipers. You want to double-check there's equal pressure in all the tyres. You stand there freezing, tugging at your coat sleeves and staring down at the bonnet. It's pitch dark outside. I catch the smell of the sea. I'm wishing like hell I wasn't standing here with you, at this filling station in the south of England. I don't know you. I don't know this place. I'm not cold enough to be merely a witness.

I'm a fellow player in this game, it suddenly dawns on me. I'm so utterly lonely here. I sit in the car waiting for you. The windows slowly steam up. I've got to be close to you. I can see no alternative, no other world where I could be. I have no choice. I've got to get under your skin.

A man died here once, you say, pointing to the cliff's edge. It's virtually impossible to see where the ground ends and the sheer drop starts. You tell me a group of ornithologists was here and their leader went right out to the edge. The others saw him standing there for a few seconds. Then the ground gave way beneath him and he plunged down onto the rocks in the sea.

I hope there will come a time when I can't even remember your name.

When we pull up on the drive in front of the garage, you tell me to keep calm. Just keep calm and everything will be fine. But I am calm. I'm ice-cold and uneasy. Something here signals danger. The house is small and well-kept. The living room has an ice-blue fitted carpet and an imitation rococo sofa. They give us cider and salted almonds. Your stepmother looks at me as if I were a saint or someone who nurses the sick. She says, 'This rumour that there are bears in Stockholm in winter isn't really true, is it? But with Russia being so close, I suppose it wouldn't be that surprising.'

All three of them insist I take a bath before we go out for a meal. Your father says this is the restaurant that never fails to please.

It is rather romantic, I have to admit. His eyes glint. Our gazes meet for a split-second. My brain's resting, in standby mode, as I make conversation, smile, make eye contact and make soft gestures with my hands. But when I go to the ladies' room, I take my time. Sit fully dressed on the toilet lid for a while, just waiting.

Pudding is a good time for confidences. If things get embarrassing, one can always ask for the bill. Your father says something about the Catholic tradition in the family: This may sound a trifle conservative to you, but . . .

You look embarrassed, but only once do you speak out: when we leave the restaurant and you ask if you can drive his sports car and he refuses. Although you're the only one who's sober. He doesn't trust you, it's a simple fact. Not in the least. And he, as a former judge, should know whom one can trust.

We follow the sports car in your car. It's misty and the roads are slippery. You say you want to thank me for coming with you. I can see you're agitated. You jerk at the gear lever, biting your lower lip the whole time. You used me as a defence, a buffer. And you introduced me to your family, after all. Now they are hoping, with a mixture of terror and delight. They can see a future for you. At the turning off to the main road, we say goodbye to your father and step-mother. No hugs, no handshakes. But I kiss them lightly on the cheek. I can see that they like it. I'm generous and disgusted. In the car on the way back to London, you suddenly scream. A helpless cry, almost like an infant. I try to make out if you're weeping, but it's too dark.

Then you explain briefly what happened. That your parents were forced to get divorced, although a lot of people disapproved. But your father, who was a judge in professional life, couldn't live with a woman who . . . with a woman who had killed a child. You tell me you had a big brother, a brother who was suffocated to death by your mother. You say: 'He was screaming and Mum stuffed his mouth full of cotton wool to make him stop.'

Later, I remember a scene in your living room. I think it was one of the first times we kissed. I'm kneeling on the floor. You're sitting on the sofa. I turn my face up to you and you lean forward so our lips meet. Your mouth turns into a cave. Your teeth are sharp rocks. A snake slithers deep inside, quick as lightning over the wet ground. Its tail lashes.

You tell me we've been invited to a party. I'll have to look my smartest. Lucky I brought my only long dress with me. It's black with full sleeves, and translucent from neck to waist. We're going to Cambridge. I've never been there, but vaguely remember the buildings from my history of architecture. I ask if you know many of the other people going. You reply evasively. You seem embarrassed by your lack of university education. I tell you I only completed a few half-hearted course units myself. That's irrelevant, you reply. After all, you're a woman.

I don't ask you to repeat that last sentence. I decide I must have heard wrong. I decide, too, that this is part of the investigation. A research project which began that night when those people in distress were standing immobile, up to their shoulders in water, pleading for help.

I long for Sonja. Her almost feline movements, her flexible intellect. Her way of talking and laughing at the same time. Our mutual understanding. But she's gone to her parents' for the weekend. We've arranged to meet on Monday morning. By then I'll have been with you for four days and nights.

On the way to Cambridge, we pick up your friend. He's much too old to be living at home. You say he doesn't want to waste his money and be lured into living a sinful life. Not like me, you say. His house is one of three in a run-down brick terrace. His parents stand still and stare at us through the kitchen window. His mother has an electric plug in her hand. For a toaster or an iron, perhaps.

Your friend comes out onto the steps in old-fashioned braces, his shirt puffing out over the waistband of his trousers. He looks at me, amused. But when we go inside after him, he tries to avoid me and can no longer look me in the eye. His whole bearing alters. He sinks inwards, becomes an elderly oddball with a stoop and dandruff in his hair. His parents watch us from the landing. They nod absently but say nothing. Their son would rather take the train to Cambridge. He says he gets car sick.

We get changed at a filling station not far from the university. I don't recognize my face in the mirror. Blue eye shadow like two black eyes; powder greenish-white on my cheeks. Feigned composure. The magic fading. But when you emerge from the gents' in your dinner jacket, strolling past the sweets and shelves of groceries under the cold strip lighting, I have to laugh.

We park the car within the college walls, in a courtyard. Flaring torches light the way to one of the entrances. On the first floor, a liveried attendant takes our coats. I'm relieved to be rid of my shabby old anorak with its patched elbows and unbecoming hood. The guests are assembling in a small lounge, sipping sherry from large glasses. The level of conversation is subdued, but punctuated now and then by loud bursts of laughter. Afterwards, the quiet is even more marked. First I arm myself with something to drink. Then I turn and survey the gathering for the first time. There seem to be about thirty of us. I'm the only woman.

I go over to you and squeeze your arm. You introduce me clumsily to the person you're talking to. All you men are in dinner jackets. I can't tell you apart any longer. I can see you're feeling embarrassed by that awkward introduction. You really want to appear chivalrous and urbane. One of the gang. A few minutes later we're able give each other a conspiratorial look, smile at the absurdity of the situation.

Then I lose you. You have to join the flock. Not let them see you're sick, otherwise you'll be cast out.

I must at least find out why we're here. I should have asked this question much earlier. But there was no reason to be suspicious. I think of your stooping friend. I scan the crowd for him. But it's he who comes up to me and kisses me lightly on the hand. His colleagues immediately look at him in surprise. I couldn't care less why he's greeting me like this. For what reason, with what ulterior motives.

The man who had to take the train.

'We're gathered here for the annual dinner of the Royal Society,' he whispers, and turns his back on me. Once again I'm standing alone with a glass in my hand.

A bell rings and it's time to file into the dining room. I feel someone tap me on the shoulder. A woman of about forty introduces herself. 'Sorry I'm late. Well, we seem to be the only representatives of the female sex here tonight. I'm a professor of mathematics. Don't worry, this is a real experience.' She smiles a wan smile. She's suffering from bad eczema, on her face. Her long dress is covered in small flowers, like a nice, safe tablecloth. I want to curl up in her arms.

I find my way to my place. I can feel the looks penetrating my dress. I don't know if I'm admired or plague-infested. I can't interpret what I see. I ought to move carefully. Creep like an Indian. I ought to play dead. But I feel something wakening within me. Something strong and supple. No, there's no reason to assume it's a tigress. It could just as well be a marten, a polecat, a shaggy terrier.

I'm seated near the high table, opposite you and with a man on my left who seems strangely distant. He looks like Napoleon, Napoleon's death mask. Down one cheek and that side of his neck he has a birthmark that looks like the Milky Way. Liver-coloured splashes and blotches. When the first course and the speech of welcome are over, I turn to my partner at the table to initiate a conversation. He flinches when I address him. Once I realize he's a librarian I feel relieved. There's the explanation for his dreamy exterior.

'Hemingway?' I ask. He suddenly turns to face me and raises his serviette to his top lip. His face is bright red. His lips greyish-white, shiny with saliva.

The white wine sends pleasant sensations through my
midriff. I feel starved, hollow. I ask the waiter for a refill. He
is attentive to my slightest signal. When I refuse the roast
beef, it's Napoleon's turn to address me. Not eating meat is
denying oneself God's generous gifts. Not accepting what is
given to you by God is a sin. He recites it like something
learnt by heart. He raises his glass in a toast to his own pro-
nouncement. As for me, I'll drink to anything.

I'm drinking almost non-stop now. I'm flirting with the
man serving me and humming a tune I've got in my head.
Napoleon has expressed his contempt for career women,
gays and foreigners. Everything's running smoothly. I can't
see properly any more. The lighted candles, the glasses of red
wine, the reflections. They all melt together into a kaleido-
scopic tapestry. By now, we've raised our glasses to every
single member of the British royal family in turn. We've
toasted Sweden's Carl XVI Gustaf and the kings of Jordan,
Monaco, Belgium and Norway. The cheers get louder as the
evening goes on. Napoleon says: 'A man who steals gets his
hand cut off. A man who commits a sin with another man
gets his you know what cut off. That's natural justice. A toast
to heterosexual royalty. Cheers.'

I turn round to the waiter and say, 'Kiss me, please kiss
me. I'll meet you out on the stairs in five minutes.' I'm too
drunk to read his expression. When he bends over to refill
my glass, I bite his arm. In the ladies', I meet the maths
professor. She pulls a comb through her hair and smiles at
me in the mirror. I want to throw my arms around her. When
I ask her why she's here, she replies simply, 'It's considered
an honour to be invited. Lots of the people here are failed academics. We've all got something to hide. The Chairman's a
homosexual. He's something high up in the Conservative
party. Our Society members have a great deal of admiration
for him, mixed with loathing of course. Festive occasions are

a rarity when you're my age. This is England, you know. Old, old England.'

I paint my lips with my kohl eyeliner pencil and rest my forehead on the mirror. I have difficulty finding my way back to my place.

Everything's floating in a sea of light. Someone tells me it's time to change places. That's what they always do after the dessert. I end up next to the Chairman. I squeeze his arm. His face is heavy and pock-marked. He has the commanding presence of some old general. 'I know who you are,' I whisper, but he turns away. On my other side there's now a young man with a shy smile. He confides to me that he's the youngest guest here tonight. He's studying music and dreams of playing in a symphony orchestra in London one day. 'You shouldn't be here,' I almost scream at him. 'They're evil, mad, deadly. Get out.

'No, on second thoughts, hold my hand. Let's hold hands under the table.' I put his damp palm between my legs. I turn to the Chairman again. I want to talk to him about homosexuality. But he gives me an uncomprehending smile. 'Here,' he says, in a rough, bass voice, 'Some port will do you good.'

I'm too drunk to keep still. I wander through the college's deserted corridors. Find my way up to the bedrooms on the top floor. I open the door to a bathroom, where the tooth mugs are standing in a row on a warped wooden shelf. I taste the toothpaste, sample a skin lotion, brush my hair with someone's brush. Then I open the window and climb out. The night air strikes raw, small raindrops brush my face. A fire has been lit down in the courtyard. People seem to be gathering there, some in rain capes, others with umbrellas. Their voices sound a long way off. I can smell the burning wood and see the night mist mingling with the smoke from the fire. I feel very calm as I gently balance my way along the narrow gutter. I support myself with one hand on the slate roof.

Turning round is harder. With extreme care, I inch my way back to the bathroom window. That's when I discover I still have my port glass in my hand. I let it fall through the air to smash to pieces on the ground.

Safely back in the bathroom, I strip it of its contents. Tooth mugs and toothbrushes, toilet paper, cracked bars of soap, towels and toilet seats, out they all go through the window. Last of all I rip down the shower curtains and send them sailing out into the night.

Then I go to seek out my composer. He's standing by the fire with the rest. It's easy to spot him. He's standing motionless, looking into the flames. The other guests drift back to the lounges for coffee and brandy. We kiss each other greedily. He's so small and slender. His blond curls are curlier still in the drizzle.

We're well aware of the danger of standing intertwined in the glow of the firelight. 'This is a play, isn't it?' I ask him, over and over again. But he looks hurt and doesn't reply. On the way in, I trip on my dress and graze my face on the ground. My cheekbone and chin are bleeding. There's a rip in my dress, a gash in my lip. I'm completely insensitive to pain. Get calmly to my feet and tear a great chunk out of my dress. My palms are covered in soil, with little bits of gravel under the skin.

I get no further than the door of the lounge before you leap up from one of the armchairs. You drag me to the car. You must hate me. It's of no consequence to me what you're feeling. You drive as quickly as you can, but I've no conception of speed. It's dark all around us. Now and then, the car is illuminated by oncoming traffic. I think we run into something on the outskirts of London. The car spins round once, the tyres squeal, then we drive on.

I can get out at any moment. I know that now. Outside us, everything's as subduing and soft as cotton wool.

translated by Sarah Death

Three Inspirational Swedes: Linnaeus, Swedenborg and Strindberg

John Fowles

from *The Tree*

A few years ago I stood in a historic place. It was not a great battlefield, a house, a square, the site of one famous event; but the site only of countless very small ones – a neat little eighteenth-century garden, formally divided by gravel walks into parterres, with a small wooden house in one corner where the garden's owner had once lived. There is only one other garden to compare with it in human history, and that is the one in the Book of Genesis, which never existed outside words. The one in which I stood is very real, and it lies in the old Swedish university town of Uppsala. Its owner was the great warehouse clerk and indexer of nature, Carl Linnaeus[20], who between 1730 and 1760 docketed, or attempted to docket, most of animate being. Perhaps nothing is more moving at Uppsala than the actual smallness and ordered simplicity of that garden (my father would have loved it) and the immense consequences that sprung from it in terms of the way we see and think about the external world. It is something more than another famous shrine for lovers of nature, like Selborne or Coate Farm or Walden Pond. In fact, for all its air of gentle peace, it is closer to a nuclear explosion, whose radiations and mutations inside the human brain were incalculable and continue to be so; the place where an intellectual seed landed, and is now grown to a tree that shadows the entire globe.

I am a heretic about Linnaeus, and find nothing less strange, or more poetically just, than that he should have gone mad at the end of his life. I do not dispute the value of the tool he gave to natural science – which was in itself no more than a shrewd extension of the Aristotelian system and which someone else would soon have elaborated, if he had not; but I have doubts about the lasting change it has effected in ordinary human consciousness.

It is not that I don't share some of my father's fertile attachment to the single tree, the tree in itself, and the art of cultivating it, literally or artistically. But I must confess my own love is far more of trees, more exactly of the complex internal landscapes they form when left to themselves. In the colonial organism, the green coral, of the wood or forest, experience, adventure, aesthetic pleasure, I think I could even say truth, all lie for me beyond the canopy and exterior wall of leaves, and beyond the individual.

Evolution has turned man into a sharply isolating creature, seeing the world not only anthropocentrically but singly, mirroring the way we like to think of our private selves. Almost

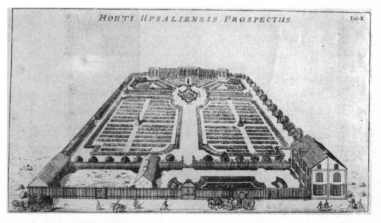

The University Botanical Gardens in Uppsala, originally laid out by Olof Rudbeck the Elder in the 1650s, later developed and supervised by Linnaeus.

all our art before the Impressionists – or their St John the Baptist, William Turner – proclaims our love of clearly defined boundaries, unique identities, of the individual thing released from the confusion of background. This power of detaching an object from its surroundings and making us concentrate on it is an implicit criterion in all our judgements on the more realistic side of visual art; and very similar, if not identical, to what we require of optical instruments like microscopes and telescopes – which is to magnify, to focus sharper, to distinguish better, to single from the ruck. A great deal of science is devoted to this same end: to providing specific labels, explaining specific mechanisms and ecologies, in short for sorting and tidying what seems in the mass indistinguishable one from the other. Even the simplest knowledge of the names and habits of flowers or trees starts this distinguishing or individuating process, and removes us a step from total reality towards anthropocentrism; that is, it acts mentally as an equivalent of the camera view-finder. Already it destroys or curtails certain possibilities of seeing, apprehending and experiencing. And that is the bitter fruit of Uppsalan knowledge.

It also begs very considerable questions as to the realities of the boundaries we impose on what we see. In a wood the actual visual 'frontier' of any one tree is usually impossible to distinguish, at least in summer. We feel, or think we feel, nearest to a tree's 'essence' (or that of its species) when it chances to stand like us, in isolation; but evolution did not intend trees to grow singly. Far more than ourselves they are social creatures, and no more natural as isolated specimens than man is as a marooned sailor or a hermit. Their society in turn creates or supports other societies of plants, insects, birds, mammals, micro-organisms; all of which we may choose to isolate and section off, but which remain no less the ideal entity, or whole experience, of the wood – and indeed are still so seen by most of primitive mankind.

Scientists restrict the word symbiotic to those relationships between species that bring some detachable mutual
benefit; but the true wood, the true place of any kind, is the
sum of all its phenomena. They are all in some sense symbiotic, being together in a togetherness of beings. It is only
because such a vast sum of interactions and coincidences in
time and place is beyond science's calculation (a scientist
might say, beyond useful function, even if calculable) that we
so habitually ignore it, and treat the flight of the bird and the
branch it flies from, the leaf in the wind and its shadow on
the ground, as separate events, or riddles – what bird? which
branch? what leaf? which shadow? These question-bound-
aries (where do I file that?) are ours, not of reality. We are led
to them, caged by them not only culturally and intellectually,
but quite physically, by the restlessness of our eyes and their
limited field and acuity of vision. Long before the glass lens
and the movie-camera were invented, they existed in our eyes
and minds, both in our mode of perception and in our mode
of analysing the perceived: endless short sequence and jump-
cut, endless need to edit and range this raw material.

I spent all my younger life as a more or less orthodox amateur naturalist; as a pseudo-scientist, treating nature as some
sort of intellectual puzzle, or game, in which being able to
name names and explain behaviourisms – to identify and to
understand machinery – constituted all the pleasures and the
prizes. I became slowly aware of the inadequacy of this
approach: that it insidiously cast nature as a kind of opponent, an opposite team to be outwitted and beaten; that in a
number of very important ways it distracted from the total
experience and the total meaning of nature – and not only of
what I personally needed from nature, not only as I had long,
if largely unconsciously, begun to feel it (which was neither
scientifically nor sentimentally, but in a way for which I had,
and still have, no word). I came to believe that this approach
represented a major human alienation, affecting all of us,

Carl Linnaeus 1707–1778

both personally and socially; moreover, that such alienation had much more ancient roots behind the historical accident of its present scientific, or pseudo-scientific form.

Naming things is always implicitly categorizing and there-fore collecting them, attempting to own them; and because man is a highly acquisitive creature, brainwashed by most modern societies into believing that the act of acquisition is more enjoyable than the fact of having acquired, that getting beats having got, mere names and the objects they are tied to soon become stale. There is a constant need, or compulsion, to seek new objects and names – in the context of nature, new species and experiences. Everyday ones grow mute with familiarity, so known they become unknown. And not only in non-human nature: only fools think our attitude to our fellow-men is a thing distinct from our attitude to 'lesser' life on this planet.

All this is an unhappy legacy from Victorian science, which was so characteristically obsessed with both the machine and exact taxonomy. I came only the other day on a letter in a forgotten drawer of the little museum of which I am curator. It was from a well-known Victorian fern expert, concerning some twenty or so specimens he had been sent from Dorset – all reducible, to a modern botanist, to three species. But this worthy gentleman felt obliged, in a welter of Latin polysyllables, to grant each specimen some new sub-specific or varietal rank, as if they were unbaptized children and might all go to hell if they were not given individual names. It would be absurd to deny the Victorians their enormous achievements in saner scientific fields, and I am not engaging in some sort of Luddite fantasy, wishing the machine they invented had been different, or even not at all. But we are far better at seeing the immediate advantages of such gains in knowledge of the exterior world than at assessing the cost of them. The particular cost of understanding the mechanism of nature, of having so successfully itemized and pigeon-holed it, lies most of all in the ordinary person's perception of it, in his or her ability to live with and care for it – and not to see it as a challenge, defiance, enemy. Selection from total reality is no less necessary in science than it is in art; but outside those domains (in both of which the final test of selection is utility, or yield, to our own species) it seriously distorts and limits any worthwhile relationship.

I caused my hosts at Uppsala, where I went to lecture on the novel, some puzzlement by demanding (the literary business once over) to see Linnaeus's garden rather than the treasures of one of the most famous libraries of Europe. The feeling that I was not behaving as a decent writer should was familiar. Again and again in recent years I have told visiting literary academics that the key to my fiction, for what it is worth, lies in my relationship with nature – I might almost have said, for reasons I will explain, in trees. Again and again

I have seen, under varying degrees of politeness, this assertion treated as some sort of irrelevant quirk, eccentricity,
devious evasion of what must be the real truth: literary influ-
ences and theories of fiction, all the rest of that purely intellectual midden which faculty hens and cocks so like
scratching over. Of course such matters are a part of the
truth; but they are no more the whole truth than that the tree
we see above ground is the whole tree. Even if we do discuss
nature, I soon sense that we are talking about two different
things: on their side some abstract intellectual concept, and
on mine an experience whose deepest value lies in the fact
that it cannot be directly described by any art . . . including
that of words.

One interrogator even accused me of bad faith: that if I sin-
cerely felt so deeply on the matter, I should write more about
it. But what I gain most from nature is beyond words. To try
to capture it verbally immediately places me in the same boat
as the namers and would-be owners of nature: that is, it exiles
me from what I most need to learn. It is a little as it is in
atomic physics, where the very act of observation changes
what is observed; though here the catch lies in trying to
describe the observation. To enter upon such a description is
like trying to capture the uncapturable. Its only purpose can
be to flatter the vanity of the describer – a function painfully
obvious in many of the more sentimental natural history
writers.

But I think the most harmful change brought about by Victorian science in our attitude to nature lies in the demand
that our relation with it must be purposive, industrious,
always seeking greater knowledge. This dreadfully serious
and puritanical approach (nowhere better exhibited in the
nineteenth century than in the countless penny magazines
aimed at young people) has had two very harmful effects.
One is that it turned the vast majority of contemporary Western mankind away from what had become altogether too

much like a duty, or a school lesson; the second is that the far saner eighteenth-century attitude, which viewed nature as a mirror for philosophers, as an evoker of emotion, as a pleasure, a poem, was forgotten. There are intellectual reasons as well for this. Darwin made sentimental innocence, nature as mainly personal or aesthetic experience, vaguely wicked. Not only did he propose a mechanism seemingly as iron as the steam-engine, but his very method of discovery, and its success in solving a great conundrum, offered an equally iron or one-sided model for the amateur naturalist himself, and made the older and more humanist approach seem childish. A 'good' amateur naturalist today merely means one whose work is valued by the professional scientists in his field.

Daniel Solander[21]

Letter to Carl Linnaeus

5 February 1761, London

Honourable Herr Archiater and Knight of the Royal Order of the North Star Worthiest Patron

When I returned home to London last Friday I had the honour of receiving Herr Archiater's letter, in which I find that Herr Archiater is planning to travel to Falun with his family. I never think of the great pleasure I had at that place without wishing for many more opportunities of partaking of the same peace.

Herr Justitierådet Leuch and I have had the benefit of fine weather during our whole tour, and were everywhere well received. The English people are generally polite to foreigners, if only you flatter them and tell them that everything you have seen in England is better than anything you have seen before; this they believe themselves and they wish all to concur. I hardly think there can be a more conceited Nation, and in this really consists the strength of the country; for though they are now pressed with the heaviest impositions and expenses as ever were imposed and many complain of total ruin, the public is content since it is used to show the nation is wealthy and capable of mighty things against her enemies. Here there is such an unnatural boasting of the success of their arms, so that you do not hear anything other than that the English could subjugate the whole world if they wanted to. The government is obliged to make the mob believe they are always victorious, otherwise they would become dissatisfied and quite furious. No mails are therefore delivered in England before the court has given its permission, for when some account of any loss or defeat comes, the mail must always be detained until they have received more pleasant news to amuse the public as well; or till they have time to plan the thing in advance as inevitable and of little consequence. It is no rarity to hear one day Prime Minister and the Generals condemned, and the next day extolled to the heavens. This goes so far that even reasonable people are equally changeable. In their newspapers that are published daily by the score, one constantly perceives the same fickleness of opinion. Their abusive opinions of Prince Ferdinand have so greatly offended him that he has twice declared that he wants to give up the command; and many suspect that henceforth he will not be so good an Englishman as he has been. They now begin to talk of their mighty secret expedition which is to perform wonders. They have certainly made rather significant arrangements for this expedition. During our tour we had a fairly good opportunity to observe this, as we travelled in those parts of England nearest the coast, from which the expedition is to depart.

I will give a short account of our excursion, which would have been much more pleasant if it could have been made in another season. We were obliged to satisfy ourselves

Dᴿ. SOLANDER.

with the creations of art and industry, which can indeed
occupy one enough in a country like England but it would
have been much more agreeable to me, if I could have
botanized and seen their tending of the land of which I
now have had little opportunity of learning any thing
except from reports. Our tour was of about 600 English
miles. We went directly from London to Buckingham
where our Christmas festivity was to look at the beautiful
Stow[e] Garden, which neither for size nor arrangement
has its equal in England; it is 12 miles in circumference and
adorned with 48 temples each built in a separate style and
dedicated to ancient gods and goddesses, to virtues and to
renowned men. Each might pass for a royal edifice, at least
the King of England can show nothing comparable with

this. From Buckingham we went to Woodstock, where steel is wrought at such a great price that few would be able to believe it. There, scissors are made up to the price of 16 to 20 ducats each; shoe and knee-ribbon buckles at 18 to 24 ducats per pair, chains for watches at 12 to 15 ducats &c. these of steel alone, without any inlaying. Then we spent some days in Oxford, which I mentioned earlier. Near Woodstock the Duke of Marlborough's palace is located, which is considered the largest building in England; it engaged us almost a couple of days just walking from one room to the other. In passing through Sudbury I got hold of a petrified *anomia testa subrotunda spinosa*, which is the finest you can imagine, for the *spinae* are longer than the diameter of the *testa* as fine as hog's bristle and fortunately the greater part of the *Spinae* are quite perfect as it lies in a loose limestone. It is the size of a hazel nut. It is *Spinosa* all over. In the same shire at Tetbury I obtained a petrified *nautilus* which I also believe to be a new species; it is the same size as a *Pompylius*. As soon as any ship sails in the spring for Stockholm they will go too. Bristol kept us almost a week, since there was quite a lot to see. My Quaker acquaintance to whom I was introduced through Mr Collinson, showed me more than I believe anyone has got to see; not only did we see all their copper and brass works, but also the whole process of blowing Crown glass, and how they prepare the materials, and I believe the whole composition. I have requested a Swede named Robsahm – a notary in the Mountain Board – now in London, to inform himself further on the subject, for I believe we in Sweden could do it better and cheaper. Our last day in Bath I had the pleasure of picking up a pocket full of *anomiis* in a field 2 miles from the town, they were lying loose in the clay. From Bath we found our way through Devizes by Stonehenge which they say ought to be reckoned among the wonders of the world. It is probably a remnant of an old heathen Druid temple; but the marvel is how they could convey there such enormous masses of granite and set them up and also how they placed them one across the other when no granite is to be found within 50 to 100 miles, and no machine is now known that could raise such big weights. At Salesbury [sic] we saw so many woollen manufacturers that I believe that more cannot be found in any other place. From there we travelled to Southampton where we saw people bathing in the sea in the middle of winter; they plunge head first, diving like the boys in Stockholm. All tell me that they are never chilled, but on the contrary get quite warm. It was exquisite to see the courage with which the most tender women rush down in the cold water, whereas I could in no way be persuaded to do so, although almost everyday I saw travellers bathing just for fun. Not far from Southampton, at Lord Petersfield's garden, I saw 4 flower pots of agate; they are probably the most beautiful of their kind, but they have also cost a lot. They were bought in Italy for £10,000 which amounts to more than 2 barrels of gold. In Portsmouth we saw the strength of England concentrated, since all their ships were now there, and a greater part of the troops and ammunition which are to be employed in this year's campaign. We were on board an English Admiral's ship at Spithead and saw the fleet which sailed for America and in the harbour all the 300 ships destined for the big secret expedition. There were frightful preparations, remarkable to watch, which we could not have seen had Mr Collinson's letter of introduction to the Quakers not procured for us such a good opportunity. The new Admiralty hospital at Gosport is one of the largest establishments I have ever seen; it far surpasses Greenwich.

Mr Ellis just now came to me. A moment ago he received a letter from Dr Garden, in which he expresses his longing for a letter from Herr Archiater, with an answer concerning the fish he has forwarded: he also says that he has collected 40 new species of fish which he will also forward to Herr Archiater as soon as he is honoured with a letter, for you must know he is an Englishman, whose greatest pleasure is to receive letters. Mr Ellis is also longing very much for a letter from Herr Archiater. He asks if it would be possible for you to send him by mail in springtime some seed of the *Rhabarbarum verum* – which he could sow in Webb's garden now under Mr Ellis' inspection. He has also now received the accompanying seed of 2 species of *Magnoliae* from Garden enclosed in wax. He has also received seeds in tallow, but they were quite spoilt as well as those put up in tallow and wax mixed together. He promises to send more seeds in the spring, but desires me to transmit these at once, lest they should be injured by delay. He presents his respects [I also send mine] to the Gracious Lady, to the young Ladies and to Herr Linnaeus and all my other patrons and friends. I have the honour to remain until my death with deepest reverence.

Honourable Herr Archiater's and Knight's most humble and most obedient servant

Daniel C Solander

Joseph Banks[22]

Letter to Johan Alströmer[23]

16 November 1784   [London?]

I blush at having for so long put off answering your letter
in which you requested biographical anecdotes about our
dear Solander. I have in haste written down the greater
part of his life, but omitted such anecdotes which are no
less known to you than to me.

Solander's journey to England seems to have been ini-
tiated by John Ellis, author of *Essay on Corallines*, and
Peter Collinson who had asked Archiater Linnaeus for a
student from Uppsala who would be capable of improving
Natural History which was then in a bad state in England.
Immediately after his arrival he got acquainted with
Philip Carteret Webb, a man of important judicial office
who was then much consulted by the administration.
Through him he became before long acquainted with
Lord Northington, Lord Chancellor of England, who,
charmed by our friend's free and pleasant manners in
company, brought him to his estate in Hampshire, when
he had not yet been one week in England. Some days
later, when the Lord's affairs forced him to remain in
London, he left Solander in the hands of his wife and
daughter, enjoining them to instruct him in the English
language and absolutely not to use any other.

In this way he became a willing prisoner there and
received daily instruction from two of the most beautiful
and wittiest women in England. It was therefore no
wonder that he made fast progress; within six weeks he
returned to London already in a certain manner master of
the English language and then distinguished himself
throughout his life with the rare gift of speaking correctly
and with a pleasant and clear pronunciation.

The position of Assistant Librarian at the British Museum, the income for which does not exceed 60 pounds a year, was chosen for him with a promise of future promotion to more advantageous conditions. His friend Webb, however, procured for him an annual salary of 100 pounds from the Trustees of the Museum and, with this benefit, on 26 February 1763 he received orders to start on a catalogue of the natural history objects in the British Museum. He was also elected a Fellow of the Royal Society of London.

When making a list of the natural history objects, he used much diligence and left beautiful transcripts of his descriptions, which became the property of the museum. It now owns a considerable number of them, which presumably will one day appear and infallibly be received by the public with much desire.

When he was free from duties at the museum, he used his time to assist his friends who much desired his help in everything that concerned natural history. In this science he was promptly considered a judge whose court was beyond appeal. He determined many plants in Pet[er] Collinson's herbarium, helped his friend Ellis in his examinations of corallines as well as his compatriot Gustaf Brander in the writing of a work that Brander published under the title of *Fossilia Hantoniensa*, and invented and set up in consultation with John Ellis, for his friend Carteret Webb, the first conservatory ever built in England.

At the time, or around 1764, when I was a student at Oxford, I first became acquainted with him and from then on our acquaintanceship was augmented more and more until it was finally transformed into a friendship [the end of which] has left me the most severe grief. Through his death I have endured a loss that could not possibly be replaced even if I could still meet a man as elevated and as magnanimous he was. At my present age the heart is not capable of receiving impressions which twenty years ago it took as easily as wax and which will not be obliterated until its final dissolution.

On 19 July 1765 he became Assistant Librarian at the British Museum with a salary. When I sailed in 1766 to Newfoundland he gave me much botanical information that was of great use to me and at my return he helped me to determine the plants I had found that were new to me; while we were occupied with this I noticed that my botanical knowledge was increasing considerably. At this time we both became acquainted with Lady Anne Monson, after whom the genus *Monsonia* was named, and with Mr Lee and several others who studied botany and entomology with much diligence and no small benefit from Solander's instruction.

When Commodore Wallis in the year of 1768 had come back from the South Seas it was decided by the Government that a ship that was intended to observe the transit of Venus across the Sun should, having carried this out, sail on in order to make new discoveries. Informed of this, I immediately applied to join it, I was given permission and began to prepare myself for the voyage.

Of this I promptly informed Doctor Solander, who received the news with much pleasure and immediately promised to provide me with complete information on all aspects of natural history which could probably be met with during such an extensive and unprecedented voyage. But some days afterwards, when we were together at Lady Monson's table and spoke about the unique opportunities I should get, Solander got remarkably fired, sprang up a short time later from his chair and asked with intent eyes: *Would you like to have a travelling companion?* I replied: *Such a person as you would be of infinite advantage and pleasure to me! If so*, he said, *I want to go with you*, and from that moment everything was settled and decided. The following day I requested of Sir Edward Hawke, First Lord of the Admiralty, that I might be allowed to bring along a traveller's companion; he more as a sailor than a philosopher refused at first, but was soon persuaded to give his consent.

During this voyage, which lasted three years, I can say of him that he combined an incomparable diligence and an acumen that left nothing unsettled, with an unbelievable equanimity. During all that time we did not once have any altercation which for a moment became heated. We often freely contested each other's opinions in all subjects, but always ended as we had begun, good-humouredly and generally being of the same opinion after one of us had accepted his opponent's reasons.

[ ]

You know Solander's way of life here in England as well as I do. The brightest part of the day he dedicated to botany, but his inclination for company would never allow him to use also the evening for the museum and, in truth, his numerous friends would have become rebellious if ever he had tried to.

Of the excellent manner in which he was generally received by the most distinguished gentlemen's families here in this country, you can testify as well as many of your compatriots of this place.

His gift to describe with taste the rare specimens of the British Museum was so unusually charming that both men and women chose the hours which they knew Solander was accustomed to display the collection.

Yes, his company was so informative, so merry, and so agreeable, that it was not only sought by all learned people, but the King himself had the grace to honour such a stranger with conversation whenever Solander was met with.

[ ]

You have probably already heard of the circumstances of Solander's death. I was a short distance from London on a pleasure trip when a message arrived with the news of his peril. I travelled by night and arrived in the morning, but there was no longer any hope. He had been quite well in the morning before his illness began and was even in company when he was attacked by paralysis. No important physician in London failed to attend of his own accord to give advice, but no one left any hope. Two years before his death he had had a violent nose-bleed which seems to have been a critical discharge; for when the head was opened after his death one observed the cause to have been a burst blood vessel in the brain.

In such a way my much lamented friend died on 12 March 1782 and was buried on the 19th. All Swedes in London were present at the Swedish Church. Among the innumerable Englishmen who wished to, none but I was allowed to escort his body to the grave. The Swedes were also numerous enough to do him this last honour and the English, although not present, mourned no less in their hearts.

This too early loss of a friend, whom I during my more mature years have loved and whom I will always miss, makes me wish to draw a veil over his death, as soon as I have ceased to speak of it. I can never think of it without feeling a mortal pain, for which mankind shudders; but if decency, justice, moderation, benevolence, diligence; if natural as well as acquired ability lays claim to a place in a better world, then nothing other than a lack of equal merit on my part can prevent us from meeting again.

Vernon Watkins[24]

Swedenborg's Skull

Note this survivor, bearing the mark of the violator,
Yet still a vessel of uninterrupted calm.
Its converse is ended. They beat on the door of his coffin,
But they could not shake or destroy that interior psalm
Intended for God alone, for his sole Creator.
For gold they broke into his tomb.

The mark of the pick is upon him, that rough intrusion
Upon the threshold and still place of his soul.
With courtesy he received them. They stopped, astonished,
Where the senses had vanished, to see the dignified skull
Discoursing alone, entertaining those guests of his vision
Whose wit made the axe-edge dull.

Here the brain flashed its fugitive lightning, its secret
    appraising,
Where marble, settled in utmost composure, appears.
Here the heirs of the heavens were disposed in symmetrical
    orders
And a flash of perception transfigured the darkness of years.
The mark of a membrane is linked with those traffickers
    grazing
Its province of princes and spheres.

Where the robbers looked, meditations disputed the legacy
Of the dreaming mind, and the rungs of their commonplace
    crime
Gave way to swift places of angels, caught up in division
From the man upon earth; but his patience now played like a
    mime,
And they could not break down or interpret the skull in its
    privacy
Or take him away from his time.

So I see it today, the inscrutable mask of conception
Arrested in death. Hard, slender and grey, it transcends
The inquiring senses, even as a shell toiling inward,
Caught up from the waters of change by a traveller who
    bends
His piercing scrutiny, yields but a surface deception,
Still guarding the peace it defends.

William Blake

from *Swedenborg. The Marriage of Heaven and Hell*

I have always found that Angels have the vanity to speak of themselves as the only wise; this they do with a confident insolence sprouting from systematic reasoning.

Thus Swedenborg boasts that what he writes is new: tho' it is only the Contents or Index of already publish'd books.

A man carried a monkey about for a shew, & because he was a little wiser than the monkey, grew vain, and conceiv'd himself as much wiser than seven men. It is so with Swedenborg: he shews the folly of churches, & exposes hypocrites, till he imagines that all are religious, & himself the single one on earth that ever broke a net.

Now hear a plain fact: Swedenborg has not written one new truth: Now hear another: he has written all the old falsehoods.

And now hear the reason. He has conversed with Angels who are all religious, & conversed not with Devils who all hate religion, for he was incapable thro' his conceited notions.

Thus Swedenborg's writings are a recapitulation of all superficial opinions, and an analysis of the more sublime, but no further.

Have now another plain fact. Any man of mechanical talents may, from the writings of Paracelsus or Jacob Bremen,

The Marriage of Heaven and Hell *by William Blake. The third of Blake's illuminated books, probably begun in 1789 and completed the following year.*

produce ten thousand volumes of equal value with Swedenborg's, and from those of Dante or Shakespear an infinite number.

But when he has done this, let him not say that he knows better than his master, for he only holds a candle in sunshine.

William Butler Yeats: the Nobel Prize in Literature 1923[25]

Acceptance Speech

'I have been all my working life indebted to the Scandinavian nation. When I was a very young man, I spent several years writing in collaboration with a friend the first interpretation of the philosophy of the English poet Blake. Blake was first a disciple of your great Swedenborg and then in violent revolt and then half in revolt, half in discipleship. My friend and I were constantly driven to Swedenborg for an interpretation of some obscure passage, for Blake is always in his mystical writings extravagant, paradoxical, obscure. Yet he has had upon the last forty years of English imaginative thought the influence which Coleridge had upon the preceding forty; and he is always in his poetry, often in his theories of painting, the interpreter or the antagonist of Swedenborg. Of recent years I have gone to Swedenborg for his own sake, and when I received your invitation to Stockholm, it was to his biography that I went for information. Nor do I think that our Irish theatre could have ever come into existence but for the theatre of Ibsen and Björnson. And now you have conferred upon me this great honour. Thirty years ago a number of Irish writers met together in societies and began a remorseless criticism of the literature of their country. It was their dream that by freeing it from provincialism they might win for it European recognition. I owe much to those men, still more to those who joined our movement a few years later, and when I return to Ireland these men and women, now growing old like myself, will see in this great honour a fulfilment of that dream. I in my heart know how little I might have deserved it if they had never existed.'

Stockholm, 10 December 1923

from *The Bounty of Stockholm*

VII

The diplomas and medals are to be given us by the King at five in the afternoon of December the tenth. The American Ambassador, who is to receive those for an American man of science, unable to be present, and half a dozen men of various nations sit upon the platform. In the body of the Hall every seat is full, and all there are in evening dress, and in the front row are the King, Princess Ingeborg, wife of the King's brother, Prince Wilhelm, Princess Margerita, and I think another Royalty. The President of the Swedish Academy speaks in English, and I see from the way he stands, from his self-possession, and from his rhythmical utterance, that he is an experienced orator. I study the face of the old King, intelligent and friendly, like some country gentleman who can quote Horace and Catullus, and the face of the Princess Margerita, full of subtle beauty, emotional and precise, and impassive with a still intensity suggesting that final consummate strength which rounds the spiral of a shell. One finds a similar beauty in wooden busts taken from Egyptian tombs of the Eighteenth Dynasty and not again till Gainsborough paints. Is it very ancient and very modern alone or did painters and sculptors cease to notice it until our day?

The Ambassador goes towards the King, descends from the platform by some five or six steps, which end a yard from the King's feet, and having received the diploma and medal, ascends those five or six steps walking backward. He does not go completely backward, but side-ways, and seems to show great practice. Then there is music, and a man of science repeats the movement, imitating the ambassador exactly and easily, for he is young and agile, and then more music and two men of science go down the steps, side by side, for they have made discoveries that are related to one another, and the prize is divided between them. As it would be impossible for two men to go up backward, side by side, without much practice, one repeats the slanting movement, and the other turns his back on royalty. Then the English ambassador receives diploma and medal for two Canadians, but as he came from the body of the Hall he has no steps to go up and down. Then more music and my turn comes. When the King has given me my diploma and medal and said, 'I thank you for coming yourself,' and I have bowed my thanks, I glance for a moment at the face of the Princess Margerita, and move backward towards the stair. As I am about to step sideways like the others, I notice that the carpet is not nailed down, and this suddenly concentrates my attention upon the parallel lines, made by the two edges of the carpet, and, as though I were hypnotised, I feel that I must move between them, and so straight up backward without any sidelong movement. It seems to me that I am a long time reaching the top, and as the cheering grows much louder

The reverse of the gold medal received by winners of the Nobel Prize for Literature and described by Yeats in The Bounty of Sweden.

when I get there, I must have roused the sympathy of the audience. All is over, and I am able to examine my medal, its charming, decorative, academic design, French in manner, a work of the nineties. It shows a young man listening to a Muse, who stands young and beautiful with a great lyre in her hand, and I think as I examine it, 'I was good-looking once like that young man, but my unpractised verse was full of infirmity, my Muse old as it were; and now I am old and rheumatic, and nothing to look at, but my Muse is young. I am even persuaded that she is like those Angels in Swedenborg's vision, and moves perpetually "towards the day-spring of her youth".' At night there is a banquet, and when my turn comes, I speak of Swedenborg, Strindberg, and Ibsen. Then a very beautiful, stately woman introduces herself with this sentence spoken slowly as though English were unfamiliar. 'What is this new religion they are making up in Paris that is all about the dead?' I wonder who has told her that I know anything of psychical research, for it must be of that she speaks, and I tell her of my own studies. We are going to change the thought of the world, I say, to bring it back to all its old truths, but I dread the future. Think what the people have made of the political thought of the eighteenth century, and now we must offer them a new fanaticism. Then I stop ashamed, for I am talking habitual thoughts, and not adapting them to her ear, forgetting beauty in the pursuit of truth, and I wonder if age has made my mind rigid and heavy. I deliberately falter as though I could think of nothing more to say, that she may pass upon her smiling road.

XI

For the next two or three days we visit picture galleries, the gallery of the National Museum, that of Prince Eugene, that of Baron Thiel. At the National Museum pictures have been taken down and lean against the wall, that they may be sent

to London for an exhibition of Swedish art. Someone exag-
gerating the influence in London of the Nobel prize-winner,
asks me to write something to get people to go and see it, and
I half promise but feel that I have not the necessary knowledge. I know something of the French impressionism that
gave their painters their first impulse, but almost nothing of
German or Austrian, and I have seen that of Sweden for the
first time. At a first glance impressionism seems everywhere
the same, with differences of power but not of sight or mind,
and one has to live with it and make many comparisons I
think, to write more than a few sentences. The great myth
makers and mask makers, the men of aristocratic mind,
Blake, Ingres in the 'Perseus', Puvis de Chavannes, Rossetti
before 1870, Watts when least a moralist, Gustave Moreau at
all times, Calvert in the Woodcuts, the Charles Ricketts of
'The Danaïdes', and of the earlier illustrations of 'The
Sphinx', have imitators, but create no universal language.
Administrators of tradition, they seem to copy everything,
but in reality copy nothing, and not one of them can be mistaken for another, but impressionism's gift to the world was
precisely that it gave, at a moment when all seemed sunk in
convention, a method as adaptable as that box of architectural
renaissance bricks. It has suddenly taught us to see and feel,
as everybody that wills can see and feel, all those things that
are as wholesome as rain and sunlight, to take into our hearts
with an almost mystical emotion what-so-ever happens
without forethought or premeditation. It is not, I think, any
accident that their art has coincided everywhere with a new
sympathy for crowds, for the poor and the unfortunate.
Certainly it arrived in these Scandinavian countries just at
the moment when an intellectual awakening of the whole
people was beginning, for I always read, or am told, that
whatever I inquire about began with the eighties, or was the
outcome of some movement of that time.

When I try to define what separates Swedish impressionism from French, I notice that it has a stronger feeling for
particular places. Monet will paint a group of trees by a pond
in every possible light, changing his canvas every twenty
minutes, and only returning to a canvas when the next day's
clock brings up the same light, but then it is precisely the
light that interests him, and interests the buyers of those
almost scientific studies. Nobody will buy because it is a
pond under his window, or that he passed in his boyhood on
his way to school. I noticed in some houses where I lunched
two pictures of the Stockholm river, painted in different
lights by Eugene Janson, and in the National Museum yet
another with a third effect of light, but much as the light
pleased his imagination, one feels that he cared very much
for the fact before him, that he was never able to forget for
long that he painted a well loved, familiar scene. I am constantly reminded of my brother who continually paints from
memory the people and houses of the village where he lived
as a child; but the people of Rosses will never care about his
pictures, and these painters paint for all educated Stockholm.
They have found an emotion held in common, and are no
longer like the rest of us, solitary spectators. I get the impression that their work rouses a more general interest than that
of other painters, is less confined to small groups of con-
noisseurs; I notice in the bookseller's shops that there seems
to be some little paper covered pamphlet, full of illustrations,
for every notable painter of the school, dead or living, and the
people I meet ask constantly what I think of this painter, or
that other, or somebody will say, 'This is the golden age of
painting.' When I myself try to recall what I have seen, I
remember most clearly a picture of a white horse on the sea-
shore, with its tints separated by little lines, that give it a general effect of mosaic, and certain portraits by Ernest
Josephson, which prove that their painter was entirely preoccupied with the personality of the sitter, light-colour, design,

all subordinate to that. An English portrait painter is some-times so preoccupied with the light that one feels he would have had equal pleasure in painting a bottle and an apple. But a preference after so brief a visit may be capricious, having some accidental origin.

XII

On Thursday I give my official lecture to the Swedish Royal Academy. I have chosen the 'Irish Theatre' for my subject, that I may commend all those workers, obscure or well known, to whom I owe much of whatever fame in the world I may possess. If I had been a lyric poet only, if I had not become through this theatre, the representative of a public movement, I doubt if the English Committees would have placed my name upon that list, from which the Swedish Academy selects its prize winner. They would not have acknowledged a thought so irrelevant, but those dog-eared pages, those pressed violets, upon which the fame of a lyric poet depends at the last, might without it have found no strong voice. I have seen so much beautiful lyric poetry pass unnoticed for years, and indeed at this very moment a little book of exquisite verse lies upon my table, by an author who died a few years ago whom I knew slightly, and whose work I ignored, for chance had shown me only that part of it for which I could not care.

On my way to the lecture hall I ask an academician what kind of audience I will have, and he replies, 'An audience of women, a fit audience for a poet'; but there are men as well as women. I had thought it would be difficult to speak to an audience in a language they had learnt at school, but it is exceedingly easy. All I say seems to be understood, and I am conscious of that sympathy which makes a speaker forget all but his own thoughts, and soliloquise aloud. I am speaking without notes and the image of old fellow-workers comes upon me as if they were present, above all of the embittered life and death of one, and of another's laborious, solitary age, and I say, 'When your King gave me medal and diploma, two forms should have stood, one at either side of me, a woman in vigorous old age and a young man's ghost. I think when Lady Gregory's name[26] and John Synge's name[27] are spoken by future generations, my name if remembered, will come up in the talk, and that if my name is spoken first their names will come in their turn because of the years we worked together. I think that both had been well pleased to have stood beside me at the great reception at your palace, for their work and mine has delighted in history and tradition.' I think as I speak these words of how deep down we have gone, below all that is individual, modern and restless, seeking foundations for an Ireland that can only come into existence in a Europe that is still but a dream.

XIII

On Friday we visit the great Town Hall which is the greatest work of Swedish art, and the most important building of modern Europe. The Royal Palace had taken ninety years to build, and been the organising centre of the art of its time, and this new magnificence, its narrow windows opening out upon a formal garden, its tall tower rising from the quay side, has taken ten years. It too has been an organising centre but for an art more imaginative and amazing. Here there is no important French influence, for all that has not come out of the necessities of sight and material, no matter in what school the artist studied, carries the mind backward to Byzantium. I think of but two comparable buildings, the Transylvania Terminus in New York, and the Catholic Cathedral at Westminster, but the Transylvania Terminus, noble in austerity, is the work of a single mind, elaborating a suggestion from a Roman Bath, a mind that – supported by the American deference to authority – has been permitted to refuse everything not relevant to a single dominating idea.

The starting hours of the trains are upon specially designed boards, of a colour that makes them harmonise with the general design, and all other advertisements are forbidden even in the stations that the trains pass immediately after leaving, or before entering the terminus. The mood of severity must be prolonged or prepared for. The Catholic Cathedral is of equal, or of greater magnificence in general design but being planted in a country where public opinion rules and the subscribers to every fund expect to have their way, is half-ruined by ignoble decoration, the most ignoble of all, planned and paid for by my country men. The Town Hall of Stockholm, upon the other hand, is decorated by many artists, working in harmony with one another and with the design of the building as a whole, and yet all in seeming perfect freedom. In England and Ireland public opinion compels the employment of the worst artists, while here the authority of a Prince[28] and the wisdom of a socialist minister of culture, and the approval of the most educated of all nations, have made possible the employment of the best. These myth makers and mask makers worked as if they belonged to one family and the great walls where the roughened surface of the bricks, their carefully varied size and tints, takes away all sense of mechanical finish; the mosaic covered walls of the 'Golden Room'; the paintings hung upon the walls of the committee rooms; the Fresco paintings upon the greater surfaces with their subjects from Swedish mythology; the wrought iron and the furniture, where all suggests history, and yet is full of invention; the statuary in marble and in bronze, now mythological in subject, now representations of great Swedes, modelled naked as if they had come down from some Roman heaven; all that suggestion of novelty and of an immeasurable past; all that multitude and unity, could hardly have been possible, had not love of Stockholm and belief in its future, so filled men of different minds, classes and occupations, that they almost attained the supreme miracle, the dream that has haunted all religions, and loved one another. No work, comparable in method or achievement, has been accomplished, since the Italian cities felt the excitement of the renaissance, for in the midst of our individualistic anarchy, growing always as it seemed more violent, has arisen once more subordination, design, a sense of human need.

Jamie McKendrick[29]

In Arcana Fidei

You had a whole shelf of books devoted to death,
most of which I now have in my keeping.
God knows they're the last things I want
though till they'd passed to me I'd hardly guessed
how scrutable to some those last things are
– since then I've learnt, for instance, that
there's a smell like the smell of flowering lilac
which Swedenborg's angels use to dissuade
anyone approaching the spirit in transit.
It must find its feet first in the other world,
then – useless all denials – its deeds and crimes
are disinterred in their entirety
down to the coded entry in the diary,
the least bit of backbiting, the wronged maiden's
tearstained roundshouldered downcast look,
the poisoned cup, the stolen funds, the secret tryst . . .

Stockholm today is like the banished zone
where the lost have found their level – and me
among them
after a sleepless night in the Blue Tower
where Strindberg died from a cancered gut, his mind gone
tortuous with alchemy and Swedenborg
– all round him poisoners: a taste from hell,
of brass and corpses. In the thin daylight here
– a narrow path between two blocks of night –

I'm free to stray from Drottninggatan's line
and chance on Swedenborg's own Minneskyrka
a small beached ark with Latin script that claims:
THE INTELLECT IS NOW PERMITTED
TO ENTER THE MYSTERIES OF FAITH
– a quaint undaunted other-worldly traffic sign
though the kirk's green spire, gilt crown and five-peaked star
make no inroads on a sky of solid cloud.

Michael Holroyd

from *Bernard Shaw*

Charlotte Shaw had no children, but increasingly, as Arnold Bennett noticed, she looked 'like the mother of a large family'. For Christmas she tucked Shaw up again in her sister and brother-in-law's house, where it was pretty well impossible for him to get into scrapes. And she kept him under her supervision and out of the country for three summer months of 1908 while the drains at Ayot were being replaced. First they went to Stockholm. To help preserve its exclusiveness, he promised to 'perpetrate the notion that Sweden is a frightful place, where bears wander through the streets and people live on cod liver oil'.

August Strindberg attending a rehearsal at his Intima Teatern in Stockholm. Drawing by Gunnar Widholm which appeared in Stockholms Dagblad *on 6 December 1909.*

[ ]

Their most curious holiday episode had been an encounter with Strindberg. 'I thought it my duty to pay my respects to a great man whom I considered one of the great dramatists of Europe,' Shaw afterwards remembered. 'People told me it was not of the slightest use. He is absolutely mad, they said, he won't see anybody, he never takes walks except in the middle of the night when there is nobody about, he attacks all his friends with the greatest fury. You will only be wasting your time.' Nevertheless, 'I achieved the impossible', Shaw wrote to William Archer[30]. 'He was quite a pleasant looking person,' Shaw recalled, 'with the most beautiful sapphire blue eyes I have ever seen. He was beyond expression shy.' Shaw had prepared some conversational material in French, but Strindberg took the wind out of his sails 'by addressing me in German'. Their exchange developed by way of some embarrassed silences, a 'pale smile or two' from Strindberg, and an undercurrent of polite French from Charlotte.

Strindberg had arranged for them to see that morning a special performance of *Miss Julie* at his Intimate Theatre, having summoned August Falck and Manda Björling back from their holiday in the archipelago to play the two protagonists. The absence of an audience and the presence of Strindberg had been unsettling – this astonishingly being 'the first time Strindberg had accepted to see the play in the 20 years of its existence,' Anthony Swerling records, 'so much did he shy from the theatre'. Though Strindberg had proudly shown the Shaws round his theatre beforehand, shortly afterwards, in a celebrated spasm of gloom, he consulted his watch and, noting that it was almost half past one, remarked in German that at two o'clock he was going to be sick. 'On this strong hint the party broke up.'

How much did they comprehend each other, the author of *Married*, which Strindberg called 'the reverse side of my fearful attraction towards the other sex'; and the author of *Getting Married*, a tentative 'conversation' with feminist implications dramatizing the economic relations of marriage? Shaw was to describe what he had seen at the Intimate Theatre as one of Strindberg's 'chamber plays'. With the emotional concentration of chamber music he had never felt easy. But generally he knew where Strindberg stood. 'I was born too soon to be greatly influenced by him as a playwright, but', he was to write 'he is among the greatest of the great'. In the Preface to *Three Plays for Puritans* he had described him as 'the only genuinely Shakespearean modern dramatist', a resolute tragi-comedian, logical and faithful, who gave us the choice either of dismissing as absurd his way of judging conduct or else, by accepting it, concluding that 'it is cowardly to continue living'.

The suffering men and women inflict upon each other in the name of love never appears in Shaw's work as it does in Strindberg's. Greatness 'implies a degree of human tragedy, of suffering and sacrifice', wrote Thomas Mann. 'The knotted muscles of Tolstoy bearing up the full burden of morality, Atlas-like; Strindberg, who was in hell; the martyr's death Nietzsche died on the cross of thought; it is these that inspire us with the reverence of tragedy; but in Shaw there was nothing of all this. Was he beyond such things, or were they beyond him?'

Shaw's tragedy lay in the need to suppress such things; Strindberg's in the need to re-enact them. But Shaw felt the force of that re-enactment. He tried to persuade Beerbohm Tree to put on *Lycko Pers Resa* at His Majesty's (the play closest to Ibsen's *Peer Gynt*), but without success. Almost none of Strindberg's plays had been translated into English before Shaw's sister Lucy, with Maurice Elvey, produced a version of *Miss Julie* that was first presented by the Adelphi Play Society in 1912. That year, the Swedish newspaper *Dagens Nyheter* circulated a letter eliciting opinions of Strindberg's role in European culture to be published in the event of his death from cancer. 'Strindberg is a very great dramatist: he and Ibsen have made Sweden and Norway the dramatic centre of the world,' Shaw replied. ' . . . Time may wear him out; but Death will not succeed in murdering him.' Strindberg died a fortnight later.

Douglas Dunn

Europa's Lover

IX

By the banks of a Scandinavian lake
We heard harness and smalltalk
As a migrating tribe came down
To water its ponies and say goodbye.

Later a picnic happened, with white cloths,
With children and jealousies and wine,
Women holding their skirts up to their knees
Tip-toeing over these same pebbles.

Then there was Strindberg or some such,
Up to his waist in lake and shivering,
Demented with ethics, maddened
By men and women and the snow falling.

Clive Sinclair[31]

from *Augustus Rex*

Prologue: 1912

'The future of Strindberg stimulates and baffles curiosity,' observed the omnipotent *Encyclopaedia Britannica* with typical gravitas, blissfully unaware that at the very moment of publication his intestines were already efflorescent with cancer. Ah, but *I* knew! How? Was I his private physician? Hardly, my dears. That honour fell to his son-in-law. Let us just say that I had *access* to various medical reports, including those of Dr Petrén of Lund who, unimpressed by talk of Benike's worm, clearly suspected malignant encrustations. I knew what that portended, being well-versed in the skills of diagnosis and prognosis, as I have to be in my line of work.

Why have you turned so white, my dears? Do you fear to dwell upon the inherent weakness of your flesh? Does the consideration of death hold too many terrors? Ah, I understand, you think I am an undertaker. Silly things! You should see me shiver when I cross the path of one of those shadowy morticians, all astink with the odour of embalming fluid. No, my job requires me to reach the moribund patient's bedside *before* the patron saint of every grave-digger, the Angel of Death, has had time to deliver the coup de grace. You could call me a travelling salesman, of sorts, specializing in a single merchandise.

What is most likely to tempt the dying? That's right, my dears, I peddle second chances. Some turn out to prefer death, of course. Others get it, whatever their predilection. Believe me, I understand the disappointment they feel as they draw their final breaths. There is nothing more frustrating, for one such as I, than to enter a sick-room full of expectation only to find the Angel of Death, already successful, with a post-coital smile on his smug face. 'Necrophiliac!' I cry. Nor am I far from the truth. Who put *mor* into a*mor*ous?

Strindberg on the balcony of his flat in 1912, shortly before his death.

The Angel of Death, called Azrael but known by most as the Don Juan at the gates of doom.

He is a handsome brute, a cold-eyed seducer; a creature of instinct whose main function is to lead the dying to their final orgasm, assist them to let go, to finally shake off the self. He is the winged harbinger of a process that is one hundred percent natural . . . unlike me. It shames me to admit it, but there have been times when I have paused on the threshold of a room in order to watch my rival at work through the key-hole.

Forgive me, my dears, the memory of those humiliations has caused me to forget my manners. I beg you to show indulgence toward one whose breeding is not all it might be and permit him to introduce himself! His name is – *my* name is Beelzebub, Lord of the Flies. Look, I don't entertain false illusions about myself, I know that most people run a mile when they hear the boom-buzz-boom that announces my arrival. To tell you the truth I wouldn't blame you if you did the same. My looks are not pretty, like Azrael's, nor is my character admirable. I would run too, if only I could. Unfortunately I possess a particular talent much appreciated by my master; I can catch souls. No, it is more than a talent, it is a gift. I was therefore spared a tedious apprenticeship among the moribund hoi-polloi and, from the outset of my career, was only despatched to obtain the immortal souls of the very great. My deeds would be less criminal, would even be *excusable*, if my master actually sought these noble beings (these Nobel prize-winners) for the sake of their company, but he neither had nor has developed any interest in their conversation whatsoever; he wants them only because of their *names*, because of their value to his eternal opponent. In short, I must sell the best minds of every generation a bill of goods.

When it became public knowledge that August Strindberg was in a bad way I was immediately shown his case history and told to prepare myself for the journey to Stockholm. Let us get something straight, I may be Lord of the Flies, but there are none on me. I knew all about Strindberg and his works long before I consulted his entry in the *Encyclopaedia Britannica*. As a matter of fact I was something of a fan. So why did I agree to conspire against him? How little you mortals know! There are some commands (as distinct from commandments) that cannot be disobeyed. Especially those of my master, whose sanctions are immoderate. To be frank, I am in thrall to a brute with no more mercy than a fatal disease. It pains me to confess to this want of courage. I'd much rather present myself as a cultivated soul, whose particular skills have been perverted by force of circumstance, but for once in my life I feel inclined to tell the truth and the truth is that they have not. I am what I am. The responsibility for my actions is mine alone. Why do I decline to exculpate myself with the time-honoured words, 'I was only obeying orders'? Because, while accurate, they avoid the uncomfortable fact that I enjoy my work immensely. This means that I went eagerly to Stockholm, as required, but with a bad conscience.

While still a healthy man Strindberg had predicted that he would breathe his last on 14 May 1912. In order to prove him wrong I had to make sure that the Angel of Death was other-wise occupied on that day. So I told him that Edvard Munch was on his last legs. Why Edvard Munch? Well, the Angel of Death has a penchant for artists, though he knows nothing about art; what he knows is that they have a talent for self-destruction. This ignorance has led to many spectacular blunders.

Allow me to introduce Marc Chagall's own account of one such, which gives you a good idea of my rival's rather dramatic working methods. 'A square, empty room. In one corner, a single bed, and me on it. It is getting dark. Suddenly the ceiling opens and a winged being descends with a crash, filling the room with movement and clouds. A rustle of trailing wings. I think: An angel!' The Angel of Death thinks: This man, Chagall, is still full of years. Embarrassed, he tries to make an inconspicuous exit, but fails. 'After rummaging about all over the place,' continued the astonished artist, 'he rises and passes through the opening in the ceiling, taking all the light and the blue air away with him.'

Franz Kafka received a similar visitation. 'Towards evening I walked over to the window and sat down on the low sill,' he wrote in a diary entry dated 25 June 1917. 'Then, for the first time not restlessly moving about, I happened calmly to glance into the interior of the room and at the ceiling . . . The tremor began at the edges of the thinly plastered white ceiling. Little pieces of plaster broke off and with a distinct thud fell here and there . . . a bluish violet began to mix with the white; it spread straight out from the centre of the ceiling, which itself remained white.' Finally the ceiling broke apart to reveal 'an angel in bluish-violet robes girt with gold cords' who sank slowly 'on great white silken-shining wings'. The Angel of Death saw the malign scars on the tips of the young writer's lungs, which looked like the clipped wings of a fallen angel, but he also saw that the tuberculosis was far from its fatal denouement. Two months later, prompted by Kafka's first pulmonary haemorrhage, Professor Pick confirmed my friend's diagnosis. Thereafter the Angel of Death kept a fatherly eye on Franz.

As planned, the credulous fellow was on a wild-goose chase while Strindberg lay adying in his room within the Blue Tower, which overlooks the intersection of Drottninggatan and Tegnérgatan. I decided to make my entrance from the balcony where The King of Poets, the People's Strindberg, had ventured for the last time the previous January to acknowledge the torchlight procession in the street below. 'There must be thousands of people down there,' he had mumbled to his daughter Anne-Marie. She had squeezed his hand. 'Happy birthday, papa,' she whispered, as one of the brass bands struck up the *Marseillaise*. Tears filled her eyes, but these may have been occasioned by the icy blast, there being a complementary drip on the end of the playwright's red nose. 'Long live Strindberg!' the workers exclaimed as they paraded past the ailing scribe, ruddy banners billowing in the easterly wind. Their champion was sixty-three, and had only four more months to live.

Enter Beelzebub, the people's hero, to the rescue. Strindberg was clearly sinking fast. His poky room reeked of disinfectant, but not even the strongest of fumes could have concealed all the olfactory evidence of corporeal dissolution. Hence the flies that congregated upon his stinking sheets. I had arrived in the nick of time. A woman in uniform kept a vigil beside his bed, like a Jewess in silent prayer at the Wailing Wall, though she brought no solace to the irascible invalid. On the contrary her obstinate adherence to such an uncomfortable wooden chair seemed to irritate him, so much so that the sting was temporarily restored to his tongue. 'Nurse Kistner,' he murmured, 'go to bed, there is no need to worry about me, I am no longer here!'

'If you are not here,' I asked after the nurse had reluctantly taken her employer's advice, 'tell me, where are you?' I can usually count on the element of surprise, the buzz-boom-buzz effect; but Strindberg, being a man of uncanny entrances and exits, was harder to impress. 'Beneath the waves,' he replied calmly, as though the devil's emissary were an everyday visitor, 'at the bottom of the sea'. 'Am I a fish?' I asked. 'No,' he conceded. 'Then you are not at the bottom of the sea,' I concluded. 'But I am badly holed,' he replied. 'My body is finished. All its innards are in revolt. It feels ready to burst, though there is precious little left of it. I am not sorry. I always suspected that my soul, my mad soul, was not fitted for confinement in such a pathetic vessel.'

My immediate task was clear; I had to prevent Strindberg from jumping ship. 'It may be a poor thing,' I agreed, 'but without it you'll be press-ganged into the diaspora of lost souls that howls in the fog outside the pearly gates. Be advised, my friend, heaven is full; even with restricted entry it resembles nothing so much as a London slum.' Strindberg looked at me curiously.

'Why do you use the word *diaspora*?' he demanded, ignoring my warning (and the subtle nod to his favourite English author). 'Are you a Yid?' 'No,' I replied, 'but the Jews named me.' 'Named you what?' he asked. 'Beelzebub,' I replied. 'Aha,' he said, 'I know all about you. The Philistine *baal-zebub*, lord of the insects, turned by the punning Israelites into *baal-zebul*, lord of the dung-hill. If I may say, you do not come smelling of roses. Have you read *The Roots of World Language* or *Ancestors of the Modern Tongue*? In them I prove, quite conclusively, that Hebrew, the sacred tongue, is the mother of all other languages. E.g. Idaho, *yehuda*. Minnesota, *minasoth*, a place of refuge. Canada, *kam*, a market town. Ad infinitum. A funny people, the Jews; even on my death bed I do not know whether I love them or hate them.'

Archimedes said, Give me a lever and I will move the world. Strindberg, in his excitement, managed a comparable miracle. He raised his emaciated frame upon his elbows so that he was, in effect, sitting up. His hair, white and sparse, was damp with the strain. 'I'm cold,' he said. So I draped a frayed dressing-gown around his shoulders. 'My clothes do not fit me any more,' he said, 'not even this'. He was correct; in his brown-check robe he looked like a scarecrow. 'Now help me walk to the piano,' he said. It was on the other side of the ill-lit chamber, against the far wall. I ferried him through the chiaroscuro, through the waves of daylight that squeezed between the cracks of the closed shutters. He was as weightless as a teacup. 'Hush,' he said, 'mustn't wake Nurse Kistner.' Then, to my amazement, he proceeded to pick out *Nearer my God to Thee* on the keyboard of the Steinway. His face, fitfully illuminated by a guttering candle, flickered like a fading photograph. 'Are you aware,' he said, 'that the orchestra on the *Titanic* insisted upon playing that when the ship went down? Look at me. The *Titanic*, c'est moi.'

'I am Beelzebub,' I said, 'my breath can melt icebergs. You do not have to die.' 'I've told you already,' he said, 'I pray to be released from this undignified corpse.' He tapped his noddle. 'Only my mind is worth saving,' he said. 'That alone, being homogeneous with the supreme intelligence, will be absorbed into the godhead, as was the *Titanic* by the mighty ocean. I yearn for death.' 'How can you, a great artist blessed with many more unwritten masterpieces, dispose of your destiny so easily?' I demanded. 'My enemies have worn me down,' he replied. 'I am weary of the fight. Like Prospero I hereby renounce my magic.' 'I am offering to restore it,' I said. 'And in return,' said the dying man, closing the piano lid, 'you'll doubtless roast my immortal remains until the last trump.'

'I'm surprised to hear such propaganda from Strindberg, of all people,' I said. 'I make an offer of celestial generosity and by way of gratitude I am pelted with fire and brimstone. Believe me, sir, hell bears no resemblance to the prophecies of your clerics. And even if it did would you choose to spend eternity in their company? Or would you prefer the society of Lucifer, Descartes, Newton and Pascal, our guiding lights? Do not look so surprised. If Pascal had truly been on the side of the angels would he have informed the Archbishop of Rouen that a certain Père St Ange was entertaining some speculative ideas on theological points that were not strictly orthodox? It seems that while he found it shocking that men who were in the right should not be tolerated, he found it even more shocking that men who were in the wrong should be.

'I freely confess that hell has its bonfires, but its general appearance resembles that of a well-tended garden; one that has been cultivated, with no little effort, from the tangled forest of human emotion and misbehaviour. It is true that anti-social insects – ah, I mean instincts, of course – and unruly inclinations can never be bred out of the species entirely; but just as the good gardener binds his honeysuckle and wisteria and forces them to grow along pre-ordained routes, so we control hysteria and similar manifestations with constant watchfulness and rigorous re-education. We see our society as a microcosm of the whole, a reflection of the universe which is – though it is often forgotten – ruled by hierarchical, regular and eternal laws. In short, we believe that truth is objective, that order descends from the higher to the lower, that humanity is raised above the animal kingdom by virtue of reason, and that the duality of mind and body symbolizes this distinction. Although you are welcome to take up residence immediately we do not necessarily encourage it, for we have no wish to over-populate hell. Rather our long-term strategy is to colonize the world by persuading carefully selected clients to stay put. You should therefore regard hell as the homeland to which you may retire when you consider that your life on earth has been properly fulfilled.'

'Are you asking me to believe that hell, far from being a place of punishment, is the ultimate rationalization,' gasped Strindberg, 'the final reduction of life to its scientific principles? Forgive my scepticism, Mr Beelzebub, but I think you are trying to sell me a bill of goods. There is no smoke without fire. Of that I am convinced!'

Before you dismiss me as a fraud, my dears, spare a moment to consider my position. I am a realist. I know that I cannot expect people to flock to hell as if it were the French Riviera. I must be able to offer something more – and, believe me, I do. Those extra years are no con. We do not have many virtues in hell, but patience is one of them. That being the case I was not offended by Strindberg's rebuff; indeed, I expected it. Most of his peers have similar reactions. However much humanity's great thinkers may prattle on about order, no one but the most deracinated of individuals really desires it; deep down, in secret places accessible only to torturers, lurks a greater dread than disorder; boredom, the fear that dares not speak its name. Therefore when Strindberg, exasperated by my persistence, cried – 'Are you deaf? Did you not hear me when I said I was finished with this vale of tears?' – I did not believe him any more than he believed me. I recognised the world-weariness of a man eaten away by cancer and responded accordingly, concentrating upon the practicalities of life rather than its theories.

'I remain unconvinced that you really consider spiritual intercourse to be superior to the bodily kind,' I remarked. 'And so I am going to set you a simple test. Do you remember what Harriet Bosse[32] said to you when you were still courting?' He remembered. Tears rolled down his wasted cheeks. 'She asked God to bless you for having written the line: "I felt like Faust regretting his youth, before this masterpiece of a woman child." Well, I can give you everything that Faust received. And more. A new dawn and a new Harriet.' 'No,' he said, shaking his head.

I was beginning to weary of his obstinacy. 'I may be deaf,' I snapped, 'but I have not been blinded by the church's calumnies. What do you think you will see when you are eventually granted admittance to the celestial sphere? God's green acres? Ha! Heaven is a cess-pit. And why? Because no one is prepared to do a minute's work up there. In heaven they think every day is the sabbath. Its characteristic sound – the flip-flop of fat feet – is echoed by its very name: *hea-ven*. Compare it to *hell*. Did you know that there have been occasions when that bell-like toll was sufficient to revive the comatose? Ding-dong hell. Listen. Hell. *Hell*. How desperately the tongue tries to free itself from the closed *h*. Fortunately, *e* (for escape) comes to the rescue. And down the double *l* you slide. To freedom. Now look at the word. Hell. The bar across the *h* is like a prison door, blocking you off from the essential pleasures of life. *E* is the key. And *ll* is the tunnel, the tunnel of love, open, unbarred and bottomless. Consider the alternative; nevermore to touch a female body, nevermore to smell womanly perfumes. No new Harriet, no new dawn. Instead you will choke upon the finite stench of your own putrefaction.' I had not used le mot juste; the whole of my carefully constructed argument was condemned by the careless placement of a single word at its end.

'The alchemists believed that putrefaction was the sine qua non of ultimate wisdom,' he replied, 'they looked upon the grave as a womb, wherein would begin the renaissance of man.' 'They were wrong,' I fibbed, 'without the body there is nothing'. Above my head I heard a rustling and, raising my eyes, saw that the ceiling was beginning to glow, as though it were suffused with ultra-violet light. 'Alas, you do not have long to make up your mind,' I said, 'the Angel of Death is fast approaching. It is, I am assured, a pleasant thing to expire in his arms. Give the word and I will leave you to his tender mercies.' I made ready to depart, hoping against hope that Strindberg, now that his final appointment was at hand, would change his mind.

'Wait!' he cried. 'It is true that I was weary and ready for death, but your cunning words have reawakened my appetite for life. Help me, Beelzebub, I am no longer prepared to forsake all earthly delights. What must I do? Help me!'

At that precise moment, as the clock on the mantelpiece struck four, the ceiling of Strindberg's bedroom parted and the Angel of Death was manifest. 'It seems that my ability to help you is at an end,' I observed. 'The Angel of Death is as beguiling as a snake-charmer. In his presence I am powerless. Poor Strindberg! You now belong irrecoverably to the dying, who do not have free-will, who have no choice but to die.' 'No!' cried Strindberg. 'Take what you want, take my immortal soul, but give me life!' 'I'll see what can be done,' I replied.

The Angel of Death has turquoise eyes, which burn like arctic ice. In order to win a reprieve for Strindberg I knew that I would have to avoid their disabling fire. I concentrated instead upon the golden buttons of his tunic. 'I was here first,' I said. 'Undeniable,' replied the Angel of Death, 'but I am here now, and unless this gentleman has unwisely signed one of your contracts I mean to have him in a matter of minutes.' *Gentleman!* Then he didn't know in whose house he was, a particular hazard of his roof-top entrances. Nor was Azrael likely to recognize his host, now that his face was covered with nothing but a butter-coloured membrane. I took heart. Meanwhile, the Angel of Death plucked Strindberg from the piano stool and returned the ragged bag of skin and bone that bore his name to its bed. 'This is a man whose time has come,' he announced. 'Listen,' I said, 'compromise on this nonentity and you'll meet no opposition the next time a celebrity nears his end.' 'For example?' he asked. 'The Great Caruso,' I replied, relying upon the angelic passion for grand opera. 'You've got a deal,' he said.

I hurried over to my client, who was growing colder by the second. I propped him up against his pillow. 'You must make a new will,' I informed him, as though I were some solicitor's articled clerk. 'To what end?' he asked. 'Here is pen, here is paper,' I replied impatiently. 'Now write the following: "My body must not be dissected or laid out in state, only shown to my relatives. No death-mask can be made, no photographs taken. I want to be interred at eight in the morning, to avoid any curious bystanders. I do not want to be buried in a crypt, much less in a church, but in the new cemetery; not in the section for the wealthy, however." Got it all?' Like Samson, that other cuckold, Strindberg somehow managed to recapture his demonic energy at the last. I saw that he had transcribed every word; nor had he forgotten that all-important addendum, his signature. 'Look,' I explained, 'you are too far gone not to die. To do otherwise would be to humiliate the Angel of Death.' 'So you failed?' he asked. 'On the contrary,' I replied, 'I have arranged for you to be spared his most fulsome embrace. You will not *actually* die, but merely enter a state of suspended animation. No warmth, no breath, shall testify, thou liv'st; each part, depriv'd of supple government, shall, stiff and stark and cold, appear like death; and in this borrow'd likeness of shrunk death you will remain for a generation or more. Until your acquaintances have all followed you to the grave. Then, *providing your instructions have been obeyed to the letter*, I shall raise you up.'

And so it happened. Strindberg died at 4.30 that afternoon. In the words of one of the few people considered close enough to attend the corpse, 'the pale face on the white pillow had a strange expression that is hard to forget, a beautiful, almost impish little smile.' I think you know why, my dears.

Three Nineteenth-Century Poets

Henry Wadsworth Longfellow

A passage from a translation of
Esaias Tegnér's 'Frithiof's Temptation' [33]

III

Spring is coming, birds are twittering, forests leaf, and
smiles the sun,
And the loosened torrents downward, singing, to the ocean
run;
Glowing like the cheek of Freya, peeping rosebuds 'gin to
ope,
And in human hearts awaken love of life, and joy, and hope.

Now will hunt the ancient monarch, and the queen shall join
the sport:
Swarming in its gorgeous splendor, is assembled all the
Court;
Bows ring loud, and quivers rattle, stallions paw the ground
alway,
And, with hoods upon their eyelids, scream the falcons for
their prey.

See, the Queen of the Chase advances! Frithiof, gaze not at
the sight!
Like a star upon a spring-cloud sits she on her palfrey white.
Half of Freya, half of Rota, yet more beauteous than these
two,
And from her light hat of purple wave aloft the feathers blue.

Gaze not at her eyes' blue heaven, gaze not at her golden hair!
Oh beware! her waist is slender, full her bosom is, beware!
Look not at the rose and lily on her cheek that shifting play,
List not to the voice beloved, whispering like the wind of May.

Tegnér's Drapa[34]

I heard a voice, that cried,
'Balder the Beautiful
Is dead, is dead!'
And through the misty air
Passed like the mournful cry
Of sunward sailing cranes.

I saw the pallid corpse
Of the dead sun
Borne through the Northern sky.
Blasts from Niffelheim
Lifted the sheeted mists
Around him as he passed.

And the voice forever cried,
'Balder the Beautiful
Is dead, is dead!'
And died away
Through the dreary night,
In accents of despair.

Balder the Beautiful,
God of the summer sun,
Fairest of all the Gods!
Light from his forehead beamed,
Runes were upon his tongue,
As on the warrior's sword.

All things in earth and air
Bound were by magic spell
Never to do him harm;
Even the plants and stones;
All save the mistletoe,
The sacred mistletoe!

Hoeder, the blind old God,
Whose feet are shod with silence,
Pierced through that gentle breast
With his sharp spear, by fraud,
Made of the mistletoe!
The accursed mistletoe!

They laid him in his ship,
With horse and harness,
As on a funeral pyre.
Odin placed
A ring upon his finger,
And whispered in his ear.

They launched the burning ship!
It floated far away
Over the misty sea,
Till like the sun it seemed,
Sinking beneath the waves.
Balder returned no more!

So perish the old Gods!
But out of the sea of Time
Rises a new land of song,
Fairer than the old.
Over its meadows green
Walk the young bards and sing.

Build it again,
O ye bards,
Fairer than before;
Ye fathers of the new race,
Feed upon morning dew,
Sing the new Song of Love!

The law of force is dead!
The law of love prevails!
Thor, the thunderer,
Shall rule the earth no more,
No more, with threats,
Challenge the meek Christ.

Sing no more,
O ye bards of the North,
Of Vikings and of Jarls!
Of the days of Eld
Preserve the freedom only,
Not the deeds of blood!

William Barnes[35]

Orra, A Lapland Tale

Illìc, ut perhibent, – intempesta silet nox
Semper, et obtentâ densantur nocte tenebræ;
Virg. Georg. Lib 1

There, as they say, perpetual night is found
In silence brooding on th'unhappy ground.
Dryden

O land of darkness, and of wintry storms,
Oft do I wish, although I know not why,
To see those hills that stretch their snowy forms
Aloft beneath thy cold and sunless sky,
While deadly chilliness is in the sigh
Of gentlest airs thy frigid winter knows;
Nor wood nor stream relieves the weary eye
But all is shrouded in accumulating snows.

They boast not there of conquests they have made,
Nor mourn the deeds their enemies have done;
The shining helmet, or the warrior's blade,
Has never glittered in that pallid sun;
They boast no trophies from the foeman won,
And none have yielded to his mightier hand:
No riches covet they – and they have none,
To lure the spoilers from a foreign land.

There in the fleet Pulkha, along the plain
They glide, exulting in the rein-deer's speed,
Nor dream of happier regions, where the rein
Controuls the gallant and the mighty steed,
Where flocks around the verdant mountains feed,
And yellow corn embrowns the fading year.

Nor are they less content, than those who lead
A life of luxury and splendour here.

Warm glows their summer, while the sky displays
The solar orb, but soon that summer flies;
The wintry air soon chills the short'ning days,
And suddenly the blasted verdure dies;
Then gathering clouds, and wintry storms arise,
And the pale sun withdraws his feeble light,
No longer striving with the gloomy skies,
But leaves the land to winter and to night.

Alfred, Lord Tennyson

from *In Memoriam*[36]

Ring out, wild bells, to the wild sky,
The flying cloud, the frosty light:
The year is dying in the night;
Ring out, wild bells, and let him die.

Ring out the old, ring in the new,
Ring, happy bells, across the snow:
The year is going, let him go;
Ring out the false, ring in the true.

Ring out the grief that saps the mind,
For those that here we see no more;
Ring out the feud of rich and poor,
Ring in redress to all mankind.

Observers of Swedish Affairs

Samuel Johnson

*The Vanity of Human Wishes. The Tenth Satire of Juvenal,
imitated by Samuel Johnson*

On what Foundation stands the Warrior's Pride?
How just his Hopes let *Swedish Charles*[37] decide;
A Frame of Adamant, a Soul of Fire,
No Dangers fright him, and no Labours tire;
O'er Love, o'er Force, extends his wide Domain,
Unconquer'd Lord of Pleasure and of Pain;
No Joys to him pacific Scepters yield,
War sounds the Trump, he rushes to the Field;
Behold surrounding Kings their Pow'r combine,
And One capitulate, and One resign;
Peace courts his Hand, but spread her Charms in vain;
'Think Nothing gain'd, he cries, till nought remain,
'On *Moscow's* Walls till *Gothic* Standards fly,
'And all is Mine beneath the Polar Sky.'
The March begins in Military State,
And Nations on his Eye suspended wait;
Stern Famine guards the solitary Coast,
And Winter barricades the Realms of Frost;
He comes, nor Want nor Cold his Course delay; –
Hide, blushing Glory, hide *Pultowa's* Day:
The vanquish'd Hero leaves his broken Bands,
And shews his Miseries in distant Lands;
Condemn'd a needy Supplicant to wait,
While Ladies interpose, and Slaves debate.
But did not Chance at length her Error mend?
Did no subverted Empire mark his End?

Did rival Monarchs give the fatal Wound?
Or hostile Millions press him to the Ground?
His Fall was destin'd to a barren Strand,
A petty Fortress, and a dubious Hand;
He left the Name, at which the World grew pale,
To point a Moral, or adorn a Tale.

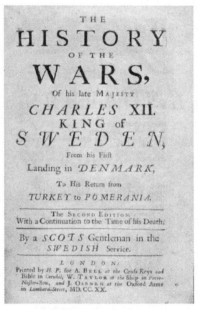

In 1717, Daniel Defoe published, anonymously, A Short View of the
Conduct of the King of Sweden, *an admiring account of Charles
XII's life and deeds up to 1714. Three years later, (after Charles's death
in 1718) a second edition appeared, this time with a detailed and
equally eulogistic description of the king's last years.*

From the Preface:
'The subject is as fruitful of great events, as any real history
can pretend to, and is grac'd with as many glorious actions,
battles, sieges, and gallant enterprizes, things which make a
history pleasant, as well as profitable, as can be met with in
any history of so few years that is now extant in the world.

The hero who makes the superior figure in this story, were we to run the parallel, might vye with the Caesars and Alexanders of ancient history; he has done actions that posterity will have room to fable upon, till they make his history incredible and turn it into romance: his enemies confess his glory, and do more than acknowledge their being unequal to him either in the camp or in the cabinet, by their stooping to all possible methods; however base or dishonourable to oppress him.

We have seen heaven punish the first breaches with an exemplar justice, and tho' for wise ends he has afflicted the Swedish nation and reduced their monarch to circumstances, not at present to do himself justice; yet if heaven should, as in justice we may render him more glorious than the first.'

William Wordsworth

Sonnets

VII: *The King of Sweden*[38]
(*Composed probably August 1802. Published 1807*)
The Voice of song from distant lands shall call
To that great King: shall hail the crownèd Youth
Who, taking counsel of unbending Truth,
By one example hath set forth to all
How they with dignity may stand; or fall,
If fall they must. Now, whither doth it tend?
And what to him and his shall be the end?
That thought is one which neither can appal
Nor cheer him; for the illustrious Swede hath done
The thing which ought to be; is raised *above*
All consequences: work he hath begun
Of fortitude, and piety, and love,
Which all his glorious ancestors approve:
The heroes bless him, him their rightful son.

XX

(Composed 1809. Published 1815)

Call not the royal Swede unfortunate,
Who never did to Fortune bend the knee;
Who slighted fear; rejected steadfastly
Temptation; and whose kingly name and state
Have 'perished by his choice, and not his fate!'
Hence lives He, to his inner self endeared;
And hence, wherever virtue is revered,
He sits a more exalted Potentate,
Throned in the hearts of men. Should Heaven ordain
That this great Servant of a righteous cause
Must still have sad or vexing thoughts to endure,
Yet may a sympathising spirit pause,
Admonished by these truths, and quench all pain
In thankful joy and gratulation pure.

XXI

Look now on that Adventurer who hath paid
His vows to Fortune; who, in cruel slight
Of virtuous hope, of liberty, and right,
Hath followed wheresoe'er a way was made
By the blind Goddess, – ruthless, undismayed;
And so hath gained at length a prosperous height,
Round which the elements of worldly might
Beneath his haughty feet, like clouds, are laid.
O joyless power that stands by lawless force!
Curses are *his* dire portion, scorn, and hate,
Internal darkness and unquiet breath;
And, if old judgements keep their sacred course,
Him from that height shall Heaven precipitate
By violent and ignominious death.

Mary Wollstonecraft[39]

from *A Short Residence In Sweden, Norway, and Denmark*

Letter Four

The severity of the long Swedish winter tends to render the people sluggish; for, though this season has its peculiar pleasures, too much time is employed to guard against its inclemency. Still, as warm clothing is absolutely necessary, the women spin, and the men weave, and by these exertions get a fence to keep out the cold. I have rarely passed a knot of cottages without seeing cloth laid out to bleach; and when I entered, always found the women spinning or knitting.

A mistaken tenderness, however, for their children, makes them, even in summer, load them with flannels; and, having a sort of natural antipathy to cold water, the squalid appearance of the poor babes, not to speak of the noxious smell which flannel and rugs retain, seems a reply to a question I had often asked – Why I did not see more children in the villages I passed through? Indeed the children appear to be nipt in the bud, having neither the graces nor charms of their age. And this, I am persuaded, is much more owing to the ignorance of the mothers than to the rudeness of the climate. Rendered feeble by the continual perspiration they are kept in, whilst every pore is absorbing unwholesome moisture, they give them, even at the breast, brandy, salt fish, and every other crude substance, which air and exercise enables the parent to digest.

The women of fortune here, as well as every where else, have nurses to suckle their children; and the total want of chastity in the lower class of women frequently renders them very unfit for the trust.

You have sometimes remarked to me the difference of the manners of the country girls in England and in America; attributing the reserve of the former to the climate – to the absence of genial suns. But it must be their stars, not the zephyrs gently stealing on their senses, which here lead frail women astray. – Who can look at these rocks, and allow the voluptuousness of nature to be an excuse for gratifying the desires it inspires? We must, therefore, find some other cause beside voluptuousness, I believe, to account for the conduct of the Swedish and American country girls; for I am led to conclude, from all the observations I have made, that there is always a mixture of sentiment and imagination in voluptuousness, to which neither of them have much pretension.

The country girls of Ireland and Wales equally feel the first impulse of nature, which, restrained in England by fear of delicacy, proves that society is there in a more advanced state. Besides, as the mind is cultivated, and taste gains ground, the passions become stronger, and rest on something more stable than the casual sympathies of the moment. Health and idleness will always account for promiscuous amours; and in some degree I term every person idle, the exercise of whose mind does not bear some proportion to that of the body.

The Swedish ladies exercise neither sufficiently; of course, grow fat at an early age; and when they have not this downy appearance, a comfortable idea, you will say, in a cold climate, they are not remarkable for fine forms. They have, however, mostly fine complexions; but indolence makes the lily soon displace the rose. The quantity of coffee, spices, and other things of that kind, with want of care, almost universally spoil their teeth, which contrast but ill with their ruby lips.

The manners of Stockholm are refined, I hear, by the introduction of gallantry; but in the country, romping and coarse freedoms, with coarser allusions, keep the spirits awake. In the article of cleanliness, the women, of all descriptions, seem very deficient; and their dress shews that vanity is more inherent in women than taste.

The men appear to have paid still less court to the graces. They are a robust, healthy race, distinguished for their common sense and turn for humour, rather than for wit or sentiment. I include not, as you may suppose, in this general character, some of the nobility and officers, who having travelled, are polite and well-informed.

I must own to you, that the lower class of people here amuse and interest me much more than the middling, with their apish good breeding and prejudices. The sympathy and frankness of heart conspicuous in the peasantry produces even a simple gracefulness of deportment, which has frequently struck me as very picturesque; I have often been touched by their extreme desire to oblige me, when I could not explain my wants, and by their earnest manner of expressing that desire. There is such a charm in tenderness! – It is so delightful to love our fellow-creatures, and meet the honest affections as they break forth. Still, my good friend, I begin to think that I should not like to live continually in the country, with people whose minds have such a narrow range. My heart would frequently be interested; but my mind would languish for more companionable society.

The beauties of nature appear to me now even more alluring than in my youth, because my intercourse with the world has formed, without vitiating my taste. But, with respect to the inhabitants of the country, my fancy has probably, when disgusted with artificial manners, solaced itself by joining the advantages of cultivation with the interesting sincerity of innocence, forgetting the lassitude that ignorance will naturally produce. I like to see animals sporting, and sympathize in their pains and pleasures. Still I love sometimes to view the human face divine, and trace the soul, as well as the heart, in its varying lineaments.

A journey to the country, which I must shortly make, will enable me to extend my remarks. –

Adieu!

Letter Five

Had I determined to travel in Sweden merely for pleasure, I should probably have chosen the road to Stockholm, though convinced, by repeated observation, that the manners of a people are best discriminated in the country. The inhabitants of the capital are all of the same genus; for the varieties in the species we must, therefore, search where the habitations of men are so separated as to allow the difference of climate to have its natural effect. And with this difference we are, perhaps, most forcibly struck at the first view, just as we form an estimate of the leading traits of a character at the first glance, of which intimacy afterwards makes us almost lose sight.

As my affairs called me to Strömstad (the frontier town of Sweden) in my way to Norway, I was to pass over, I hear, the most uncultivated part of the country. Still I believe that the grand features of Sweden are the same every where, and it is only the grand features that admit of description. There is an individuality in every prospect, which remains in the memory as forcibly depicted as the particular features that have arrested our attention; yet we cannot find words to discriminate that individuality so as to enable a stranger to say, this is the face, that the view. We may amuse by setting the imagination to work; but we cannot store the memory with a fact.

As I wish to give you a general idea of this country, I shall continue in my desultory manner to make such observations and reflections as the circumstances draw forth, without losing time, by endeavouring to arrange them.

Travelling in Sweden is very cheap, and even commodious, if you make but the proper arrangements. Here, as in other parts of the continent, it is necessary to have your own carriage, and to have a servant who can speak the language, if you are unacquainted with it. Sometimes a servant who can drive would be found very useful, which was

The town of Kvistrum in western Sweden, close to the Norwegian border, around the time of Mary Wollstonecraft's visit in 1795.

our case, for I travelled in company with two gentlemen, one of whom had a German servant who drove very well. This was all the party; for not intending to make a long stay, I left my little girl behind me.

As the roads were not much frequented, to avoid waiting three or four hours for horses, we sent, as is the constant custom, an *avant courier* the night before, to order them at every post, and we constantly found them ready. Our first set I jokingly termed *requisition* horses; but afterwards we had almost always little spirited animals that went on at a round pace.

The roads, making allowance for the ups and downs, are uncommonly good and pleasant. The experience, including the postillions and other incidental things, does not amount to more than a shilling the Swedish mile.

The inns are tolerable; but not liking the rye bread, I found it necessary to furnish myself with some wheaten before I set out. The beds too were particularly disagreeable to me. It seemed to me that I was sinking into a grave when I entered them; for, immersed in down placed in a sort of box, I expected to be suffocated before morning. The sleeping between two down beds, they do so even in summer, must be very unwholesome during any season; and I cannot conceive how the people can bear it, especially as the summers are very warm. But warmth they seem not to feel; and, I should think were afraid of the air, by always keeping their windows shut. In the winter, I am persuaded, I could not exist in rooms thus closed up, with stoves heated in their manner, for they only put wood into them twice a day; and, when the stove is thoroughly heated, they shut the flue, not admitting any air to renew its elasticity, even when the rooms are crowded with company. These stoves are made of earthenware, and often in a form that ornaments an apartment, which is never the case with the heavy iron ones I have seen elsewhere. Stoves may be economical; but I like a fire, a wood one, in preference; and I am convinced that the current of air which it attracts renders this the best mode of warming rooms.

We arrived early the second evening at a little village called Kvistrum, where we had determined to pass the night; having been informed that we should not afterwards find a tolerable inn until we reached Strömstad.

Advancing towards Kvistrum, as the sun was beginning to decline, I was particularly impressed by the beauty of the situation. The road was on the declivity of a rocky mountain, slightly covered with a mossy herbage and vagrant firs. At the bottom, a river, straggling amongst the recesses of stone, was hastening forward to the ocean and its grey rocks, of which we had a prospect on the left, whilst on the right it stole peacefully forward into the meadows, losing itself in a thickly wooded rising ground. As we drew near, the loveliest banks of wild flowers variegated the prospect, and promised to exhale odours to add to the sweetness of the air, the purity of which you could almost see, alas! not smell, for the putrifying herrings, which they use as manure, after the oil has been extracted, spread over the patches of earth, claimed by cultivation, destroyed every other.

It was intolerable, and entered with us into the inn, which was in other respects a charming retreat.

Whilst supper was preparing I crossed the bridge, and strolled by the river, listening to its murmurs. Approaching the bank, the beauty of which had attracted my attention in the carriage, I recognized many of my old acquaintance growing with great luxuriancy.

Seated on it, I could not avoid noting an obvious remark. Sweden appeared to me the country in the world most proper to form the botanist and natural historian: every object seemed to remind me of the creation of things, of the first efforts of sportive nature. When a country arrives at a certain state of perfection, it looks as if it were made so; and curiosity is not excited. Besides, in social life too many objects occur for any to be distinctly observed by the generality of mankind; yet a contemplative man, or poet, in the country, I do not mean the country adjacent to cities, feels and sees what would escape vulgar eyes, and draws suitable inferences. This train of reflections might have led me further, in every sense of the word; but I could not escape from the detestable evaporation of the herrings, which poisoned all my pleasure.

After making a tolerable supper, for it is not easy to get fresh provisions on the road, I retired, to be lulled to sleep by the murmuring of a stream, of which I with great difficulty obtained sufficient to perform my daily ablutions.

The last battle between the Danes and Swedes, which gave new life to their ancient enmity, was fought at this place 1788: only seventeen or eighteen were killed; for the great superiority of the Danes and Norwegians obliged the

Swedes to submit; but sickness and scarcity of provisions proved very fatal to their opponents, on their return.

It would be very easy to search for the particulars of this engagement in the publications of the day; but as this manner of filling my pages does not come within my plan, I probably should not have remarked that the battle was fought here, were it not to relate an anecdote which I had from good authority.

I noticed, when I first mentioned this place to you that we descended a steep before we came to the inn; an immense ridge of rocks stretching out on one side. The inn was sheltered under them; and about a hundred yards from it was a bridge that crossed the river, whose murmurs I have celebrated; it was not fordable. The Swedish general received orders to stop at the bridge, and dispute the passage; a most advantageous post for an army so much inferior in force: but the influence of beauty is not confined to courts. The mistress of the inn was handsome: when I saw her there were still some remains of beauty; and, to preserve her house, the general gave up the only tenable station. He was afterwards broke for contempt of orders.

Approaching the frontiers, consequently the sea, nature resumed an aspect ruder and ruder, or rather seemed the bones of the world waiting to be clothed with every thing necessary to give life and beauty. Still it was sublime.

The clouds caught their hue of the rocks that menaced them. The sun appeared afraid to shine, the birds ceased to sing, and the flowers to bloom; but the eagle fixed his nest high amongst the rocks, and the vulture hovered over this abode of desolation. The farm houses, in which only poverty resided, were formed of logs scarcely keeping off the cold and drifting snow; out of them the inhabitants seldom peeped, and the sports or prattling of children was neither seen nor heard. The current of life seemed congealed at the source: all were not frozen; for it was summer, you remember; but every thing appeared so dull, that I waited to see ice, in order to reconcile me to the absence of gaiety.

The day before, my attention had frequently been attracted by the wild beauties of the country we passed through.

The rocks which tossed their fantastic heads so high were often covered with pines and firs, varied in the most picturesque manner. Little woods filled up the recesses, when forests did not darken the scene; and vallies and glens, cleared of the trees, displayed a dazzling verdure which contrasted with the gloom of the shading pines. The eye stole into many a covert where tranquility seemed to have taken up her abode, and the number of little lakes that continually presented themselves added to the peaceful composure of the scenery. The little cultivation which appeared did not break the enchantment, nor did castles rear their turrets aloft to crush the cottages, and prove that man is more savage than the natives of the woods. I heard of the bears, but never saw them stalk forth, which I was sorry for; I wished to have seen one in its wild state. In the winter, I am told, they sometimes catch a stray cow, which is a heavy loss to the owner.

The farms are small. Indeed most of the houses we saw on the road indicated poverty, or rather that the people could just live. Towards the frontiers they grew worse and worse in their appearance, as if not willing to put sterility itself out of countenance. No gardens smiled round the habitations, not a potatoe or cabbage to eat with the fish drying on a stick near the door. A little grain here and there appeared, the long stalks of which you might almost reckon. The day was gloomy when we passed over this rejected spot, the wind bleak, and winter seemed to be contending with nature, faintly struggling to change the season. Surely, thought I, if the sun ever shines here, it cannot warm these stones; moss only cleaves to them, partaking of their hardness; and nothing like vegetable life appears to cheer with hope the heart.

So far from thinking that the primitive inhabitants of the world lived in a southern climate, where Paradise spontaneously arose, I am led to infer, from various circumstances, that the first dwelling of man happened to be a spot like this which led him to adore a sun so seldom seen; for this worship, which probably preceded that of demons or demi-gods, certainly never began in a southern climate, where the continual presence of the sun prevented its being considered as a good; or rather the want of it never being felt, this glorious luminary would carelessly have diffused its blessings without being hailed as a benefactor. Man must therefore have been placed in the north, to tempt him to run after the sun, in order that the different parts of the earth might be peopled. Nor do I wonder that hordes of barbarians always poured out of these regions to seek for milder climes, when nothing like cultivation attached them to the soil; especially when we take into the view that the adventuring spirit, common to man, is naturally stronger and more general during the infancy of society. The conduct of the followers of Mahomet, and the crusaders, will sufficiently corroborate my assertion.

Approaching nearer to Strömstad, the appearance of the town proved to be quite in character with the country we had just passed through. I hesitated to use the word country, yet could not find another; still it would sound absurd to talk of fields of rocks.

The town was built on, and under them. Three or four weather-beaten trees were shrinking from the wind; and the grass grew so sparingly, that I could not avoid thinking Dr Johnson's hyperbolical assertion 'that the man merited well of his country who made a few blades of grass grow where they never grew before', might here have been uttered with strict propriety. The steeple likewise towered aloft; for what is a church, even amongst the Lutherans, without a steeple? But to prevent mischief in such an exposed situation, it is wisely placed on a rock at some distance, not to endanger the roof of the church.

Rambling about, I saw the door open, and entered, when to my great surprise I found the clergyman reading prayers, with only the clerk attending. I instantly thought of Swift's 'Dearly beloved Roger', but on enquiry I learnt that some one had died that morning, and in Sweden it is customary to pray for the dead.

The sun, who I suspected never dared to shine, began now to convince me that he came forth only to torment; for though the wind was still cutting, the rocks became intolerably warm under my feet; whilst the herring effluvia, which I before found so very offensive, once more assailed me. I hastened back to the house of a merchant, the little sovereign of the place, because he was by far the richest, though not the mayor.

Here we were most hospitably received, and introduced to a very fine and numerous family. I have before mentioned to you the lillies of the north, I might have added, water lillies, for the complexion of many, even of the young women seem to be bleached on the bosom of snow. But in this youthful circle the roses bloomed with all their wonted freshness, and I wondered from whence the fire was stolen which sparkled in their fine blue eyes.

Here we slept; and I rose early in the morning to prepare for my little voyage to Norway. I had determined to go by water, and was to leave my companions behind; but not getting a boat immediately, and the wind being high and unfavourable, I was told that it was not safe to go to sea during such boisterous weather; I was therefore obliged to wait for the morrow, and had the present day on my hands;

which I feared would be irksome, because the family, who possessed about a dozen French words amongst them, and not an English phrase, were anxious to amuse me, and would not let me remain alone in my room. The town we had already walked round and round; and if we advance farther on the coast, it was still to view the same unvaried immensity of water, surrounded by barrenness.

The gentlemen wishing to peep into Norway, proposed going to Halden, the first town, the distance was only three Swedish miles. There, and back again, was but a day's journey, and would not, I thought, interfere with my voyage. I agreed, and invited the eldest and prettiest of the girls to accompany us. I invited her because I liked to see a beautiful face animated by pleasure, and to have an opportunity of regarding the country, whilst the gentlemen were amusing themselves with her.

I did not know, for I had not thought of it, that we were to scale some of the most mountainous cliffs of Sweden, in our way to the ferry which separates the two countries.

Entering amongst the cliffs, we were sheltered from the wind; warm sun-beams began to play, streams to flow, and groves of pines diversified the rocks. Sometimes they became suddenly bare and sublime. Once, in particular, after mounting the most terrific precipice, we had to pass through a tremendous defile, where the closing chasm seemed to threaten us with instant destruction, when turning quickly, verdant meadows and a beautiful lake relieved and charmed my eyes.

I have never travelled through Switzerland; but one of my companions assured me, that I should not there find any thing superior, if equal to the wild grandeur of these views.

As we had not taken this excursion into our plan, the horses had not been previously ordered, which obliged us to wait two hours at the first post. The day was wearing away. The road was so bad, that walking up the precipices consumed the time insensibly. But as we desired horses at

each post ready at a certain hour, we reckoned on returning more speedily.

We stopt to dine at a tolerable farm. They brought us out
ham, butter, cheese, and milk; and the charge was so mod-
erate, that I scattered a little money amongst the children
who were peeping at us, in order to pay them for their
trouble.

Arrived at the ferry, we were still detained; for the people
who attend at the ferries have a stupid kind of sluggish-
ness in their manner, which is very provoking when you
are in haste. At present I did not feel it; for scrambling up
the cliffs, my eye followed the river as it rolled between the
grand rocky banks; and to complete the scenery, they were
covered with firs and pines, through which the wind rus-
tled, as if it were lulling itself to sleep with the declining
sun.

Behold us now in Norway; and I could not avoid feeling
surprise at observing the difference in the manners of the
inhabitants of the two sides of the river; for every thing
shows that the Norwegians are more industrious and
more opulent. The Swedes, for neighbours are seldom the
best friends, accuse the Norwegians of knavery, and they
retaliate by bringing a charge of hypocrisy against the
Swedes. Local circumstances probably render both unjust,
speaking from their feelings, rather than reason: and is
this astonishing when we consider that most writers of
travels have done the same, whose works have served as
materials for the compilers of universal histories. All are
eager to give a national character; which is rarely just,
because they do not discriminate the natural from the
acquired difference. The natural, I believe, on due consideration, will be found to consist merely in the degree of
vivacity or thoughtfulness, pleasure, or pain, inspired by
the climate, whilst the varieties which the forms of government, including religion, produce, are much more
numerous and unstable.

A people have been characterized as stupid by nature; what a paradox! Because they did not consider that slaves, having no object to stimulate industry, have not their faculties sharpened by the only thing that can exercise them, self-interest. Others have been brought forward as brutes, having no aptitude for the arts and sciences, only because the progress of improvement had not reached that stage which produces them.

Those writers who have considered the history of man, or of the human mind, on a more enlarged scale, have fallen into similar errors, not reflecting that the passions are weak where the necessaries of life are too hardly or too easily obtained.

Travellers who require that every nation should resemble their native country, had better stay at home. It is, for example, absurd to blame a people for not having that degree of personal cleanliness and elegance of manners which only refinement of taste produces, and will produce every where in proportion as society attains a general polish. The most essential service, I presume, that authors could render to society, would be to promote inquiry and discussion, instead of making those dogmatical assertions which only appear calculated to gird the human mind round with imaginary circles, like the paper globe which represents the one he inhabits.

This spirit of inquiry is the characteristic of the present century, from which the succeeding will, I am persuaded, receive a great accumulation of knowledge; and doubtless its diffusion will in a great measure destroy the factitious national characters which have been supposed permanent, though only rendered so by the permanency of ignorance.

Arriving at Halden, at the siege of which Charles XII lost his life, we had only time to take a transient view of it, whilst they were preparing us some refreshment.

Poor Charles! I thought of him with respect. I have always felt the same for Alexander; with whom he has been

Charles XII of Sweden

classed as a madman, by several writers, who have rea-
soned superficially, confounding the morals of the day
with the few grand principles on which unchangeable
morality rests. Making no allowance for the ignorance and
prejudices of the period, they do not perceive how much
they themselves are indebted to general improvement for
the acquirements, and even the virtues, which they would
not have had the force of mind to attain, by their individual exertions in a less advanced state of society.

The evening was fine, as is usual at this season; and the
refreshing odour of the pine woods became more percep-
tible; for it was nine o'clock when we left Halden. At the
ferry we were detained by a dispute relative to our Swedish

passport, which we did not think of getting countersigned in Norway. Midnight was coming on; yet it might with such propriety have been termed the noon of night, that had Young ever travelled towards the north, I should not have wondered at his becoming enamoured of the moon. But it is not the queen of night alone who reigns here in all her splendour, though the sun, loitering just below the horizon, decks her with a golden tinge from his car, illuminating the cliffs that hide him; the heavens also, of a clear softened blue, throw her forward, and the evening star appears a lesser moon to the naked eye. The huge shadows of the rocks, fringed with firs, concentrating the views, without darkening them, excited that tender melancholy which, sublimating the imagination, exalts, rather than depresses the mind.

My companions fell asleep: – fortunately they did not snore; and I contemplated, fearless of idle questions, a night such as I had never before seen or felt to charm the senses, and calm the heart. The very air was balmy, as it freshened into morn, producing the most voluptuous sensations. A vague pleasurable sentiment absorbed me, as I opened my bosom to the embraces of nature; and my soul rose to its author, with the chirping of the solitary birds, which began to feel, rather than see, advancing day. I had leisure to mark its progress. The grey morn, streaked with silvery rays, ushered in the orient beams, – how beautifully varying into purple! – yet, I was sorry to lose the soft watery clouds which preceded them, exciting a kind of expectation that made me almost afraid to breathe, lest I should break the charm. I saw the sun – and sighed.

One of my companions, now awake, perceiving that the postillion had mistaken the road, began to swear at him, and roused the other two, who reluctantly shook off sleep.

We had immediately to measure back our steps, and did not reach Strömstad before five in the morning.

The wind had changed in the night, and my boat was ready.

A dish of coffee, and fresh linen, recruited my spirits; and I directly set out again for Norway; proposing to land much higher up the coast.

Wrapping my great coat round me, I lay down on some sails at the bottom of the boat, its motion rocking me to rest, till a discourteous wave interrupted my slumbers, and obliged me to rise and feel a solitariness which was not so soothing as that of the past night.

Adieu!

Thomas Thomson

from *Travels in Sweden during the Autumn of 1812*

The principal merchants in Gothenburg are Scotsmen. In consequence of letters of introduction which we carried to several of them, we experienced from that liberal and respectable body a profusion of kindness and politeness which it was impossible to surpass, and which would be very difficult to equal. The want of inns, and our ignorance of the Swedish language, would have made it very difficult for us to have procured dinner while we stayed at Gothenburg, but this difficulty was obviated by the merchants, with one or other of whom we dined every day during our stay in that city. The entertainments which they gave, were in the Swedish style, and possessed a degree of splendour at which I was not a little surprised. As the mode of dining in Sweden is very different from the mode followed in Great Britain, I shall give a general description of a dinner, that my readers may form some notion to themselves of the customs of that country.

The houses in Sweden are fitted up with great magnificence. The public rooms are usually on the first floor, and vary from three to seven or more according to the size of the house and the wealth of its master. These rooms always open into each other, and constitute a very elegant suit of apartments. The furniture though very handsome is not similar to ours. You seldom see mahogany chairs; they are usually of birch or of some other wood painted. As the table cloth is never removed they have no occasion for our fine mahogany tables, and as the dishes are brought in one by one, and the dessert and wine put upon the table before the company sit down, they have but little occasion for a side-board. Accordingly, except in the house of Mr Lorent, who had a very splendid side-board made in London, I do not recollect to have seen one in Sweden, even in the houses of men of the first rank. The rooms are not provided with bells. This I am told is owing to the extreme cheapness of servants in Sweden, which enabled every person to keep such a number as rendered bells unnecessary. This reason, which I do not consider as a very good one, exists not at present, for since the loss of Finland the wages of servants have considerably increased. Bells, therefore, might now be introduced with the greatest propriety; and to a foreigner, from Britain at least, they would constitute a great convenience. I have sometimes been obliged to go three times to the kitchen during the course of my breakfast, to ask for things that had been neglected or forgotten by the servants.

The Swedes are fond of great parties. I have more than once sat down to table with nearly 50 people in a private house. The hour of dinner is two o'clock. After the company are assembled they are shown into a room adjoining the dining-room. In the middle of this room there is a round table covered with a table-cloth, upon which are placed bread, cheese, butter and corn-brandy. Every person eats a morsel of bread and cheese and butter, and drinks a dram of brandy, by way of exciting the appetite for dinner. There are usually two kinds of bread; namely, wheat-bread baked into a kind of small rolls, for I never saw any loaves in Sweden: and rye, which is usually baked in thin cakes, and is known in Sweden by the name of nickebroed. It is very palatable but requires good teeth to chew it.

After this whet, the company are shown into the dining-room, and take their seats round the table. The first dish brought in is salmagundy, salt fish, a mixture of salmon and rice, sausages, or some such strong seasoned article, to give an additional whet to the appetite. It is handed round the table, and every person helps himself in succession to as much of it as he chooses. The next dish is commonly roasted or stewed mutton, with bacon ham. These articles are carved by some individual at table, most commonly the master of the house, and the carved pieces being heaped upon a plate are carried round the company like the first dish. The Swedes like the French eat of everything that is presented at table. The third dish is usually soup, then fowls, then fish (generally salmon, pike or streamlings), then pudding, then the dessert, which consists of a great profusion of sweet-meats, in the preparation of which the inhabitants of Gothenburg excel. Each of these dishes handed about in succession. The vegetables, con-

Gothenburg in the early nineteenth century

sisting of potatoes, carrots, turnips, cauliflowers, greens &c. are handed about in the same way. During the whole time of dinner a great deal of wine is drunk by the company. The wines are claret, port, sherry, and madeira. What they call claret at Gothenburg does not seem to be Bordeaux wine. It is a French wine with a taste intermediate between claret and port. At Stockholm I drank occasionally true claret; but scarcely in any other part of Sweden. As all the wine used in Sweden is imported from Great Britain, our wine merchants can probably explain this circumstance though I cannot.

The Swedes employ the same articles for seasoning their food as we do, salt, pepper, mustard, vinegar &c. I was struck with one peculiarity which I had never seen before: they always mix together mustard and sugar: I had the curiosity to try this mixture, and found it not bad. The dinner usually lasts about two hours. On a signal given the company all rise together, bow with much solemnity towards the table, or rather towards each other, and then adjourn into the drawing-room. Here a cup of coffee is served up immediately to every individual. It is but doing the Swedes justice to say that their coffee is excellent, greatly preferable to what is usually drunk in England. This is the more remarkable because the Swedes import all their coffee from Britain: its quality therefore is not different from that of our own, and its superiority owing solely to their understanding better how to make it. You can get coffee in the meanest peasant's house, and it is always excellent. It is usually about five o'clock when coffee is over. The company separate at this time, either going home to their own houses, or sauntering about in the fields if the weather be good.

Evelyn Waugh

The Scandinavian Capitals: contrasted post-war moods

Daily Telegraph and Morning Post, 11 November 1947

In this third year of the Occupation[40] it is more bitter than sweet to read of the delights of travel, but it would be insincere and ungrateful to write of the problems of the Scandinavian countries without some mention of the beauty and ease which they offer the privileged visitor.

The politician, the journalist and the commercial traveller – most fortunate of modern Englishmen – may find in Stockholm and Copenhagen two of the most pleasant cities in the world: Stockholm, fatuously dubbed the 'Venice of the North' (it is as much like Rangoon), where in summer the low sun casts huge shadows before one and blinds the oncoming cyclists, where every street ends in a glitter of water, where the classic Mediterranean orders are crowned with eastern cupolas of green copper and rise amid funnels and rigging, where lovely women are still undefiled by the fashions of Hollywood, where the cooks are among the best in Europe and only the waiters are vile; Copenhagen, flat, open, clean, gay and decorous, encircled by palaces, where ancient quays and sailor-streets lead straight into rococo squares, where Italian pantomime of the time of Bomba is still played nightly in the public gardens and unique cherry brandy is distilled in the original eighteenth-century mansion of the family who guard its secret; these cities leave memories to warm the tourist through many winters of discontent.

And Oslo – poor Oslo, one is inclined to think: all trams and shirt-sleeves and ice-cream cones, noisy, inelegant younger sister – Oslo has not the least need of our compassion. She is radiant with civic pride and rapidly completing a prodigious town hall which, inside and out, promises to be the most hideous in the world.

Very recent history has determined the mood of each of the Scandinavian capitals.

The Norwegians are conscious of having done well in the war. They fought and suffered and conquered, and in the process have been entirely cured of the inherited sense of inferiority which in the past sometimes rendered them less companionable than their neighbours. Their physical conditions are, of course, better than our own, but not vastly better. The difference is that they were very bad two years ago, have improved and are improving.

Alone among western peoples the Norwegians believe in progress, and this archaic illusion somewhat restricts mutual understanding, but their interest in English culture is boundless. In their bookshops, as in those of all Scandinavia, one can find the English books long rumoured to exist but quite forgotten rarities in their land of origin – poems, novels, manuals of child psychology, the fruit of a bloody and destructive decade. It is to us that the Norsemen look for culture. National pride swells at the display and then (dare one hint it?) suffers a deflation. So here they all are, those books we saw reviewed! This is what we were missing! Somehow we hoped it was rather more imposing.

It would be too much to say that Norwegian writers take the English as their models. They have grave troubles of their own, chief of which is their lack of any formal tongue. The battle of fifty years ago between the Danish-derived town-tongue and the rural folk-tongue resulted in no decision. It merely lost its fierceness. Now children return from school speaking a patois which is often strange to their parents. Most writers employ varieties of the town-language, pleasing themselves in their choice of spelling, grammar and vocabulary. The Norwegians await a genius to give their language definite shape. It is natural, therefore, that much of their exuberance for self-expression should take plastic and visual form. Vigeland, of whom more hereafter, and Munch, the two masters are lately dead, but under generous patronage by the state a new generation is painting acres of wall and carving tons of granite. It is perhaps not the adornment we should choose for our own ancient cities, but a good time is being had by all.

The Swedes, by contrast, seem a weary and cynical people, the children of endemic neutrality. The socialists order things better in Sweden, and at first glance they seem to have attained their paradise. The state is supreme, but humane; hereditary class distinctions barely exist, and taxation has brought the level of diminishing returns so low that the only serious labour problem is middle-class absenteeism. Domestic service has been abolished, and with it the private house. Almost everyone in Stockholm inhabits a tiny flat: the most conspicuously self-indulgent employ daily maids who decamp before dinner. Few have cars, many have sailing boats; nudists employ ample opportunities for their fun. Nothing except the changing of the royal guard is at all disorderly. At the universities technology is dominant; there are no debating societies.

I suppose that it was some such state as this which the English voter dimly aspired to create at the general election. And yet even here there are signs that physical well-being is not enough. The favourite authors of the young are Kafka and Sartre, there is a low birth-rate and a high suicide-rate, a thriving Communist Party and the most repressive liquor restrictions in Europe.

For the Danes the war was a bitter experience. At first they suffered humiliation without tragedy. Normal life went on; the occupying forces were discreet. Oppression developed gradually; the Resistance was in the main conservative. It produced its heroes and martyrs, but the Danes lack, or seem to lack, that sense of a national war of liberation brought to a victorious end which characterizes the Norwegians. Their hatred of the Germans is unappeased. They are shocked by the stories of Anglo-German fraternization which reach them in distorted form from across their frontier. They do not respect what they know of American habits and resent their infiltration through films and magazines. But when all this is said they remain the most exhilarating people in Europe, for the reason that they are not obsessed by politics, national or international. More civilized than the Norwegians, more humorous and imaginative than the Swedes, they are a people for whom the Englishman feels a spontaneous, reciprocated sympathy.

The observer in passage who seeks a quick glimpse of Danish manners should visit the Tivoli gardens. Here in summer all Copenhagen has resorted for more than a century, children and elders, bourgeois and proletarian.

It costs a shilling to enter. There is a fun-fair, a concert hall, a little theatre, a circus, fireworks, beer gardens, cafés, restaurants: there are very few drunks and no hooligans; those who have an occasion to celebrate can dine luxuriously without arousing resentment. Such a place could perhaps have prospered in London fifty years ago. Could it today?

Scandinavia Prefers A Bridge To An Eastern Rampart

Daily Telegraph and Morning Post, 13 November 1947
Today it is not of art or cooking or domestic habits that the returning traveller is expected to give an account. There is one grim question set him: what about Russia? And it is particularly pertinent to the Scandinavian countries.

The Swedes are nearest to danger and most scared. The destruction of the Baltic states and the conquest of Finland – lands intimately associated with them – impressed them more deeply than the spate of pro-Russian propaganda with which we sought to reassure them during the war. Now they see no advantage in being overrun in a third world war. Oblivious of the fact that it is usually in small countries that great wars begin, they behave like children at a party who do not wish to get involved in the rough games of the older boys.

A conservative Swede remarked to me that *I Chose Free-dom*[41] had enjoyed a record sale in Stockholm. 'It is a terrible thing,' he said.

'Why? Do you think it is false?'

'I know it to be quite true. But it will be a terrible thing if ill-feeling is aroused against Russia. Spiritually, of course, we belong to the West, but we must live in friendship with the East. We must be a bridge, not a rampart.'

I forebore to press the question which way he expected the traffic to flow on his bridge. The Swedes keep intent watch on Finland, where Russian tactics seem to differ greatly from the normal. Gen. Mannerheim, for example, lives unmolested, as would not happen in any other of Russia's recent conquests. Finnish industry works for Russia, but industrialists enjoy considerable freedom and privilege. Swedes can easily visit friends across the border. An attempt was made this summer to make Helsinki a cultural centre. A congress of young northern writers was convened there which proved remarkable for a grave outbreak of typhus and a ferocious attack on the American *Reader's Digest* as the organ of international Fascism.

Both in Norway and Sweden the Communist party forms a vigorous minority among the dominant socialists. In Denmark it is losing prestige among manual labourers, but still attracts Bohemians. Nowhere in the world is Communist policy in doubt; nowhere does its numerical voting power indicate the feasibility of the policy. The chance of any country's chance of survival is the awareness of those outside the party of the true character of the enemy. In this test both Norway and Sweden seem signally to fail.

The Swedes have made a trade agreement which makes them virtually a Russian workshop. They resent it, not because it ties them to the soviet system, but because it does so on disadvantageous terms. Their own days of imperial ambition are so remote and proved so disastrous, their imagination is so dulled by long and lucrative neutrality, that they simply cannot conceive that any one can be so silly as to inconvenience themselves for Glory or Power. 'Dollar diplomacy' they understand, or think they do. It seems reasonable enough to want money and they are easily convinced that America has sinister designs in her philosophy. But the conception of a cosmic order to be imposed for its own sake and at all costs is meaningless to them. They believe very firmly in their own sanity. The word 'mad' is often on their lips, applied to individuals and peoples. They cover by this general charge most of the motive forces which history shows have in fact proved most potent for good and ill.

The tiny populations of Scandinavia can never hope to oppose aggression with physical force. If they are to survive it must be through spiritual strength, and there, alas, for all their charm and good humour and good sense, they are woefully enfeebled. When my friend said that 'spiritually' he belonged to the West, he meant, I am afraid, almost nothing except that he spoke perfect English, for Scandinavia has in the past century suffered a vast apostasy and no longer forms part of Christendom. Foreign readers of Mass Observation's *Puzzled People* might be tempted to declare this of England also, but that penetrating and highly significant inquiry was made solely among English men and women who had been educated by the state. The report gave a devastating picture of the results of the system which the politicians seek to make universal, but there is in England a small but still influential body who had the good fortune to be taught by monks and nuns or to have spent their formative years at the public schools and older universities which are permeated by traditional Christianity.

No such society exists in Scandinavia. They are secularized from infancy by the omnipotent state and as a result are unique in history in having no religion at all. A few eloquent pastors can attract congregations. Dr Buchman's 'Oxford' group has its adherents and, indeed, publishes a handsome magazine in Oslo. Each of the larger cities has a very small, very devout Roman Catholic community. But for the vast majority of Scandinavians, and in particular for the 'intellectuals' who throughout the West are now turning to formal Christianity in a degree unknown since the Renaissance, the religious conception of life, of man existing in relation to his Creator, of the world existing in relation to Heaven and Hell, is totally and, humanly speaking, irretrievably lost.

Michael Frayn

Frayn's Sweden

The Observer Review, 21 April 1974

Useless, I suppose, to tell you that the suicide rate in Sweden is in fact lower than in (for instance) merrily waltzing Austria, or that the Swedes in fact drink less per head than (for instance) the sober, dog-loving British. You have your own ideas about Sweden. You know that all their famous wealth and peace and social justice have, gratifyingly, led to nothing but drunkenness and the highest suicide rate in the world.

So you'll be pleased to hear that within a few days of arriving in Sweden I was sitting comfortably and watching a new Swedish film about a man attempting suicide after a drinking bout. He had received a crushing tax-demand, and had also been mugged. The suicide attempt failed ludicrously, and the film ended in a very long, passionate embrace – the hero kissing the receipt for the tax he had finally paid off.

I must add that the director of the film who also played the lead, was thirteen years old. He had mastered not only all the basic technology and visual vocabulary of the cinema, but also a very funny right-angled running turn on one foot derived from Chaplin. It was a funny film.

This was one Sunday in the country, after a great Sunday lunch with eleven of us at table, including children and grandparents. It was an old wooden house on the edge of the forest, all odd angles and unexpected rooms. Painted country furniture glowed dark green and red against the cool grey floor timbers. The old tiled stove in the corner filled the room with a sleepy warmth. The younger children played quietly. The projector murmured hypnotically on.

Outside – the long winter night, the empty leagues of snowbound forest, and all the moral ghosts we were laughing at within. *Trygghet* – security; the warm enclosing uterine reassurance against all ills to which the whole of Swedish politics seems bent on giving expression.

Or so it seemed to me. But into the mild transparent complexity of Sweden you can read almost any interpretation you like.

The Social Democrats have been in power continuously now for forty-two years. While I was there Gunnar Sträng, the Finance Minister, presented his nineteenth budget. The trains leave on time, and run quietly past neat wooden houses painted dark Dalarna red, past concrete cliffs of habitation rising from landscapes of trees and rock outcrops, where no streetlamps are broken and no old cars lie dying, past inviolate forest and lakes and ploughland. There are no waste lots, no vague areas on the edge of towns, no slums, no derelict industrial landscapes, no nothingness. Everything (as Bishop Butler said) is what it is, and not another thing.

But this air of changeless prosperity is deceptive, for the whole experience of modern Sweden has been one of continuous and dislocatingly rapid change. God did not create Sweden rich and progressive. Until far on into the nineteenth century it was one of the very poorest and most backward countries in Europe – the Balkans of the North. Between 1860 and World War I nearly a fifth of the population fled hunger by emigrating to America.

The common shared experience of this century has been the bewildering move off the land into the towns. The drift continues, particularly out of the economically bleak North; up there the initials AMS, which designate the Swedish equivalent of the Department of Employment, are said to stand for *Alla Måste Söderut* – Everyone Must Go South.

It was only in the 1940s that Sweden caught up with the rest of Europe. Well over half the housing in the country has been built since then. Progressive social ideals – in marriage, in pensions, in education – have been applied almost as fast as the flats have been built. 'Social democracy,' said the Prime Minister, Olof Palme, in a speech once, 'has been able to be radical because it represents stability. That is not a contradiction in terms.' In Sweden change has been the norm, the status quo.

A lot has changed even since I was first here in the 1950s. The awkwardness and stiffness have gone out of social life. (I used to think then that the British disliked Sweden because they saw in the Swedes people just like themselves only disconcertingly more so.) The complex sequence of toasts which had to be observed at dinner-parties has disappeared (though some people told me their parents never failed to notice the moments when the glasses should have been raised to them and weren't). So has the curious usage whereby strangers were addressed by their 'title' in the third person ('Would Writer Strindberg like another cup of coffee?') though in the telephone directory, maddeningly, *Svensson* Lennart Bus-driver would still be listed as alphabetically prior to *Svensson* Arvid Cabinet Minister. The polite plural form of 'you', moreover, has completely vanished from social life, and '*du*' has become almost universal. I couldn't help thinking of the leftists I met in Germany who were struggling to call strangers '*du*', but who confessed privately to feeling very awkward about it. In Sweden change is wholesale.

A certain old-fashioned country quality persists, all the same – a certain thrifty homeliness. I went to see an old friend of mine who now lives in one of the new suburbs of Stockholm – Tyresö, a twenty-five-minute ride aboard an uncrowded bus out beyond carefully preserved forest. Tall blocks among pines; hard-packed snow; a short day; then only the neighbourhood policeman patrolling the shopping centre with his Alsatian and children playing ice-hockey on little rinks among the pedestrian walkways and woodlands of the estates, beneath floodlights that swung and creaked in the wind.

But all around you, through the trees, like little illuminated stage-sets, domestic interiors uncurtained against the winter night; a thousand theatres side by side, or stacked above one another, each playing the warm, bright drama of *trygghet*.

Foreigners misconceive Swedish domestic style. They have a picture of pale bland functional objects made of birchwood and stainless steel against a background of austere white emptiness. But these rooms *glow*. Their keynote is solid masses of warm colour – deep reds, and the dark flowered greens of traditional painted country furniture. Silver and steel are reflected in dark veneers. Bowls of tulips stand beside blue armchairs. Climbing plants cover walls and half-obscure windows.

My friend flung her arms round me when I arrived and hugged me impulsively (Swedish nature is as misunderstood abroad as Swedish décor.) But a little later she was reminding me candidly that I owed her 9.50 crowns which I'd borrowed as change for fares last year, plus 1.40 for a stamp.

Money – this is what we talked about. We did everywhere I went, and half the stories in the papers seemed to be about money, too. I don't mean in any coarsely materialistic way. We talked frankly about how much we earned, and how much we paid in tax. We talked thriftily about how much things cost, and how certain cunning savings could be made.

When we talked about politics it seemed to be almost entirely in terms of contributions and subsidies.

[ ]

Money, it seemed to me, was the medium of all political thought and action. Sweden is the richest nation in Europe, of course, and a high proportion of her wealth passes through the fiscal system – over 45 per cent of the gross national product is absorbed in taxes and social service premiums. Two schoolteachers who went through their accounts with me in some detail were earning £5,000 and £6,000 a year, and repaying 44 per cent and 50 per cent of it in tax respectively. Almost everything – including the arts and even the practice of politics itself – has become dependent upon the closely negotiated redistribution of these central funds.

The political parties (including the Communists) are subsidised by the State in proportion to their electoral strength; a supporter of the new Lapp party, *Samernas väl*, whom I met in the North, explained to me that it couldn't be expected to make much headway because it was too small to qualify for an adequate subsidy. Anyone recognized by the appropriate committee as a professional writer receives a guaranteed income, from State compensation for library loans equalised out and supplemented by additional grants, of £2,400, and a Royal Commission has just recommended that publishers should be required to distribute 1,250 copies of each book they publish at the State's expense before normal sales commence.

Even the funds of the unions must sometimes come to seem to their members to be part of this same financial system; the contributions are levied on a progressive sliding scale like tax, and like tax deducted at source by the management, who also pay the local branch chairman and provide an office for him.

Now the State has begun to accumulate huge sums in the pension funds. The pensions paid out are large by any

standards – two-thirds of your income averaged over your fifteen best years. But the contributions levied (chiefly from the
employers – 10 per cent of the wages bill) outbalance them.
A Social Democratic party official told me that the party saw
the surplus very much as an instrument of State influence
over the economy. By the beginning of last year the funds
had reached £5,600 million. Already they have outstripped
the commercial banks as a source of credit, and they are now
beginning to move into the risk capital market. By the end of
the century they are expected to have reached about £70,000
million.

The community provides; the individual is provided for.
My friend in Tyresö showed me round a new church youth
club. It could have been the headquarters of some successful
progressive advertising agency – suites of conference rooms
and offices, each with its own carefully chosen warm colour
scheme, its own complete set of matching furniture and
equipment. The children hadn't yet been admitted; when
they were, they wouldn't need to think about a thing.

She also showed me the school where she taught; another
warmly stylish new building. Here there were children, but
only 250 of them in a building which in Britain would have
housed two or three times that number. They were taught
mostly in groups of not more than fifteen, in warm-coloured
classrooms with fitted carpets and house phones. The fitted
carpets were clean; when the discreet chimes sounded at the
end of a lesson and the pupils moved out of a room, a team
of cleaners moved in. The phones had not been vandalized.
Nothing had been vandalized. There was very little sign, good
or bad, of the children's presence.

When we came out into the snow at the end of the morning, however, and saw the bus we wanted just leaving the
stop, there was a spontaneous scream of jeering laughter
from two fourteen-year-old girls who happened to be passing, which struck a rather more familiar note. Later my
friend showed me a newspaper cutting about the excesses of

drunkenness and vandalism which had greeted the end of the last school year in various parts of the country. At one festivity ('arranged by a child welfare committee') in the west of Sweden, complained the writer, 'some intoxicated and naked pupils had public intercourse with each other'.

'None the less,' he added, 'a social worker said that "the result of our arrangements was better than expected"'.

They don't drink much in Sweden by international standards, but, as in all North European countries, the drinkers drink to get drunk. In Stockholm they then accumulate, perhaps by a natural process of gravitation, in the underground. In the evenings and at weekends the air down there is heavy with the exhaled fumes of grain alcohol. Old beer cans roll under foot. Long-haired young policemen patrol in twos and threes and fives. Small groups of men transport fragile private worlds of geniality about with them like huge invisible parcels, staggering under the comical awkwardness of the load. But I couldn't help feeling, as I watched one young drunk with blond hair over his shoulders aggressively bum a light for his cigarette, then struggle halfway up the platform, against some powerful magnetic field which seemed to be trying to divert him from his goal, in order to dutifully deposit the empty cigarette packet in a rubbish bin, that there was something rather homely about even these deviations from decorum.

In a restaurant one night I sat at the next table to a very respectable middle-class couple in their late forties who were both helplessly drunk. I had to eat with my left hand, because at frequent intervals the lady fell sideways and grabbed at my right arm, urging me to dance with her, or to come home with them for the night, and scrabbling about in my lap looking for a napkin to dab at the confusion of slopped coffee, beer, and akvavit which was accumulating on their table.

'Inga-Lisa, Inga-Lisa!' moaned the man, trying to catch glasses as they somehow lost their balance. She stumbled up to various tables in the restaurant, presumably with the same propositions. Everywhere she went, wine turned over, coffee ran into laps. She persuaded a bald young man with side-boards to hold her up for a few minutes on the dance-floor. Then she insisted, with determined wrong-headedness, on getting back to her place by squeezing round the side of the table against the wall, where no gap had been left. She was a tubby little lady, with thick spectacles and warm red socks. The table heaved and swayed. 'Inga-Lisa, Inga-Lisa!' complained the gentleman sadly, performing a dream-like slow-motion juggling act with the tumbling cups and glasses, the saucers full of cold coffee. Then they argued about which of them was paying. Then she somehow slipped down on to the floor, and disappeared between the tables. The discreet silver-haired maître d'hôtel, whom you would have taken to be the chairman of the Stockholm Enskilda Bank, raised a mildly disapproving eyebrow, but did nothing else. About half an hour after they were finally assisted to the door I passed them in the street outside. They were propped up against a shop, still arguing. And still about money, of course.

A year ago, a lawyer told me, brothels were taking full-page advertisements in the papers; but this was felt to be a breach of the traditional Swedish moderation in all things, and stopped after a new establishment run as a producers' co-operative in the elegant Östermalm district was successfully prosecuted. *Dagens Nyheter,* the leading quality daily, still carries advertisements for night-clubs offering 'Live show every hour', or 'non-stop on four different screens – animal-homo-spanking'. But most of the films on offer seem to be American, and the newspaper in its editorial columns is worried about the increasingly open allusion to intercourse which Swedish advertisers are learning from current British practice. And even in the sex-clubs there is a note of cosy good taste. 'Our sex-hostesses,' claims Sexy House, in an advertisement for its porno-shop, 'demonstrate everything in a beautiful porn-environment.'

There is something touchingly homely, too, about a lot of the public sexual frankness. I was struck by a letter in the advice column of one of the Stockholm evening papers from a woman who claimed that she had enjoyed 'hundreds of orgasms' simply by imagining herself naked when men looked at her in the street – a handy knack which, she couldn't resist adding, was 'free of charge'. Alongside was a letter from a man who was a little worried about a strange new technique he described which his wife had suddenly started trying out on him after thirty years of marriage. (It was fellatio, as the paper's medical correspondent explained.) She had first sprung this on him, he said, when she came home one night after hearing the ladies discussing it at a meeting of her sewing-circle. He signed himself 'Regular Reader'.

Some of the announcements in the Births column of *Dagens Nyheter,* too, have a certain broad rustic humour which seems remote from *The Times.* A friend of mine at Gothenburg University showed me a collection which she and her children had made to amuse friends in Denmark. I liked the verses best. Difficult to do them justice in translation, but here are one or two:

'We're so pleased we could shout/Now ULRIK'S come out.'

'That bulge in his mother/Is now Sven's LITTLE BROTHER.'

'Let the bells tinkle/It's one with a pinkle.'

My friend's favourite was this one, celebrating the arrival of a daughter in a family presumably much taken up with boats and outboard motors:

'What did the long cold winter bring?/3.25 kilograms/Without a starter-string.'

The British Council in Sweden

Jim Potts

Recollections of T. S. Eliot in Sweden, 1942

Peter Ackroyd, in his book *T. S. Eliot* (Hamish Hamilton, 1984), writes: 'At the end of this month (February 1942) he travelled to Sweden on a tour organized by the British Council; it lasted five weeks, and he gave a number of readings in Stockholm, Uppsala, Lund and elsewhere.'

The British Embassy's wartime weekly newspaper, *News from Britain* (*Nyheter från Storbritannien*) advertised, in April 1942, 'a volume of translations of T.S. Eliot edited by Ronald Bottrall and Gunnar Ekelöf with the help of Erik Mesterton, who, with Karin Boye, had first introduced Eliot to Sweden with their translation of *The Waste Land*. The translations were all by leading Swedish poets including Eric Blomberg, Karin Boye, Johannes Edfelt, Gunnar Ekelöf, Erik Lundgren, Artur Lundkvist, Mesterton himself, Vennberg and Anders Österling, the Secretary of the Swedish Academy.' (Peter Tennant, *Touchlines of War*, University of Hull Press, 1992).

Erik Lindegren and Karl Vennberg both revealed echoes of Eliot in their own poetry, according to the Swedish literary historian Anneli Jordahl (*Swedish Literature in the 20th Century*, The Swedish Institute, 1998). A doctoral thesis by Mats Jansson (in Swedish) on the impact of Eliot in Sweden, entitled *Tradition och Förnyelse, Den svenska introduktionen av T. S. Eliot*, was published in 1991 (Brutus Östlings Bokförlag Symposion AB, Stockholm/Skåne). Chapter V, 'In i 40-talet', gives a comprehensive account of Eliot's 1942 tour of Sweden, his various lectures and poetry readings.

I would like to quote from two letters I received in answer to my enquiries in October 2000, from Professors Emeritus Claes Schaar and Carl Fehrman of Lund University.

Professor Schaar wrote to me on 10 October 2000:

> Eliot came to Lund in April 1942. He gave one lecture in our large auditorium, which was packed with eager listeners (and spectators). I heard it, and though I was a twenty-two-year-old undergraduate I remember the occasion very vividly. He talked about drama. What he had to say was not very remarkable, but I was fascinated by the voice and indeed by the man's presence. He later read *The Waste Land* to a more select audience, to which I naturally did not belong.
>
> I should perhaps also say that it was a very tough thing to do, to cross the North Sea in a flimsy aeroplane in 1942. We were much impressed by that.
>
> Modernism was certainly of great importance in Sweden at that time (Lindegren, Ekelöf, and others; all influenced by Eliot). Britain of course was our sole hope in the early 1940's, and people who hoped for a Nazi victory were *very* few (though you may have been told otherwise).

Professor Fehrman wrote to me on 18 October 2000 and on 15 August 2002:

> Eliot's signature is in the 'Lundensiska literatursällskapets' book, where lecturers wrote their name and the title of their lectures; the date is 29.4.1942, on the occasion of his lecture, *Poetry in the Theatre*. I remember the lecture as an ordinary university lecture, given in the main University building to a fully packed audience.
>
> The University lecturer in English was Arthur H. King (later in the British Council). It was he who organized the Lund days for Eliot. In his lectures and seminars he had, from the early Thirties, introduced and interpreted Eliot's poetry to his pupils with great success (I studied English as his pupil from 1935 to 1937). My copy of Eliot's *Collected Poems* was bought at Foyles in 1937, when I studied in London, writing a paper on some of Shakespeare's sonnets.
>
> The lecture mentioned above was official. A more private meeting with Eliot was arranged in the students' building,

'Akademiska Föreningen', to which King had invited some scholars, professors, *docents* [ed. senior lecturer] and students. A meal was served, and Eliot was supposed to read some of his poems. From this session I remember his reading of *What the thunder said*, efficiently stressing the thunder-imitating words and sounds, similarly when reading from *Burnt Norton*: 'Quick said the bird, find them, find them', painting the twittering efficiently but with discretion at the same time – a memorable performance for those of us who had read but never heard the poems recited.

Asta Kihlbom, then *docent* in English in Lund (later professor in Norway) took the chance to thank him, stressing the political implications of his work as an author and of his visit to Sweden in April 1942. I remember her words: 'For *your* cause is *our* cause'. I am not sure he liked being reminded of his political mission at *this* moment. To all initiated the situation was self-evident and did not need to be stressed officially.

A third occasion when Eliot met Lund people was at the Bishop's house; his interest in Anglo-Catholicism was well known. Here he met our outstanding Lund theologian, Bishop Edvard Rodhe and some other theology professors well-oriented in the Anglican tradition, and the then well-known Professor Anders Nygren (author of *Eros and Agape*). I was not present at this occasion, arranged by Arthur King, but I guess that this meeting made a deep impression on all who were present.

Finally I remember a dinner where Olle Holmberg, Professor of Literature, was the host and prominent University people were guests, among them the *Rector* of the University, the Latin scholar, Einar Löfstedt. In his speech at the dinner table Holmberg, thinking of the bombing of Coventry Cathedral, alluded to the ongoing war as 'the murders in the Cathedrals'. Literary discussions took place. Löfstedt judged the French poets, Paul Claudel and Paul Valéry, as 'very artificial'. I am not certain that Eliot appreciated the judgement, knowing that a good poem might well be an 'artefact'.

I was given the honorary task of accompanying Eliot from his hotel to the station and the train to Stockholm. I really do not think I made any impression at all on our guest, and his own conversation was, as in one of his poems, restricted to

T. S. Eliot receives his Nobel Prize from Sweden's Crown Prince Gustaf Adolf in December 1948.

'What precisely, and If and Perhaps and But'. I had some contacts with Gunnar Ekelöf, who was busy translating *The Love Song of J. Alfred Prufrock*, probably in spring 1942. I suppose that Ekelöf met him in Stockholm, and the other poets who prepared *Dikter i urval*.

It should be added that Arthur King played an important role in making Eliot known both in Lund and Uppsala, as a teacher; among his pupils was the journalist Allan Fagerström, of *Aftonbladet*, and Claes Schaar.

In Stockholm, Peter Tennant (British Press Attaché at the Embassy; later Sir Peter Tennant) took Eliot sailing on Lake Mälaren.

One of my most memorable outings was with T.S. Eliot. He had come over to lecture and jumped at the opportunity of a sail as he had never sailed in his life. We had a fascinating afternoon in very stormy weather. I steered and he baled and talked of the poets who had most influenced him in his life – Kipling, Lear and Lewis Carroll. I took him home to dry and have tea in front of our big open log stove and he charmed the children with stories and sent them later what he said was his best book, *Old Possum's Book of Practical Cats*.

Following the first publication of this article in the British Council's Newsletter for Sweden (*Agenda*) in September 2002, I have received an intriguing e-mail from Michael Srigley in Uppsala (19 September 2002), who informed me that 'Professor Gunnar Sorelius, my colleague, tells me that there was a rumour circulating in Uppsala that the purpose of Eliot's visit was to pick up a cargo of ball bearings and take them to England'. He goes on to say that Eliot (according to Uppsala poet Carl-Erik af Geijerstam) on the way back to his hotel, after a lecture on chiaroscuro in Renaissance art, spoke of the nightmarish flight he had had from England because of his bad lungs, caused by his heavy smoking and the fact that the plane flew at a great altitude and had no oxygen available . . . The most interesting thing I learnt was that Eliot was accompanied to Sweden by the Bishop of Durham who was on a secret mission to Germany to meet the German opposition and learn more about their plans to assassinate Hitler. Eliot, knowingly or not, was to be the cover for this mission by making it seem that their arrival in Stockholm was a cultural one on his part and a theological one on the Bishop's part. The Bishop would then slip off and fly to Berlin.'

Leaving aside these unconfirmed rumours of secret missions, and concentrating solely on the cultural and literary significance of the visit, what were the outcomes of this British Council tour of Sweden? What was the impact? I leave you to consider the performance indicators, the criteria for evaluation and assessment of impact, the methods of measurement of press coverage, audience size, perception change. Cultural relations work is also about long-term impact and personal contact. Sixty years seems sufficient time in order to declare a visit a success.

As Eliot said in his 1948 acceptance speech for the Nobel Prize in Literature:

> To enjoy poetry belonging to another language is to enjoy the understanding of the people to whom that language belongs, an understanding we can get in no other way. Partly through his influence on other poets, partly through translation, which must be also a kind of recreation of his poems by other poets, partly through readers of his language who are not themselves poets, the poet can contribute toward understanding between peoples . . . I think that in poetry people of different countries and different languages – though it be apparently only through a small minority in any one country – acquire an understanding of each other which, however partial, is still essential. And I take the award of the Nobel Prize in Literature, when it is given to a poet, to be primarily an assertion of the supra-national value of poetry.

Peter Tennant[42]

from *Touchlines of War*

Chapter XVII: The British Council

When I went to Sweden at the end of September 1939, the British Council asked if I would handle their cultural business alongside that of the Ministry of Information and the Foreign Office. For a long while they kept me well supplied with photographs and articles which the Ministry of Information failed to do.

My employers agreed I should work for them and I did my best. It was not too difficult and I got the help of a Mr Charlesworth, a lecturer at the Swedish Workers Educational Organisation which covered the whole of Sweden. I had contacts in Stockholm's *Högskola*, the predecessor of the present university, and I made my number in the Universities of Uppsala and Lund. We ran a cultural shop window in Stockholm with books and photographs but had no separate office.

In due course I found it difficult to combine my information activity with the work of lectures for the Council. In 1941, when I visited London, I asked them to send out a representative. They agreed but suggested I should find one. I put up a friend of mine from Cambridge, Ronald Bottrall, a poet with some experience as a lecturer in Finland. He was languishing from boredom as a Principal in the Ministry of Aircraft Production. He was immediately hired and he and his charming wife Margaret flew out to Sweden. The Swedes found it difficult to accept this giant who looked more like a retired boxer with his broken nose, than an emissary of British culture. They were convinced for a time that he was the Head of the Secret Service just as was the case with the French Cultural Attaché who represented the Deuxième Bureau. They also confused the British Council with the British Consul. Ronald did a superb job and we all gave him as much support as we could. He worked with Swedish writers and together with Gunnar Ekelöf, one of the foremost Swedish poets of the period, produced a translation of some of T.S. Eliot's poetry.

The cost effectiveness and cost benefits of the British Council are continuously a matter of debate and it has suffered as the whipping boy of the Treasury and of the *Daily Express*, particularly in the days of Lord Beaverbrook. But it has survived. There are ways in which its effectiveness can be measured but they are often not sufficiently convincing for the Treasury or for Parliament who make a virtue of cutting expenditure by measuring the cost and rarely the value of an undertaking. The value of the British Council in projecting the image of British life abroad provides a strong foundation for our policies in many other fields.

In Sweden during the war we had one example of a benefit which must have saved thousands of lives. On 18 July 1944, Victor Mallet, our Minister, drove the Swedish Minister for Foreign Affairs, Christian Günther, to Sigtuna to

attend a British Council event at a summer school for teachers where they were having their last night concert and
supper. On the way Victor tackled Günther about the V2
rocket which had landed in Southern Sweden. The experts in
Farnborough had asked to be allowed to fly it home for a thor-
ough inspection. Mallet pointed out the carnage these
ghastly weapons might wreak among the civilian population
even though we were over-running at that time the launching
sites of the far less formidable V1s. Victor writes in his
unpublished memoirs:

> Günther said he would have to think about my request but
> refused to make a decision. At the Summer school Ronald
> Bottrall laid on an admirable concert of Elizabethan songs and
> madrigals ending with a very congenial supper. On the way
> back Günther said he had been much moved by the music
> and the happy atmosphere of this Anglo-Swedish school. It
> had made him reflect on the subject of the bomb and he had
> decided that it would not be right for him to deprive us of the
> opportunity of counteracting such a devilish weapon which
> might be used to destroy thousands of innocent British civil-
> ian lives. I might telegraph to the Foreign Office and say that
> we could take it away as long as this was done with the great-
> est secrecy. The next day the bomb was collected and flown
> home.

Victor tells how a few days after the end of the war, Air Mar-
shal Lord Tedder flew from Copenhagen to Stockholm with
the object of personally thanking General Nordenskiöld, the
Head of the Swedish Airforce, for the great help he had given
us in this matter by immediately telling our Air Attaché of
the extraordinary find the Swedes had made.

'Years afterwards,' Victor wrote, 'I reminded Mr Günther
(they were then both colleagues as Head of their missions in
Rome) of our talks on the way back from Sigtuna and of the
momentous decision which he had taken then. I said to him
"Your decision was something of which you can always be

proud". The dear modest man merely answered "Not proud but thankful".'

Many of us felt that Günther was miscast as Foreign Minister, but we have reason to be thankful to him for this decision and to the British Council for its contribution. The cost to Britain would have been incalculable if the decision had not been made.

Michael Roberts[43]

Retrospect

In all periods of English history the competition was fierce; and vested interests existed upon which it would be presumptuous for a beginner to intrude. Much more promising prospects seemed to open in the field of European history; for at that time not many of us ventured upon it, no doubt because of the linguistic attainments which it obviously demanded. I looked around, therefore, to see where there was an obvious lack of information available to an almost monoglot English readership. There was no difficulty in identifying three or four such areas. For a time I was tempted by eighteenth-century Portugal; or again, by eighteenth-century Tuscany; but in the end the choice seemed to reduce itself to some seventeenth-century topic in the history of either Poland or Sweden. Poland was in fact better provided for than I suspected; but Sweden was scarcely provided for at all. I took what seemed to me a practical step towards resolving my hesitation. One Friday I went into Blackwell's bookshop and simultaneously bought myself a *Teach Yourself Polish,* and a *Teach Yourself Swedish.* A weekend's inspection of these volumes was sufficient: by Sunday evening I had decided that Poland was not for me. And since it was to be Sweden, I determined, with the self-confidence of youth, to plunge in at the deep end and write a book on Gustav Adolf.

There was no lack of Swedish books to buy: to start with, Ahnlund's *Gustav Adolf den Store* had appeared, most opportunely, in 1932. I bought all I could afford, and slowly learned to stumble through them by the light of nature, untroubled as yet by any aspiration to speak the language.

So, more or less by accident, I had cast myself for the part of a writer on Swedish history. But then came another accident, quite unforeseen, which seemed to cancel out the former. In 1935 I found myself translated to the Chair of Modern History at Grahamstown. Rhodes University College (as it then was) was at that time no bigger than a large Oxford College, and not much assistance in the department was available, so that I found myself saddled with a very heavy lecturing and teaching load. I did indeed continue to buy Swedish books and printed sources as opportunity offered – more as a hobby, now, than with any idea of prosecuting a project; but I could not disguise from myself that in the existing circumstances the whole Swedish venture must probably be written off. And since it seemed very unlikely that the English-reading public would within a foreseeable future be edified by my observations on Gustav Adolf, it occurred to me that it would be a useful service (and, incidentally, a useful exercise) to do a translation of *Gustav Adolf den Store*. The American-Scandinavian Foundation turned out to be willing to publish it; Ahnlund himself was not dissatisfied; and in 1940 the book duly appeared. But if it thus represented the interment of one aspiration, it sowed the seed of another; for it planted in me that fascination with the craft of translation which has never relinquished its hold, and has encouraged me to ventures which have broken out intermittently ever since.

Then came the war, and it was time to forget about such things. I found myself in the S.A. Intelligence Corps. It was not very exciting; and when one day a notice came round from the British Council enquiring whether anybody would be interested in teaching English to the offspring of Arab sheiks somewhere in the Middle East I put in an application, and began to look round for a *Teach Yourself Arabic*. Luckily for myself (and for the sheiks) I was never to be reduced to such a desperate enterprise; for one day when I was being intelligent in Asmara there came a signal from Defence Headquarters to the effect that the Council had changed its mind, and would be obliged if I would go as its Representative to Stockholm. And that was the final accident that determined where my interests would have to lie.

And so, in the summer of 1944, my wife and I flew (somewhat hazardously) from Prestwick to Bromma, took up our quarters in Askrikegatan, and confronted the demands of the job. The presupposition was that it was the mission of the Council to familiarize the country to which its Representatives were assigned with what was then called 'the British way of life'; though life as the Representative in Stockholm lived it – under the shelter of the Legation, and with many semi-diplomatic privileges – bore few resemblances to life as it was lived in Britain in 1944. Still, we were to expound what *had* been, and, we hoped, what might one day be again. English literature, English music, British institutions, British social assumptions and social policies – these we were to make known, in as advantageous a light as possible, to any who might be prepared to listen. But before we could begin we had ourselves to be educated. The first few days of our stay in Stockholm were devoted to careful instruction on such matters as Swedish social habits and customs, the elements of good manners, tricky questions of precedence, and the correct form of address: we were still in the age of obligatory titles and the third person singular. At first it all seemed complicated and strange, and no doubt we blundered before it came to feel like second nature: I still recall with shame an occasion when at a large formal dinner I delivered a thank-you speech when it was not my place to do so. For obvious reasons, Sweden was at that time one of the Council's more important spheres of activity, and we had to be careful to consult the Legation if any plausible gentleman with a Hungarian name suggested that we meet for lunch. We had our office in Birger Jarlsgatan, as the Germans had theirs in Kungsgatan, and our display-window offered what we hoped were attractive pictures of the British way of life: photographs of prominent artists, authors or musicians and their works; historic buildings; landscapes to make the lucklessly-isolated Swedes dream of post-war travel; no politics. The window was looked at: its effect was doubtful; and on one dreadful occasion it was hard not to think that our seductive picture of Salisbury Cathedral must be making less impact on the public than the simultaneous display in Kungsgatan of the bombing of Dresden. We gave such advice as we could to those who came to us for information; we ran a reading-room, a small library and a record-collection. We participated, when invited to do so, in the activities of Folkhögskolor and the ABF. We arranged occasional scholarships. And we held an agreeable summer school at Sigtuna: that of 1945 made memorable by the enthusiastic participation of Professor Henry Donner, whose perfect Oxford English rather put the rest of us to shame.

But by far the most interesting and demanding work consisted in trying to serve the Anglo-Swedish Societies. Of these there were by 1944 rather more than a hundred. They met, as a rule, once a month during the autumn and winter, they were scattered over the whole of the country: and for every meeting they turned to us for a lecturer. Many of the members were no doubt impelled by their political sympathies; but many also by their simple desire to hear English spoken. In the near-total isolation in which Sweden then was, it was not easy for a Swede outside the major cities to hear and speak any other language than his own; and the sense of deprivation was perhaps curiously reflected in a temporary interest in Esperanto. To provide them with what they wanted was a demanding task: there were a few members of the office in Birger Jarlsgatan who could be made available at need; but the main burden fell on the Representative – with useful assistance on occasion from his wife.

The Societies were very appreciative of the lectures that we gave them, though many members did not greatly care whether we were telling them about the novels of Jane Austen, the career of the younger Pitt, English nursery schools, the British Empire, the peculiarities of Oxbridge, or the English sense of humour. Nothing came amiss to them, subject to one essential proviso: they must be able to hear, and hearing to understand. Some of them were grammatical precisions: I remember being taken to task (I think it was in Jönköping) by a woman who remarked that I had spoken of 'Dickens's works', though, as she drily observed, she had always been taught that when a substantive ended in s the apostrophe followed the s, and hence the correct form was surely 'Dickens' works'. She may very well have been right; but to encourage any doubt about the purity of one's own English would have been destructive of morale. But if a member came up after it was over and told you, 'Do you know, I understood every word', then the lecture (on whatever subject) was a success. Not otherwise.

All this entailed a great deal of travelling by rail; and I early began to arrange matters so that I never returned by the same route as that upon which I had set out. I had until recently – but have now, alas, lost it – an SJ map of the Swedish railway system as it stood in 1946; and on that map I marked in red the lines over which I had travelled. When I left Sweden in 1946 well over three-quarters of the total rail network was so marked. The only outstanding blank area was eastern Östergötland: I never succeeded in doing the line from Linköping to Kalmar by way of Vimmerby; and though on later visits I came determined to fill that gap, somehow it never got done. But otherwise I managed to range from Kiruna to Ystad, from Sollefteå to Borås, from Östersund to Landskrona, from Lysekil to Valdemarsvik – memorable for the gift, by a kind and discerning host, of Alfred Västlund's *Guldregn*. Only once, for some reason, was I constrained to take to the road, and it was with the aid of a *gengas* [ed. wood gas] car that I struggled from Sundsvall to Kramfors: all very well on the flat, but heavy going on the hills. But the trains were a never-failing joy: the little narrow-gauge lines of Västergötland, which might have served as models for 'Emmet' in his *Punch* drawings; the movable armchairs which welcomed the traveller on the train to Riksgränsen (they made their last appearance, I believe, in some first-class coaches between Stockholm and Uppsala); the exciting experience of doing the whole length of Inlandsbanan, with an overnight stop at Vilhelmina. SJ in those days took some care for the standard of behaviour of those who used its facilities: I used to cherish the notice which it affixed in its compartments, and which I feloniously appropriated. That notice reminded travellers that conversation on political or religious topics was better avoided, for fear of wounding the susceptibilities of one's companions; it pointed out to any who might stretch themselves out on the seat that their ticket entitled them to one place only, and exhorted them, in the event of another passenger's entering, to *'stå utan vidare opp: låtsas ej att Ni sover'* [ed. 'stand up immediately: do not pretend to be asleep']; and rounded it all off by austerely proclaiming that *'eder och svordomar äro motbjudande för de flesta människorna'* [ed. 'swearing and cursing are offensive to most people']. One of these trips brought me to Lund on 30 April 1945, when I saw (but imperfectly understood) that year's apex, heard with astonishment the Rektor being instructed in his duties by the student body, and with equal astonishment beheld him recruiting himself afterwards in a *skål* to Spring from a Venetian glass nine inches tall. It was on this occasion that I bought myself, with some hesitation, Petrus Laesta-dius's[44] *Journal*. In some doubt I asked a Swedish friend 'Is this any good?' and was answered with appropriate asperity 'It is a classic'. As indeed I found it to be; making Linné's *Iter Lapponicum* look somewhat lightweight in comparison. But then I am no botanist. That memorable visit finished in Malmö at a historic moment; for on the quay Folke Bernadotte's Red Cross buses stood lined up ready for departure.

The hospitality offered by the Societies was delightful, and in the circumstances miraculous. But it could on occasion be exhausting. I shall not easily forget Luleå. Arriving around two-thirty p.m., I was whisked away to a Society whose improbable name appeared to be 'W-6'; and there, with unre-lenting hospitality, was plied from a perennial spring of alco-holic refreshment for the entire period between my arrival and dinner-time – a space of nearly four hours – by way of prelude to my discoursing on the Structure of the British Empire. This experience was in no way lessened by the dinner that followed. I survived it somehow, delivered the lecture, and was ardently longing for bed, when there arose a questioner in the audience who demanded that I confess that India paid enormous sums in direct taxation to the British exchequer. It was in vain to attempt to rebut this allegation; for my interlocutor proved to be Redaktör Brick of *Norrskens-flamman*[45],and he knew better; moreover he had with him his brother, just home from emancipated America, who confirmed his statement in every particular. There being no way of resolving this difference of opinion, and the rest of the audience having already had as much as they could conve-niently assimilate, the meeting was dispersing, when to my surprise the brothers Brick came forward and with the utmost cordiality suggested that what we all needed now was a *sängfösare* [ed. nightcap]. I sagged at the prospect, but it would have been uncivil to refuse, and craven to decline the

battle for the British Empire; so we adjourned to resume liba-
tions which had already proved excessive. At some time in
the small hours I managed to get away, ruefully reflecting
that I was due to catch an early train for Kiruna. I awoke to
the consciousness that the brothers Brick were sitting on
either side of my bed. They greeted me warmly, and at once
proposed a *magborstare* [ed. hair of the dog]. This I somehow
contrived to avoid, caught the train by the skin of my teeth,
and abandoned the British Empire to its fate. But it had been
a formidable experience. The next day made amends: it was
early September, the first light snow had fallen, but the dwarf
birches showed red against it, the sun shone from a cloudless
sky, and it was very beautiful.

All this meant that Sweden for the first time became real,
rather than simply a country with an interesting history that
one read about in books; and perhaps nothing could have
impressed that reality on me so well. Stockholm of course
provided easy access to such places as Skokloster, Gripsholm
and Ängsö; but I have the Anglo-Swedish Societies to thank
for Läckö, Vadstena, Kalmar, Borgholm, Kristianstad, and
many other places of interest to the historian; and – not least
– for some idea of that leading constituent of Swedish
humour, the small provincial town, immortalised in
Grönköping (though I cannot recall that Hjo boasted an
Anglo–Swedish Society, I managed to get there somehow –
perhaps by the ferry which then ran from Vadstena). And
this was perhaps why I devoured volume after volume of
Hjalmar Bergman with such relish. I still think of that world
with some nostalgia. Certainly the 1940s were a good period
for a foreigner to begin reading Swedish literature: it was the
period of Gustaf Hellström, Ludvig Nordström, Eyvind Johnson, Sigfrid Siwertz, Pär Lagerkvist, and above all of Piraten
and F.G. Bengtsson.

[ ]

It was a good period too for music: Hilding Rosenberg,
Lars-Erik Larsson, Dag Wirén, Atterberg were new experi-

ences. The Stockholm Opera, despite war conditions, seemed remarkably flourishing: Brita Hertzberg and Einar Beyron were great in *Tristan;* Hjördis Schymberg was irresistible in Mozart; *Lycksalighetens Ö* impressed me – as it impressed William Walton when he came over soon after the war: is it still performed, I wonder? *Värmlänningarna* was disarming; *Arnljot* rather less so. *The Beggar's Opera,* alas, proved a failure. And there was older Swedish music, at that time still almost unknown in England: Roman, Berwald (I became an early convert), Alfvén, Stenhammar. I remember listening to a broadcast of a violin sonata, and saying to myself, 'This is a new romantic voice! I must find out more about this chap'. It proved to be Stenhammar's op. 15. I duly prosecuted my enquiries, and they have proved rewarding.

Despite these distractions I found it possible to do a little work. Among our friends at this time few were historians: Yngve Lorents and Maj, both committed anglophiles even in the darkest days; Folke Lindberg; Gunnar Ahlström; Eli Heckscher, with his great collection of English detective stories: one of the only two men I have ever met (the other was G.D.H. Cole) who were familiar with the novels of Frances Trollope; Nils Andrén; Ragnar Svanström. Ahnlund I met only once or twice, on ceremonial occasions. But one could always buy books: then and for some years afterwards second-hand books were surprisingly cheap. When at last it was time for us to return to Grahamstown we sailed – luxuriously – in *Kolmaren,* heavily freighted with literature and gramophone records. For my spell with the Council had in one respect been decisive: I was at last firmly committed to the idea that what I had to do was to write about Swedish history, and persuaded that I had become sufficiently well acquainted with the country to make the idea less of an absurdity than it had seemed in the late 1930s. Even so, there remained formidable bibliographical problems, and small chance of returning to Sweden to fill the gaps within a reasonable time. For the moment, the difficulty was relieved by the extraordinary benevolence of Uppsala university library, which for three or four years after the war was generous and trusting enough to send me consignments of books on loan, a dozen at a time, with the sole proviso that I should not keep them for more than a month. That meant, of course, hard labour on the arrival of each parcel. But what other library anywhere, at any time, would have been liberal enough to lend books to a reader 6,000 miles away?

Memoirs and Biography

Michael Holroyd

from *Basil Street Blues*

My mother's beginning was dramatic. In 1916 her parents were living at Örebro, 200 kilometres west of Stockholm. They had been married three years, had a two-year-old son Karl-Åke, and my grandmother was over five months pregnant with her second child. On 19 November Karl-Åke was playing in the kitchen where his nurse was cooking – simply boiling water it seems at the fireplace. Some say the child knocked over an oil lamp and started a fire; others that he tipped the boiling saucepan over himself. He was rushed to hospital, lingered there almost three weeks, then died on 9 December. The shock caused my grandmother to give birth prematurely to a tiny daughter on the day after the accident and in the hospital where her son was dying. They called their daughter Ulla. This was my mother.

I knew none of this until my mother wrote it down for me. I am not certain how much she knew of it herself before then – perhaps it is the sort of knowledge we suppress. But while preparing her account she told me that Greta, a neighbour of her mother in Stockholm, 'is trying to pump her without her knowing so, to keep her mind off her health – let's see what we'll get.' In other words Greta was doing what I was doing.

What we got was to be one of the main sources of my mother's rapid narrative. She wrote on lined paper, twenty centimetres long, and with forty-six narrow lines to the page which her fast-flowing handwriting often overlapped. She wrote in pencil, suggesting the impermanence of the past, yet with great speed and dash, almost violence, underlining words – names, dates, countries, towns, as well as words that needed special emphasis, such as *all* and *dead*. Her writing appears full of activity, as if responding to the urgency of these events which streamed confusingly in and out of each other until they came to an end at the top of the thirteenth page. Then she started again, from somewhere near the middle, ending this time with notes of her various dogs; another fourteen pages. My mother had little time for the past. What absorbed her was the eternal present. Nevertheless, as she wrote, and then as I read, an unusual interest in these events seemed to grow up between us.

She noted that her father, a major in the Swedish army, had died in 1945. That surprised me. I had thought it was very much earlier. Only when I came to write this book did I realize he actually died several years later. I never met him. 1945 was the year I began making regular sea journeys with my mother to visit our Swedish relatives in Borås and Stockholm, Göteborg and a holiday island nearby called Marstrand.

My understanding at the time was that, despite being in one of the country's safest professions, the Swedish army, my grandfather had died young. I imagined him, sword in hand, falling gloriously from a horse during hectic manoeuvres in a northern forest.

From my mother's notes I see that he was son of Knut Johansson, a director of the Växjö Match Company in southern Sweden and his wife Amanda Hall who came from a family that ran the Kreuger Match Company. On her marriage certificate my mother was to give her maiden name as Ulla Knutsson-Hall. Evidently, her father took, or was given, his father's first name, a second syllable to remind us that he was the son of his father, and finally his mother's maiden name. He is Karl Knutsson-Hall.

Karl (or Kalle as he was usually called) had a good voice and had once dreamed of being an opera singer. He did sing in a few amateur productions, but his parents wanted him to take over the family's match empire. Eventually, by way of compromise, he went into the army which was thought to provide a respectable career.

My mother's maternal family had come from southern Germany, and her great-grandfather, Gustav Jagenburg, worked in Moscow early in the nineteenth century before settling down with his wife at Rydboholm, near Borås. He was a textile manufacturer and his son Rudolf was said to have invented a wondrous dye that never faded. In the 1880s Rudolf married the daughter of the prison priest at the Castle of Varberg. The second of their six children was my grandmother. Her formal name was Karin though we all called her Kaja.

How Karl and Kaja first met I do not know. But I do know that the Jagenburgs considered themselves socially superior to Karl's match-making family which was lower-middle class. They strongly opposed the marriage of this handsome couple on the grounds that Kaja could do better for herself. There was no money to be made in the army and Karl's excellent horsemanship did not particularly impress them. But Kaja in those days was a headstrong, passionate girl. A photograph of her in her early twenties among my mother's possessions shows a sweet face, with watchful slanting eyes, a rather sensuous but determined mouth, her expression provocative and full of character. No one was going to tell her whom to marry. She was in love with this charming officer, and that was enough.

So, in 1913, she married Lieutenant Karl Knutsson-Hall and went up to Boden in the north of Sweden where he was stationed. She was twenty-one and could marry without parental consent; he was four years older.

It seems probable that the marriage never recovered from the burning to death of their infant son Karl-Åke at the end of 1916. They had no more children after my mother Ulla and by the 1920s, when the family moved to Stockholm and my mother was old enough to notice things, Karl was spending more time with his brother officers than with his wife. They seemed to regard him still as a romantic bachelor. 'A more gentlemanly officer than Karl Hall could not be found in 1920s Sweden,' wrote one of his subordinates who recalled this 'idyllic warrior' during their company's 'legendary manoeuvres in Trosa during 1922 . . . and the merry ball in Trosa's grand hotel where Karl Hall reigned over the dusty recruits and young beauties . . . a generous, chivalrous heart-breaker.'

Ulla went first to the Margaretha School in Stockholm and then to Franska Skolan at 9 Döbelnsgatan where she began to learn her many languages. In the holidays she often went to Växjö where the Hall family had a large country house. Her most enduring memory was of twin earth-closets in a red building with white gables where 'I used to sit with my cousin'. Her father being the eldest of nine children, there were plenty of these cousins with whom to play. At the end of the garden stood a lake where they would all swim ('trod on a snake once on the way down the slope', my mother wrote). What she most enjoyed were the children's suppers by this lake in the endless summer evenings – sandwiches made from freshly baked brown bread with delicious fillings. 'I once ate 15!' my mother boasted. 'A record.' She was looked after during those early holidays by Karin – not her mother (who disliked the Hall family and didn't often go to Växjö) but one of her in-laws whom she thought of as her 'nanny'.

At the age of twelve Ulla was sent to a French family in the Haute Savoie for three months to practise her French. But there was another reason for removing her from Stockholm. Her parents had decided to separate. This was not a friendly arrangement but a stubbornly fought duel that lasted almost four years and according to the family was to lead to a change in the Swedish divorce laws. Up till that time 'we lived in various nice flats', my mother wrote. But after she returned from France everything changed. Mother and daughter moved rapidly between small apartments and boarding houses pursued by Karl. Sometimes at night there were drunken brawls in the street and on one memorable occasion Karl staggered towards them shouting and waving a revolver.

Kaja was determined to win her divorce. But though Karl was apparently drinking heavily and had, Kaja told her daughter, contracted venereal disease from an extra-marital liaison, there seemed no way for her to obtain a legal divorce unless her husband consented to it. His condition of consent was a million kronor, which he calculated Kaja's father (he of the miraculous unfading dye) could afford to pay him. There was a prolonged and bitter feud that my mother found unnerving. 'I suffered,' she wrote. But what struck me as strange when reading her brief account was that she didn't appear to blame her father for those dreadful years. Perhaps she romanticized him, not knowing him so well, and missing him. Kaja had never been very 'understanding' with her as a child and was, Ulla felt, too 'demanding' with her husband.

Eventually Kaja won the divorce battle largely because one of her uncles was Riksmarskalk of Sweden (equivalent of Lord High Chamberlain in England). After 'Lex versus Hall' was settled in 1932 it became easier for women to get divorced in Sweden.

Following their divorce Karl retreated into a home for alcoholics where he was nursed by the daughter of a priest (the home was apparently managed by the Church). Then in her mid-twenties, Marianne was half Karl's age, but 'understanding and kind which was what he *needed*', my mother insisted. So they married. As a bonus she was 'very good-looking', my mother observed. This suggests that she must have seen Marianne, but gets her name wrong (Margareta instead of Marianne) which suggests she did not actually know her. Perhaps they met only at Karl's funeral. In my mother's speedy narrative, the happy couple are disposed of rather brutally: 'My father died of T.B. and god knows what else,' she wrote. 'He caught T.B. from his wife who was later killed by being squashed by a lorry against a wall whilst walking with a girlfriend in Stockholm – five years after Papa died.' This must have been based on what Kaja was telling her neighbour, Greta. In fact Karl's cause of death is given as a respectable heart attack ('Infartus cordis kardiosclerasis').

In her teens Kaja had done some sewing and cutting in her father's textile workshops in Borås. Then, arriving in Stockholm as a married woman, she persuaded her father to introduce her to Countess Margareta von Schwerin, known as Marg, who in 1927 was to open the celebrated fashion house Märthaskolan where elegant ladies had their dresses made. Before long Kaja became a consultant there and was coming into contact with Swedish high society. She took her work seriously and, she would tell her daughter, was never late, not even by five minutes, for an appointment. 'I can see Kaja entering the salons well aware of the impression she made, so sure of herself and her beauty,' a friend of my mother's wrote to me. 'Everyone had to admire her, and then entered Ulla, pretty, laughing and much more warm at heart, everybody felt.'

Kaja soon floated free from the disreputable business of her divorce and settled into her work as a couturier for Märthaskolan. This was a school of dress as well as a fashion house and in those days the greatest single influence in the creation of Swedish femininity. The Countess Margareta von Schwerin herself was really a fashion reporter with strong opinions as to what would be useful for young girls. She travelled widely and dealt with most of the French couturiers. But she did not promote a single style or confine her interest to high fashion. She was an ambitious woman and wanted to dress all women in Sweden, whatever their age or status. She

*Michael Holroyd, seated on the floor, with his Swedish relations,
August 1946. His grandmother is sitting three from the left, his mother
three from the right.*

saw herself as an educator. Her mission was to give Swedish
women confidence in the home and at work by the way they
presented themselves.

Among the bits and pieces my mother left after her death
are a few photographs of our trips together to Sweden from
the late 1940s and the 1950s. There I am sitting on the floor
with my pretty cousin Mary. She is smiling, blonde and
lively; I, aged nine or ten, am blank-faced and bird-like,
decked out in foreign tailoring, with blue and yellow Swedish
cufflinks, a frilled handkerchief and bow tie (my God! What
would my schoolfriends in Surrey have said?). Behind us, sitting and standing in rows, a contingent of the family has
formed up for the photograph. I can recognise my grandmother Kaja, a formidably handsome woman looking frankly
at the camera; and I can see my mother, unsmiling, with a
similar gingham frock and hair neatly arranged like my
grandmother's – she is on her very best behaviour. But I
cannot identify anyone else. Which is Elis? Where is Inga?

But with my mother's written account before me I can at last make some sense of this family group. My grandmother was in her mid-fifties at the time these photographs were taken, though she looks younger. And these are her brothers and sisters, their husbands and wives and children, who have lined up before the camera. There is a bank manager, an engineer, a doctor, a businessman: all respectable middle-class people. Of course there are some lapses of respectability. One of the brothers, for example, an import-export manager, imported syphilis from a Hamburg brothel and has never quite recovered. My grandmother believes it must have addled his brain – why else would he have married a waitress from a Borås hotel? My mother likes Kristina, her waitress-aunt, who has always been kind to her. But my grandmother cannot stand her and makes pointed remarks such as, when Kristina comes into the room with some drinks: 'You must be used to carrying trays.'

My grandmother is a snob. Snobbishness is her form of authority. It cows other people, and this suits her. That is why she looks so young in the photographs and my mother so ill-at-ease. My grandmother believes in appearances and, living up to her beliefs, she appears splendidly superior.

Kaja always walked, sat, spoke and generally carried herself with soldierly precision. She had the unquestioning air of an officer – more so than her ex-husband. She assumed the posture of high command, straightened her back, raised her chin, yet somehow retained her attractiveness. This is a determined and successful couturier we see in the photographs.

Kaja revelled in this work and felt proud of being part of the Countess's team at Märthaskolan. She allowed herself one acknowledged admirer, Birger Sandström, a middle-aged gentleman with a brilliant white moustache, whose presence breathed respectability. He escorted her to parties and she employed him almost as a fashion accessory. It was a discreet arrangement which became easier to manage after 1934 when Ulla sailed for England.

Ingmar Bergman

from *The Magic Lantern. An Autobiography*

In 1970, Laurence Olivier had persuaded me to stage *Hedda Gabler* at the National Theatre in London, with Maggie Smith in the title rôle. I packed my suitcase and left, with considerable inner resistance and full of forebodings.

My hotel room was dark and dirty, the traffic noisy outside, shaking the building and rattling the windowpanes. There was a smell of damp and mould and the radiator to the right of the door made rumbling noises. Some small shiny insects, beautiful but out of place, lived in the bath. The supper with the new Lord Olivier and the actors to welcome me turned out badly, the food Javanese and inedible. One of the actors was already drunk. He told me that Strindberg and Ibsen were unplayable dinosaurs, which simply went to prove that bourgeois theatre was on its way out. I asked why the hell he was taking part in *Hedda Gabler*, and he said that there were 5,000 unemployed actors and actresses in London. Lord Olivier smiled a little wryly and told me that our friend was an excellent actor, and the fact that he became revolutionary when drunk was nothing to worry about. We broke up early.

The National Theatre was provisionally playing in rented premises while the new theatre was being built on the south bank. The rehearsal room was a concrete and corrugated iron shed in a spacious yard containing stinking garbage bins. When the sun blazed down on the metal roof, the heat was almost unbearable. There were no windows. Iron pillars every five metres held up the roof, so the scenery had to be placed behind and in front of these stanchions. There were two lavatories between the rehearsal room and the temporary administration hut. They were forever overflowing and stank of urine and rotten fish.

The actors were excellent, some of them outstanding. Their professionalism and speed frightened me a little and I at once realized their working methods were different from ours. They had learnt their lines by the first rehearsal. As soon as they had the scenery, they started acting at a fast tempo. I asked them to slow down a little and they loyally tried to, but it bewildered them.

Lord Olivier had cancer, but appeared in his administration hut every morning at nine o'clock, worked all day and played Shylock several times a week, two performances on some days. One Saturday I went to see him in his cramped and uncomfortable dressing room after the first performance. He was sitting in his underclothes and a ragged make-up overall, deathly pale and sweating profusely. Some unappetizing sandwiches were floating about on a dish. He was drinking champagne, one glass, two glasses, then a third. Then the make-up person came and touched him up, the dresser helped him on with Shylock's worn frock coat, he inserted the rôle's special false teeth and reached for his bowler hat.

I could not help thinking about our young Swedish actors complaining about having to rehearse in the daytime and perform at night. Or even worse, having to perform at a matinée and then again at an evening performance. What hard work! How bad for their artistry! How difficult the next day! How disastrous for their family life!

I high-handedly moved to the Savoy Hotel and swore I was prepared to pay whatever it cost. Lord Olivier offered me his pied-à-terre at the top of a high-rise in one of the more genteel areas of the city. He assured me I would not be disturbed. He and his wife, Joan Plowright, lived in Brighton, and he might spend the odd night in London occasionally, but we would not embarrass one another. I thanked him for his thoughtfulness and moved in, to be welcomed by a Dickensian character who was his housekeeper. She was Irish, four feet tall and moved crabwise. In the evenings she read her prayers so loudly, I first thought it was a service being broadcast through a loudspeaker in her room.

At first sight, the apartment was elegant, but turned out to be dirty, the expensive sofas grubby, the wallpaper torn, and there were interesting damp formations on the ceilings. Everything was dusty or stained. The breakfast cups were not properly washed up, the glasses had lip marks on them, the wall-to-wall carpets were worn out, the picture windows streaky.

Practically every morning, I met Lord Olivier at breakfast. For me, it was instructive. Laurence Olivier held seminars over our cups of coffee and lectured me on the subject of Shakespeare. My enthusiasm knew no bounds. I asked questions, he answered, taking his time, occasionally 'phoning to say he could not attend some morning meeting, then sitting down and having yet another cup of coffee.

That singularly modulated voice spoke from a lifetime with Shakespeare, about discoveries, adversities, insights, and experiences. Slowly but with joy I began to understand English actors' profound intimacy with and straightforward practical handling of a force of nature which could have crushed them or bound them to slavery. They lived fairly freely within a tradition – tender-hearted, arrogant, aggressive, but free. Their theatre, the short rehearsal times, the severe pressure, the compulsion to reach their audience, was direct and unmerciful. Their contact with their tradition was multidimensional and anarchic. Laurence Olivier carried on the tradition but also rebelled. Thanks to constant collaboration with younger and older colleagues, who lived under the same severe but creative circumstances, his relationships within his overwhelming professional life were constantly changing. His rapport with his art became fathomable, managable, and yet always dangerous, exhausting and surprising.

We met several times, but then that all came to an end. Lord Olivier had just filmed his production of *Three Sisters*. I thought the film sloppily made, badly edited and wretchedly photographed. It also lacked close-ups. I tried to say all this as politely as possible, praising the quality of the performances and the actors,' especially Joan Plowright, a matchless Masha. It was no use. Laurence Olivier suddenly turned very formal. Our earlier cordiality and common professional interest changed into mutual squabbling over minor details.

He came to the *Hedda Gabler* dress rehearsal half an hour late, made no apology, but aired some sarcastic (if true) opinions on the weaknesses in the production.

On the day of the premiere, I left London, which I had hated with every fibre in my body. It was a light, May evening in Stockholm. I stood down by the North Bridge looking at the fishermen in their boats and their green scoop nets. A brass band was playing in Kungsträdgården. I had never seen such beautiful women. The air was clear and easy to breathe, the cherry blossom fragrant and an astringent chill rose from the rushing water.

translated by Joan Tate

Ingmar Bergman's 1970 National Theatre production of Ibsen's Hedda Gabler *with Maggie Smith, Robert Stephens and Sheila Reid.*

Laurence Olivier

from *Confessions of an Actor*

[1969]

One of my greatest managerial ambitions for the National [Theatre] was to persuade the famous Ingmar Bergman to give us an English production of *Hedda Gabler*; I heard he was staying at the Savoy on a short visit and so I asked him and the lovely Liv Ullman to lunch with me at their hotel (Liv in Swedish means 'life' – I'll drink to that). It is to be expected that in matters of business a great genius is apt to play hard to get, and so I was not surprised by his skilful evasions. When there were only a few minutes left and I was beginning to give up the ghost, I was rescued by a lightning life-saving job by the lovely Liv. 'How can you be so naughty?' she said to him in her enchanting accent. 'You know perfectly well you are going to do it, why don't you put the poor man out of his misery and tell him so?' And that is how, giddy with incredulity, I realized that I was to be the first manager to persuade the great man to do an English production in London, a place he clearly detested.

I had lined up for him a brilliant cast, headed by Maggie Smith; the company and he got on so well that when, in most unusual custom after one week, he told me he had done all the work that was needed and that now the company could get on perfectly well by themselves, they were undismayed, provided he would come back to see them through the dress rehearsals and on for the first night. They made it quite clear that they didn't want me around trying to pinch-hit for him, and neither did he. A mite hurtful though this may have been, I had just wisdom enough to leave things as they were; back he came as promised, and the show was one of the great prides of my time at the National.

Nicholas Shakespeare

from *Bruce Chatwin*

Until he was fourteen, Bruce's experience of abroad consisted in family sailing holidays to France. Then at the end of his first year at Marlborough, he was offered the chance to spend the summer in Sweden with a Swedish boy of his own age.

The Bratt family contacted Charles through a friend. Would Bruce like to stay the summer at their lake-house south of Stockholm and teach English to their son, Thomas?

In June, Margharita saw him off at Tilbury on the SS *Patricia* with a box of liqueur chocolates for Mrs Bratt. He shared a cabin with a young man who was hoping to become a monk and who said his prayers through the night in Latin. 'And another who I think was a Polish Jew who snored all night,' he wrote. 'What with snoring and Latin I did not get much sleep.' On landing he was searched for contraband cigarettes by a Swedish customs officer who mistook him for a Frenchman.

Lennart Bratt's family was well known in Sweden. His father Ivan, a physician, had initiated a programme to control Swedish drinking habits. The Bratt 'system', in place for forty years, rationed alcohol consumption to four litres a month. Bruce's destination had been used by Ivan Bratt as his summer resort.

Bruce spent nearly two months at the farm of Lundby Gård on the edge of Lake Yngaren. The farm was remote. He wrote to Margharita: 'There is not a shop for miles and everything has to be ordered, so my £10 may come back unmolested.' The estate comprised several houses around a white flag-pole and seemed more like a village than a farm. Built in the early nineteenth century, the pine houses were painted blood red with iron oxide from the copper mine mixed with water. One day Bruce would paint his own house near Nettlebed with the same Swedish oxide. 'It's a pity I didn't bring my camera because it is so beautiful a country.' He responded to the northern architecture: the clean lines of the roofs, like upturned hulls, the clear, simple colours decorating the woodwork and the scrubbed pine floors of the interiors. 'I understood his sense of colour when I visited Sweden,' says Elizabeth. 'Pale grey and pale green and ochre, not primary colours. You can see it in all his flats.'

Bruce and Thomas shared a room which had not long before been used as a gaol. Bruce wrote, 'I had expected Thomas to be fair-haired etc, but he has jet black hair and dark skin which makes him look like an Italian.' Bruce's task seemed simple enough: to talk to him in English. They ate meals of pike, perch and Ryvita; they visited Viking graves under the ash trees; they sailed in the square-rigged dinghy, *Terna*. But to Mrs Bratt's dismay, they did not get on. She says: 'I tried in every way to make them do things together. I even hired a canoe. Such a mistake!' The two boys paddled the canoe fifteen miles without exchanging a word.

According to Bruce, Thomas was only interested in gramophone records and detective novels. According to Thomas's younger brother Peter, the fault lay with Bruce. 'I remember an extremely dull boy running around with a net,' says Peter Bratt. 'It's a strange thing, a boy of fourteen mostly interested in collecting butterflies and putting needles through them. We thought it was disgusting. It occurred to us to put a snake in his bed, a black and yellow snake, but they can bite and my mother would have been angry. Just to tease him we put nettles in his bed, but he never complained. He never said anything. We were a bit disappointed.'

Having nothing in common with the boys, Bruce sought the company of their great-uncle, Percivald.

In many respects, Percivald Bratt filled the space left by Bruce's grandfather Sam, who had died a year before in a London hospital. Percivald had trained to be a dentist, but his nerves failed him and he had spent the greater part of his salaried life as an actuary. 'Work is the hell of your life,' he said – a refrain taken up by Bruce, who described employers as 'professional time-wasters'.

Percivald never dressed before three. He wore a monocle, a brown Manchester-tweed suit like Sam, and carried a watch on a gold chain. Most of the time, he read. He had no academic qualification, but he was a man of wide erudition and his tastes ranged from the poetry of Karl Feldt to the *Spectator*, which arrived each week. He kept his books upstairs, in a glass cabinet on legs. He made Bruce read Duff Cooper's biography of Talleyrand and Chekhov in Constance Garnett's translation.

Cut off from time and space, Percivald was old-fashioned, quiet-voiced and fanatically tidy. He was always combing the gravel outside his gate in the Bratt 'village' and once after Thomas marked his walls with greasy hands, he changed the wallpaper. He loved porcelain and he owned twelve plates from the time of Charles XII, the Warrior King. When his daughter dropped one of them, he talked about it every day for three weeks until Great Aunt Eva just smashed them all. After that no one mentioned plates.

Partial to acting, Percivald's idea of charades was to perform *The Panama Canal*.

Soon Bruce was spending all his afternoons with Percivald, drinking tea out of gold cups (which Percivald claimed had been rescued from a sunken boat in the Atlantic) and learning the secrets of Swedish chandeliers (the Swedes were the only people who understood about chandeliers, said Percivald, because they understood about ice). One afternoon, Bruce was permitted to handle Percivald's wooden casket with mother-of-pearl inlay. Percivald had bought this in North Africa as a young man. Once, in a fit of intense depression, he had abandoned his wife and his comfortable life and travelled into the Sahara, filling the casket with fine sand. No one was allowed to touch it, but on occasions he would open the box to sift its contents. Ten years later, under similar stress, Bruce would take a similar journey into the desert.

For Thomas Bratt, the summer exchange had been a wash-out – the following year, instead of staying with Bruce at Brown's Green he opted for another family in the Isle of Wight – but for Bruce it was a turning point. 'He came back years older,' said his mother, whom he had bought a simple white porcelain dish. 'That summer opened his eyes to abroad.' Hugh remembered his brother arriving home with 'the MAD, MAD eyes of a nineteenth-century explorer'.

Bruce Chatwin

from *What Am I Doing Here?*

A Coup

The Africa I loved was the long undulating savannah country to the north, the 'leopard-spotted land', where flat-topped acacias stretched as far as the eye could see, and there were black-and-white hornbills and tall red termitaries. For whenever I went back to that Africa, and saw a camel caravan, a view of white tents, or a single blue turban far off in the heat haze, I knew that, no matter what the Persians said, Paradise never was a garden but a waste of white thorns.

'I am dreaming,' said Jacques, suddenly, 'of perdrix aux choux.'

'I'd take a dozen Belons and a bottle of Krug.'

'No speak!' The corporal waved his gun, and I braced myself, half-expecting the butt to crash down on my skull.

And so what? What would it matter when already I felt as if my skull were split clean open? Was this, I wondered, sunstroke? How strange, too, as I tried to focus on the wall, that each bit of chaff should bring back some clear specific memory of food or drink?

There was a lake in Central Sweden and, in the lake, there was an island where the ospreys nested. On the first day of the crayfish season we rowed to the fisherman's hut and rowed back towing twelve dozen crayfish in a live-net. That evening, they came in from the kitchen, a scarlet mountain smothered in dill. The northern sunlight bounced off the lake into the bright white room. We drank akvavit from thimble-sized glasses and we ended the meal with a tart made of cloudberries. I could taste again the grilled sardines we ate on the quay at Douarnenez and see my father demonstrating how his father ate sardines *à la mordecai*: you took a live sardine by the tail and swallowed it. Or the elvers we had in Madrid, fried in oil with garlic and half a red pepper. It had been a cold spring morning, and we'd spent two hours in the Prado, gazing at the Velasquezes, hugging one another it was so good to be alive: we had cancelled our bookings on a plane that had crashed. Or the lobsters we bought at Cape Split Harbour, Maine. There was a notice-board in the shack on the jetty and, pinned to it, a card on which a widow thanked her husband's friends for their contributions, and prayed, prayed to the Lord, that they lashed themselves to the boat when hauling in the pots.

How long, O Lord, how long? How long, when all the world was wheeling, could I stay on my feet . . . ?

Michael Holroyd

from *Lytton Strachey*

Swedish Experiment, French Solution
Summer 1909

Lytton started out on his quest for health in mid-July. With him went two female attendants – an eccentric aunt of Duncan Grant's[46] called Daisy McNeil who ran a private nursing home in Eastbourne for the infirm members of well-to-do families; and one of her elderly affluent patients, a woman by the name of Elwes, 'a poor dried-up good-natured old stick with an odd tinge of excitability, alias madness'. Both ladies were extraordinarily obliging, offering to mend Lytton's socks, presenting him at all times of the day with cups of weak tea, and insisting that he read the out-of-date newspapers before themselves. He repaid them by cracking polite jokes and elaborately admiring, for their benefit, the scenery. 'Even La Elwes's conversation has its charms,' he reported back to Duncan (1 August 1909). 'At first I was terrified by her hatchet nose and slate-pencil voice – and I still am occasionally – but on the whole I now view her with composure. Never have I met a more absolutely sterile mind – and yet how wonderfully cultivated! It's like a piece of flannel with watercress growing on it.'

On their arrival in Stockholm, Daisy McNeil, who spoke Swedish, arranged for Lytton to have some medical tests – fearful intimate encounters carried on in broken French. 'Pas de laxatifs, monsieur!' were the doctor's first and last words; and he sent Lytton down with his retinue of ladies to Badanstalten, a health sanatorium for 'physical therapeutics' at Saltsjöbaden, by the sea, not far from Stockholm. This sanatorium specialized in the treatment of heart conditions, nervous illnesses, stomach, intestinal and digestive complaints and was presided over by a charming cello-playing Dr Zander who attended personally to Lytton.

The water was undoubtedly the best feature of Salt-sjöbaden, and if he had only owned a small sailing boat, life might have been tolerable. He saw a great many boats, but they were all private and it seemed out of the question to hire one. 'I believe I'm the only person of our acquaintance who could do what I'm doing,' he boasted to his brother James.

'The dullness is so infinite that the brain reels to think of it, and yet I might almost be called happy . . . I had quite a shock when I entered the dining-room for the first time and saw the crowd of middle-aged and middle-class invalids munching their Swedish cookery. For complete second-rateness this country surpasses the wildest dreams of man. I sometimes fear that it may be the result of democracy, but imagine really that it's inborn, and brought to its height by lack of cash. All the decent Scandinavians, no doubt, left the place a thousand years ago, and only the dregs remain. Yet they're amazingly good-looking; and the sailors in Stockholm, with their décol-leté necks, fairly send one into a flutter. The bath-attendants, however, so far, have not agitated me, and this in spite of the singular intimacies of their operations. Even the lift boys leave me cold. My health seems to be progressing rather well, but my experiences have been more ghastly than can be con-ceived, medical experiences, I mean – oh heavens!'

It was the improvement in his health that made the tedium supportable. He had started off the first week with nothing more strenuous than some insignificant baths ('Finsenbad'), but almost immediately he began to gain in weight, his diges-tion improved – also his temper – and other departments. 'Conceive me if you can a healthy and pure young man,' he wrote to Maynard Keynes (13 August 1909). 'My only terror is that none of it'll last.' After the first successful week he graduated from the bathroom to the gym. 'I hope when I get on to the mechanical gymnastics, etc., that I shall swell out of my clothes,' he told Duncan. By the third week his female attendants were letting out his waistcoats.

Saltsjöbaden, Badhotellet.

The spa hotel at Saltsjöbaden outside Stockholm where Lytton Strachey spent the summers of 1909 and 1910.

The regime now grew more formidable. At eight o'clock each morning Lytton was called by sister Fanny who brought him a glass of 'Carlsbad water' – a mild tonic. Half an hour later he breakfasted off a locally concocted simulacrum of porridge and sour cream. At nine-thirty he paraded at the gym for a thirty-minute period of mechanical exercises – gadgets and appliances of a gruesome medieval appearance. 'The hall where one does them [the exercises] looks exactly like a torture chamber,' he explained to his mother (3 August 1909), '– terrific instruments of every kind line the walls, and elderly gentlemen attached upon them go through their evolutions with the utmost gravity'.

When the sun shone, the air would glow miraculously light and clear, and he was able to sit out on his special deck-chair among the pines and the perspiring Swedish patients, dreaming and doing nothing. At the back of every dream stood the heroic figure of George Mallory. To his friends he poured out a stream of letters describing the rigours and incongruities of this 'Swedish experiment'. And when he had wearied of writing, he would read Tolstoy, Saint-Simon, Voltaire, Swinburne. 'I only regret that I forgot to bring a copy of the Holy Bible,' he wrote to his mother. He eagerly devoured imported copies of the *Gloucester and Wilts Advertiser* and began to get quite heated over far-off local affairs. Swedish politics also tried to claim his attention when, early in August, a general strike was called. However, there was scarcely a ripple of disruption in the medicinal halls.

It was during these morning periods of reading and writing letters, that Lytton conceived a plan for compiling an anthology of English heroic verse. 'One might get a great many good extracts which people don't know of,' he wrote to his mother (21 August 1909). 'The interest would be to trace the development up to Pope, etc., and then the throw back with Keats and Shelley.

'I think Pope made more advance on Dryden – in the mere technique of the line – than is usually recognized. Dryden's line, though of course it's magnificent, lacks the weight of Pope's. I once analysed some passages in the Dunciad, and found that the number of stressed syllables in each line was remarkable – sometimes as many as seven or eight. It's difficult to believe that this is the same metre as Epipsychidion which rushes along with three stresses to a line at most. I've written to Sidgwick proposing to do this. I hope he'll accept.'

Nothing came of this plan, though fifteen years later Lytton incorporated some of his reflections on the heroic couplet into his Leslie Stephen Lecture on Pope.

Lunch took place at one o'clock, and once the patient was judged to have properly digested his food, he was plunged into a medicinal bath. These were rather strict affairs, meticulously supervised by stewards and officials, and always too cold for pleasure. After tea at four, Lytton was allowed two hours' rest until dinner which, to his disgust, was served at the unbelievably *bourgeois* time of six o'clock. Communal walks were permitted after dinner, under the pallid sky and among the mangy conifers of the so-called 'English Park'. It was a shocking experience to be hedged in on these slow expeditions by the elderly inhabitants. There were so many of them – all Swedes or Finns – and, despite their middle-class habits, suspected by Lytton of being counts and countesses incognito, as in a comic opera. Wherever he looked he saw them: dotted across the nondescript countryside, wandering in the scrubby woods or bobbing about in boats, streaming endlessly through the corridors to their various meals and cures, or chattering over their symptoms in the 'Salong'. There was no escaping them.

In the later evening, after promenading around in the park, Lytton usually played a few games of billiards with Daisy. He soon gained an immense reputation as a billiards expert among the inmates. 'Directly we begin to play,' he informed his mother (21 August 1909), 'crowds enter the room, and take seats to watch the Englishman playing "cannon-ball" as they call it. As the table is very small and the pockets are very large I occasionally manage to make a break of 15 or 20 which strikes astonishment in the beholders. Apparently the Swedish game consists entirely of potting the red ball with great violence, so that cannons and losing hazards brought off with delicacy appear to these poor furriners wonderful and beautiful in the extreme.'

At half-past nine play was interrupted for an evening bowl of pseudo-porridge; and an hour later Lytton retired upstairs to his bedroom, drew down his special blinds and went off into dreamless sleep. He had experienced nothing like this since his schooling at Abbotsholme. After six weeks he became so attuned to the monotony that he could hardly believe in any mode of living which did not comprise dinner-at-six, mechanical gymnastics, porridge and cold baths, and perambulations with dubious Scandinavian countesses. It was not the unremitting hell it sounded, but rather a purgatory where he had absolved himself through suffering.

Early in September Daisy McNeil and 'La Elwes' gave up the struggle and fled to England; but James bravely came out to stay with his brother for the remaining days of his treatment. 'It was very fortunate,' Lytton explained to Maynard (17 September 1909), 'as otherwise I should have been alone and moribund in this ghastly region'.

The brothers left Saltsjöbaden on 23 September, arriving back in London two days later. After a week in Belsize Park Gardens, suffering from piles and carrying an air cushion, Lytton travelled down with his mother and Harry Norton to Brighton, where he set about trying 'to recover from the effects of Sweden'.

Summer 1910

Lady Strachey had run out of new ideas to contend with her son's illnesses, and the only remedy that anyone could think of was a second sojourn at the Saltsjöbaden sanatorium. Accordingly Lytton set off in the second week of July for another ten weeks' spell in Sweden accompanied by his sister Pernel and Jane Harrison, the fifty-nine-year-old classical anthropologist and scholarly spirit behind the Cambridge Marlowe Society and Rupert Brooke's Garden-City Neo-Pagans, who was using this pharmaceutical holiday 'to get new heart' for the writing of *Themis*, her celebrated study on the social origins of Greek religion. When he entered the clinic, there, to welcome him, was the veteran brigade of patients going through the same hectic programme of porridge and baths. 'I already feel as if I'd been here for twenty years,' he began a letter to James written on his first day (18 July 1910).

While Jane Harrison took advantage of her stay to learn Swedish, principally from the writings of Selma Lagerlöf, Lytton concentrated on mastering Italian – for his dreams had revived of travelling south. He was going through the same pantomime of billiards, gymnastics and massage, but this time the medical treatment was more stringent. He was placed under the care of Dr Olof Sandberg, a specialist in digestive complaints, who insisted that Lytton should eat a great deal – 'as much as possible and sometimes a little more' – and who favoured a liberal use of the stomach pump. By the middle of August he reported to Pippa: 'My cure has been going very well.'

For Jane Harrison, suffering under a similar course of treatment, there were no redeeming features. She could not attune herself to the colourless oddity of the place; and Pernel fared little better. 'They both find the place very singular,' Lytton explained to his mother (5 August 1910), 'and I should think the place returns the compliment so far as Jane is concerned – she makes a strange figure among the formal Scandinavians, floating through the corridors in green shawls and purple tea-gowns, and reciting the Swedish grammar at meals.' Before long the two women surrendered and hastened back to England. 'This is the last anyone will hear of my health,' remarked Jane Harrison ruefully.

Lytton's invalidism was made of sterner stuff, and for him the rigorous cure continued unchecked. He was joined by his sister Pippa, but even she could only endure a fortnight of the sanatorium. Yet still Lytton stayed on. Then he suffered a relapse, the cause of which none of the specialists could diagnose. 'I've stayed on here week after week,' he complained to Maynard (26 September 1910), 'lured by the hope of attaining eternal health: on Friday I shall drag myself away . . . I feel that this has been a wasted summer for me.'

Summer 1928

To avoid the hammering commotion Lytton carried off Roger Senhouse[47] for a short Scandinavian holiday. 'We have had all sorts of meals in all sorts of restaurants – have spent hours in second-hand bookshops, with no result – have walked through endless streets and gardens – and so far have seen no sights,' he wrote to Carrington from Copenhagen (8 August 1928). ' . . . The inhabitants are pleasant, but oh!

so lacking in temperament! Duty seems to guide their steps, and duty alone.'

At the end of the week they moved on to Stockholm. The fearsome medicinal halls at Saltsjöbaden, to which Lytton paid a brief nostalgic visit, appeared unchanged from when he had been there eighteen years before, but Stockholm itself was more evidently a capital city. 'There is a great deal of water in every direction – broad limbs of the Baltic permeating between the streets – so that there really *is* some semblance to Venice,' he wrote to Carrington (14 August 1928). 'The blueness of the water in this northern light is often attractive, and there are quantities of white steam ferry boats moving about, which adds to the gaiety of the scene.

'The best building to my mind is the royal palace, which stands on the central island of the town – a large severe square pale brown 18th century structure, dominating the scene. Then, slightly remote on a broad piece of water, is the new Town Hall – distinctly striking – very big – and of an effective bigness, built in dark red brick, with one very high tower at the junction of two wings – one (facing the water) longer than the other . . . The worst of it is, however, that in spite of a certain grandeur of conception, there is no real greatness of feeling about it. It is extremely clever and well thought out, but the detail is positively bad – in bad taste, and sometimes actually facetious – and there is no coherency of style – classical, gothic, oriental, byzantine, modern Viennese, etc. etc., so that one has no sense of security or repose. It is a pity, as the site is so good, and the hulk *is* impressive – which is certainly something; but the more I looked the more certain I became that it was infinitely far from real goodness.'

Evelyn Waugh

from *The Diaries*

Stockholm, Sunday 17 August 1947

A very hot day in London and Stockholm where I arrived at 11 at night, found a note directing me to the Carlton Hotel, a small, modern, noisy place in a main shopping street. But the restaurant was still open and I had half a bottle of champagne and a beautifully cooked sole.

Monday 18 August 1947

I spent the day looking at Stockholm, a city of startling beauty, water on all sides, bridges, trees, some lovely buildings. My change of address necessitated rewriting to all to whom I had sent letters of introduction. An admirable luncheon at Opera Keller. In the evening to an expensive restaurant called Bellmansro where I was too tired to eat. The *Telegraph* agent came to see me. A cheerful, civil good-looking fellow who is sick of Stockholm and wants to go to Berlin. First impressions of Stockholm Paradise, second Limbo. Girls very pretty and not disfigured by paint and hairdressing. All look sexually and socially satisfied.

Tuesday 19 August 1947

More sightseeing. Splendid German woodcarving of St George and princess. The town hall the last building of importance in Europe designed to be picturesque. Not my taste but everything carefully designed with aesthetic intent. I lunched with Viklund, the *Telegraph* correspondent and the literary editor of his paper – an ugly man enormously well informed about modern English writers. After luncheon a dull young woman, fat, came to interview me. Later when the interview appeared it was headed 'Huxley's Ape makes hobby of graveyards'. That evening Mrs Holmquist, to whom I was introduced by both Victor Mallet and Ran-

Stockholm City Hall, designed by Ragnar Östberg and completed in 1923, was one of the foremost European architectural undertakings of the era. Lytton Strachey, W. B. Yeats and Evelyn Waugh all formed strong, if diverging, opinions of the building on visits to Stockholm.

dolph, dined with me at Opera Keller. Very pretty, shy, gluttonous. I should think passionate. She said Randolph had greatly alarmed her by his bad temper. She has a beautiful little flat at the top of a building in Strandvägen and from her I began to get some impression of the straightened circumstances of the upper class. After dinner we walked through the old town and had beer in a cellar where a man was singing Bellman to the lute.

Wednesday 20 August 1947
More sightseeing. Luncheon with Assarsson, head of the Foreign Office, an old pansy with a pretty modern bungalow full of works of art. With us Grafström, head of political department FO. Assarsson had no car, but he had caviare and a Hepplewhite table.

Thursday 21 August 1947
Three invitations to dinner of which I accepted the first, Karl Asplund, a poet antiquaire. Mrs Holmquist came to lunch-

eon with me bringing a son and daughter and picking up a pert tart. We went first to the House of the Nobility, one of the finest exteriors in the city but modern renovations inside (pretty chimneys). A great hall full of coats of arms. Mrs H.:'But this is funny. I find here the names of so many friends I did not know were nobles.' Arplund's (*sic*) dinner was in an old inn some way out of town. Delicious food and drink. Pen Club company all most knowledgeable about English books. They apologized for Prince Wilhelm's absence (his uncle Eugen the painter is just dead).

Friday 22 August 1947

A day's outing with my publisher, a dull fellow. Swedes are bloody dull. He said: '*I Chose Freedom* has sold 35,000 copies. A great sale.'

'That is good.'

'It is very bad.'

'Why? Do you not think it truthful?'

'I know it is quite truthful but it will be a terrible thing if it caused feeling here against Russia.'

The Swedes have a very disadvantageous trade agreement with Russia. They resent it being disadvantageous, not on other grounds. Communism to them is simply Russian aggression. They cannot conceive its mystique. Eighteen per cent of town council are Communist.

We saw Gripsholm Castle, a pretty building with masses of portraits. A drive through rich farmland and lakes. Insolently bad service in the hotel at Gripsholm.

In the evening Arplund had invited me to join a little party for the French Legation to see the pavilion Haga (Gustav III) which is being renovated very carefully by a French enthusiast. I found it included a dinner party. Again delicious food and wine but a great lack of imagination and curiosity in the conversation. A French woman with carmine lips tried to be the life and soul of the party. I was weary and glad when the restaurant closed. Drink regulations here are not oppressive.

Saturday 23 August 1947

To Uppsala by train to visit Engströmer, the Chancellor who lives in a tiny Park West flat. The Professor of English joined us and we went to visit the Faculty House, full of English and American books. The Chancellor told me without reserve that most of the girl students live in concubinage. The town is delicious and many of the buildings good. Cathedral awful. Queen Christina's silver bell is still rung daily for her 'luck'. I am astonished by the lack of curiosity displayed by all types of Swedes in all subjects.

Sunday 24 August 1947

In the evening my publisher asked me to dine to meet two young poets. One was my age and very drunk. They call themselves the '40 group', admire Kafka, Sartre.

Oslo, Monday 25 August 1947

Left Stockholm by the morning aeroplane and arrived at Oslo at 1 o'clock.

Notes

1. Ales Stenar (Ale Stones), a monumental, ship-shaped stone formation of 59 large boulders, 67 metres in length. It is situated high on a ridge near the fishing village of Kåseberga in Skåne, southernmost Sweden. Very little is known of the history of the stones, which are now thought to date from pre-Viking times.
2. Students and readers of the great Old English epic, *Beowulf*, will be familiar with the references to the Danes, Geats and Swedes. The Anglo-Saxon poet was not necessarily very precise in his geographical references, but it is clear that Beowulf's people, the Geats, lived in what is now Southern Sweden. The Geats were traditional enemies of the Swedes. As Seamus Heaney says in the introduction to his translation, 'The poem called Beowulf was composed some time between the middle of the seventh and the end of the tenth century of the first millennium'. Mr Heaney has adjusted this excerpt for this anthology.
3. Ronald Bottrall (1906–86) emerged as a notable poet in the early 1930s, when F. R. Leavis praised his early work. He was the first British Council representative in Sweden.
4. Carol Rumens was British Council writer-in-residence at Stockholm University in 1999. Carol Rumens has published 11 collections of poetry, including *Holding Pattern* (Blackstaff Press, 1999) and *Hex* (Bloodaxe Books, 2002). 'Kings of the Playground', inspired by a demonstration against the bombing of Belgrade which the poet witnessed in Stockholm, was a runner-up in the 2001 Cardiff International Poetry Competition.
5. King Aun, legendary Norse king who lived to the age of 200 by sacrificing nine of his ten sons to Odin.
6. Robyn Bolam, professor of English literature and language at St Mary's College, University of Sussex, is a former British Council writer-in-residence at Stockholm University. She previously published as Marion Lomax. Her interests include contemporary poetry; Renaissance drama and women's poetry.

7. Dr Dannie Abse, born in Cardiff, Wales in 1923, is a medical man and one of Britain's greatest contemporary poets. He took part in 'The Great Poetry Exchange' in Stockholm, in March 2002, with Jamie McKendrick, Katherine Pierpoint and Sophie Hannah. His most recent novel, *The Strange Case of Dr Simmonds and Dr Glas* (Robson Books, 2002) was, in part, inspired by Hjalmar Söderberg's *Dr Glas*. Dannie Abse's *New and Collected Poems* was published in February 2003 by Hutchinson.

8. In 1956, James Kirkup was appointed by the Swedish Ministry of Education to a one-year travelling lectureship in English language and literature that took him the length and breadth of Sweden. He was teaching pupils of all levels, with widely varying degrees of English comprehension. In his teaching he often used his own children's poems as well as new poems inspired by the life and landscapes of Sweden.

9. Raman Mundair, who lectures in South Asian literature in English at Loughborough University, is a former British Council writer-in-residence at Stockholm University. Raman Mundair was born in India and raised in England; she is a writer, playwright, lecturer and performer. Her collection of poetry, *Lovers, Liars, Conjurors and Thieves*, is published by Peepal Tree Press. She is currently working on her first novel.

10. Dag Hammarskjöld (1905–1961), Swedish diplomat who was General Secretary of the UN from 1953 until his death in a plane crash in Northern Rhodesia on 18 September 1961 during mediations with the warring factions in the Congo. He was awarded the Nobel Prize for Peace posthumously the same year. *Markings (Vägmärken)*, Hammarskjöld's spiritual diary, was first published four years after his death.

11. Leif Sjöberg was a distinguished Swedish scholar, teacher and translator who spent most of his academic career in the USA. Dismayed by the reluctance of US and British publishers to venture into Swedish literature, his answer was to collaborate with well-known British and American poets on interpretations of leading Swedish poets. W. H. Auden writes in his introduction to *Markings* that he himself knew no Swedish.

12. Johannes Edfelt (1904–97), leading Swedish poet, translator and essayist, was a member of the Swedish Academy and its Nobel Committee.

13. Harry Martinson (1904–78) shared the 1974 Nobel Prize in Literature with his fellow Swede, Eyvind Johnson. Martinson escaped the poverty of his boyhood in southern Sweden by

running away to sea. Many of his literary themes reflect the six years he spent at sea.

14. Pär Lagerkvist (1891–1974) was one of the major Swedish writers of the first half of the 20th century. He was a member of the Swedish Academy and was awarded the Nobel Prize in Literature in 1951.

15. Gunnar Ekelöf (1907–68). Ekelöf is regarded by many as Sweden's greatest lyric poet. He studied oriental languages in London and Uppsala, and although his early work is influenced by the French surrealists, the mysticism and themes of much of his later poetry reflects his love of the Middle East and the Orient. This extract is from *Dīvān over the Prince of Emgión* (1965), most of which he wrote in Istanbul.

16. Per Wästberg (born 1933) is a poet, novelist and journalist, an authority on Africa and leading anti-Apartheid activist who was president of International PEN 1967–78. He is a member of the Swedish Academy and of the Nobel Committee for Literature and has published some 50 books – novels, poetry and non-fiction – including, in English translation: *The Air Cage*, 1972, and *Love's Gravity*, 1977.

17. Werner Aspenström (1918–76), leading poet, dramatist and prose writer; member of the Swedish Academy. 'Colour' appeared in the collection *Sorl* (1983). In the years up to her death on 7 January 1963, the poet Sylvia Plath had been living in Primrose Hill, London, and had paid regular visits to the nearby London Zoo with her children.

18. Eva Ström was born in Sweden in 1947. A medical doctor, she has been a full-time writer since 1988. She was awarded the Nordic Council Prize for Literature 2003 for Revbensstaderna (Rib Cities), her latest collection of poetry. *A to Zed* refers to a walk to Fitzroy Road in Primrose Hill, London, the last address of poet Sylvia Plath. A plaque on the wall tells that the house had previously been the home of W. B. Yeats. Sylvia Plath's own memorial plaque can be found on the wall of her penultimate home in nearby Chalcot Square, a place less associated than Fitzroy Road with the tragedy of her early death. The quotations in *A to Zed* and *He* are from W. B. Yeats.

19. Johanna Ekström (born 1970) is a writer and visual artist who has published novels, poetry, short stories and is at present living in London and working on a film script.

20. Carl Linnaeus (1707–78), Sweden's most famous natural historian and father of the modern method of classifying the

natural world. In Uppsala he was professor of medicine and vice-chancellor of the university and was also in charge of the botanical gardens. He founded the Royal Swedish Academy of Sciences, based on the Royal Society in London, and sent his students on ambitious voyages of botanical discovery to the far corners of the earth. After his death his collection was sold to an English collector and formed the basis for the Linnean Society of London.

21. Daniel Solander (1733–82) was a protégé of Carl Linnaeus, under whom he studied natural history at Uppsala University. Solander went to England in 1760 and made his home there, becoming keeper of the natural history collections at the British Museum, a member of the Royal Society and one of the most important naturalists of his age. He sailed with James Cook on his first circumnavigation of the world. *Archiater* was an honorary medical title used in Sweden at the time.

22. Joseph Banks (1743–1820), wealthy naturalist and explorer who became head of the Royal Botanical Gardens in Kew, a trustee of the British Museum and president of the Royal Society. Together with Solander he was a member of Captain Cook's first voyage of discovery to the South Seas 1768–71.

23. Johan Alströmer (1742–86), industrialist who continued the work of his father, agricultural reformer Jonas Alströmer, in promoting the cultivation of the potato in Sweden.

24. Vernon Watkins (1906–67) was a leading Welsh poet. A close friend of Dylan Thomas, he spent most of his working life in a Swansea bank. Emanuel Swedenborg (1688–1772), Swedish scientist, theologian and mystic, died in London and was buried there. In 1908 it was decided that he should be reburied in Uppsala Cathedral. When his body was exhumed it was discovered that the head was missing. It appeared that Swedenborg's skull had been stolen some 50 years after his death. The skull was eventually discovered in a second-hand shop in Wales and bought by Swedenborg's family.

25. In December 1923, W. B. Yeats (1865–1939) travelled to Sweden to receive the Nobel Prize in Literature. Two years later he published *The Bounty of Sweden*, a volume containing his impressions of Stockholm as well as the lecture he delivered to the Swedish Academy. Yeats apparently heard later that the

Swedish royal family had 'liked him better than any previous Nobel Prize winner'.

26. Lady Augusta Persse Gregory (1852–1932) of Coole Park, Ireland, was a writer and folklorist who became Yeats's patron.

27. J. M. Synge (1871–1909), controversial Irish dramatist and admirer of Yeats who in 1906 became head of the Abbey Theatre in Dublin.

28. The prince Yeats refers to is Prince Eugen (1865–1947), a leading landscape painter and influential figure in Swedish cultural life. He was responsible for the famous frescoes in Stockholm's City Hall.

29. Jamie McKendrick is a former writer-in-residence at Gothenburg University. His first book of poems, *The Sirocco Room*, appeared in 1991 and his latest, *Ink Stone*, will be published in 2003.

30. Shaw's friend William Archer was a drama critic, playwright and translator of Ibsen.

31. Novelist and short-story writer Clive Sinclair was British Council writer-in-residence at the University of Uppsala in 1988. From 1983–7 he was literary editor of the *Jewish Chronicle*. His first book of short stories, *Hearts of Gold*, won the Somerset Maugham Award. His latest work is *Meet the Wife* (Picador 2002).

32. In 1901, Strindberg married Harriet Bosse, a 23-year-old, Norwegian-born actress. They divorced three years later.

33. The verse epic *Frithiof's Saga* (1824) by Swedish romantic poet Esaias Tegnér (1782–1846) and based on an Icelandic saga from around 1300, attracted a great deal of attention after publication and was quickly translated into a number of languages. The story is about the love between Frithiof and Ingeborg, the daughter of King Bele.

34. *Drapa*, a poem in many verses about or addressed to a person of high rank. Balder was a Norse god, son of Oden and Frigg. Balder's mother obtained promises from all things on earth except the mistletoe that they would not harm her son. Cunning Loke, who knew of this, tricked the blind Höder into using an arrow of mistletoe one day when the gods were using the unwoundable Balder for target practice. Balder died.

35. The Rev William Barnes (1801–1886) was a Dorset dialect poet, linguist, philologist and artist/engraver. His early work,

Orra: A Lapland Tale (1822), is a narrative poem of 65 stanzas, influenced by Ambrose Philips' *A Lapland Song* and by Giuseppe Acerbi's *Travels through Sweden, Finland and Lapland to the North Cape* , London, 1802. Acerbi travelled through Lapland in 1798–1799.

36. *In Memoriam* (1850), these three verses (CVI, stanzas 1–3) from the poem with which Tennyson established his reputation, have become an integral part of the open-air New Year celebrations in Stockholm.

37. Charles XII (1682–1718), Swedish warrior king who spent most of his reign in the field or in exile, attempting to defend Sweden's great power status. His greatest victory was the battle of Narva against Tsar Peter in 1700. His defeat by Peter nine years later at Poltava in the Ukraine signalled the end of Sweden's Baltic empire. He spent the next five years in the little town of Bender (today in Moldavia), intriguing against Russia with the Turks, before finally returning to Sweden in 1715. Charles eventually died at Fredriksten in Norway in November 1718. England had originally sided with Sweden in the Nordic wars, but under its new Hanoverian king, George I, ships from the British fleet were used in the blockade of Swedish Stralsund. Posterity has held widely diverging views of Charles XII. For some he was the heroic monarch who fought to the last for his country. For others he was a madman whose folly brought down a whole empire.

38. King Gustav IV Adolf (1778–1837) reigned from 1792 until 1809, when he was forced to abdicate after Sweden's defeat in the 'Finnish War' against Russia. In sonnets XX and XXI, Wordsworth contrasts the newly abdicated Swedish monarch with the 'intoxicated despot', Napoleon.

39. Mary Wollstonecraft's Scandinavian journey lasted from June to October 1795. She travelled with a lady's maid and her infant daughter Fanny, although they remained in Gothenburg while she travelled north into Norway. The letters are written to an anonymous correspondent in London. We now know that they were addressed to Gilbert Imlay, the father of her daughter. Wollstonecraft and the American Imlay had lived together in France, and their troubled relationship had been the cause of her first attempt at suicide. The purpose of Mary's journey seems to have been to resolve a dubious business affair in which Imlay was involved.

40. The 'Occupation' to which Waugh refers here was the Labour government elected in 1945.

41. *I Chose Freedom: The Personal and Political Life of a Soviet Official*, by Victor Kravchenko, was published in 1946 (New York, Charles Scribner's Sons).

42. Sir Peter Tennant (1910–96) read Modern Languages at Cambridge and went on to lecture in Scandinavian languages. He worked as Press Attaché at the British Embassy in Stockholm during the war, and later at the embassy in Paris. From 1950 to 1952 he was Deputy Commandant of the British Sector in Berlin. He then left the Foreign Service for the Federation of British Industry and later the CBI, and spent the rest of his career working to promote British trade interests. He retained a lifelong interest in Scandinavian literature, especially the works of Ibsen and Strindberg.

43. Michael Roberts, Professor of Modern History at the University of Belfast until his retirement and author of some noted works on Swedish history, was the second British Council Representative in Sweden. The son of a Lancashire engineer, he won a scholarship to read modern history at Worcester College, Oxford. After graduating he spent a year as a visiting fellow at Princetown before returning to England and an assistant lectureship in Liverpool. He had intended to continue his research in English history but, as the extract begins, he has realised that he would be wise to venture into a less competitive academic field.

44. Petrus Laestadius (1802–41) was a priest and missionary in Lapland, who in 1833 published one of the most important literary accounts of life in the far north of Sweden.

45. *Norrskensflamman* was a Communist newspaper founded in Luleå in 1906.

46. Duncan Grant was Lytton Strachey's cousin.

47. Lytton Strachey's friend Roger Senhouse was a publisher and translator.

Acknowledgements

For permission to reprint copyright material we gratefully acknowledge the following:

Peter Ackroyd: from *T. S. Eliot* (Hamish Hamilton 1984). Copyright © Peter Ackroyd 1984. Reproduced by permission of Penguin Books Ltd.

Werner Aspenström: 'Colour' from *The Wind Itself. Werner Aspenström Selected Poems* translated by Robin Young. (Planet, Aberystwyth 1999). Reprinted by permission of Robin Young.

'What I noticed in London' translated by Robin Fulton and reproduced by kind permission of the translator.

Ingmar Bergman: from *The Magic Lantern* by Ingmar Bergman, translated by Joan Tate. Copyright © 1988 by Joan Tate. Original copyright © 1987 by Ingmar Bergman. Used by permission of Viking Penguin, a division of Penguin Putnam Inc.

Robyn Bolam: Copyright © Robyn Bolam. Reprinted by kind permission of the author. 'Two Springs' first appeared in *Poetry Review*, vol 91 (2) summer 2001, edited by Peter Forbes.

Ronald Bottrall: 'Nordica' from *The Collected Writings of Ronald Bottrall* (Sidgwick & Jackson 1961).

Malcolm Bradbury: from *To the Hermitage* (Picador 2000). Reproduced by permission of Macmillan Publishers Ltd.

Alan Brownjohn: 'Avalanche Dogs' from *The Cat Without E-Mail* (Enitharmon Press 2002). Copyright © Alan Brownjohn. Reproduced by permission of Enitharmon Press.

Humphrey Carpenter: from *W. H. Auden. A Biography* (Allen & Unwin 1981).

Bruce Chatwin: 'A Coup' from *What Am I Doing Here?* copyright © 1989 by The Estate of Bruce Chatwin. Used by permission of Viking Penguin, a division of Penguin Putnam Inc.

Douglas Dunn: 'Europa's Lover, IX' from *Douglas Dunn. Selected Poems 1964–1983* (Faber and Faber). Reproduced by permission of Faber and Faber Ltd.

Paul Durcan: 'The 24,000 Islands of Stockholm' from *Cries of an Irish Caveman* by Paul Durcan (Harvill Press 2001). Used by permission of The Random House Group Limited.

Johannes Edfelt: 'Summer Organ' translated by W. H. Auden and Leif Sjöberg. From *Modern Scandinavian Poetry 1900–1975* (The Anglo-American Center, Mullsjö, Sweden, 1982). Copyright © Martin Allwood. Reprinted by kind permission of Kristin Allwood.

Gunnar Ekelöf: from *Gunnar Ekelöf. Selected Poems translated by W. H. Auden and Leif Sjöberg* (Penguin Books 1971). Reproduced with permission of Curtis Brown Group Ltd, London, on behalf of the Estate of W. H. Auden. Copyright © W. H. Auden 1971.

Johanna Ekström: *Cotton Wool* (original Swedish title *Bomull*) from Johanna Ekström's short story collection *Vad vet jag om hållfast-het* (*What Do I Know of Stability*) (Wahlström & Widstrand, Stockholm 2000). Reprinted by kind permission of the author and the translator.

John Fowles: from *The Tree* (Aurum Press 1979). Copyright © John Fowles. Reproduced by permission of Aurum Press.

Michael Frayn: 'Frayn's Sweden' from *The Observer*, 21 April 1974. Copyright © Michael Frayn 1974. Reproduced by permission of Greene & Heaton Ltd.

Robin Fulton: 'Remembering an Island' from *The Faber Book of Twentieth-Century Scottish Poetry* (Faber and Faber 1992). Copyright © Robin Fulton. Reprinted by kind permission of the author.

Graham Greene: from *England Made Me* (Vintage 2001). First published by William Heinemann 1935. Copyright © Graham Greene 1935. Reproduced by permission of David Higham Associates Ltd.

Graham Greene: from *Ways of Escape* (The Bodley Head 1980). Copyright © Graham Greene 1980. Reproduced by permission of David Higham Associates Ltd.

Dag Hammarskjöld: from *Markings*, edited and translated by W. H. Auden and Leif Sjöberg (Faber and Faber 1964). Reproduced by permission of Faber and Faber Ltd.

Seamus Heaney: 'Ales stenar' reproduced by kind permission of the author. Extract from *Beowulf: A New Translation by Seamus Heaney* (Faber & Faber 1999). Reproduced by kind permission of the author.

Michael Holroyd: from *Basil Street Blues* (Abacus 2000). First published by Little, Brown and Company 1999. Copyright © Michael Holroyd. Reproduced by kind permission of the author.

Michael Holroyd: from *Lytton Strachey* (Chatto and Windus 1994). Copyright © Michael Holroyd. Reproduced by kind permission of the author.

Eva Ström: 'A to Zed' and 'He' are translations of prose poems from the collection *Revbensstäderna* (Rib Cities) (Albert Bonniers förlag, Stockholm 2002). Reproduced by kind permission of the author and the translators.

Peter Tennant: *The Touchlines of War* (University of Hull Press, 1992).

Per Wästberg: reprinted by kind permission of the author and the translator.

Vernon Watkins: 'Swedenborg's Skull' from *Cypress and Acacia* (Faber and Faber 1959). Copyright © G. M. Watkins. Reproduced by kind permission of G. M. Watkins.

Evelyn Waugh: *The Essays, Articles and Reviews of Evelyn Waugh*, edited by Donat Gallagher (Penguin Books 1986). The articles 'The Scandinavian Capitals: Contrasted Post-War Moods' and 'Scandinavia Prefers a Bridge to a Rampart' by Evelyn Waugh are reproduced by permission of PFD on behalf of the Estate of Laura Waugh.

The Diaries of Evelyn Waugh, edited by Michael Davie (Penguin Books 1979). First published by Weidenfeld & Nicolson.

W. B. Yeats: *The Bounty of Sweden* (Cuala Press, Dublin 1925). Reprinted by permission of A. P. Watt Ltd on behalf of Michael B. Yeats.

Illustrations

Pages xi and 187 Michael Holroyd; Pages xvi and 166 © Pressens bild, Stockholm; page 4 Jim Potts; page 2 The British Council; pages 50, 53 and 93 © Nobel Foundation, Stockholm; page 58 Johanna Ekström; pages 102 and 107 © Strindbergsmuseet, Stockholm; page 192 © Zoë Dominic.

The editors apologize for any errors or omissions. Please notify us of any corrections that should be entered in further editions of this work.

Index of Authors and Translators

General Index